Now or Never

Now or Never

Hazel Ro

www.urbanbooks.net

Urban Books, LLC
300 Farmingdale Road, N.Y.-Route 109
Farmingdale, NY 11735

Now or Never Copyright © 2024 Hazel Ro

ISBN 13: 978-1-64556-598-7
EBOOK ISBN: 978-1-64556-599-4

First Trade Paperback Printing June 2024
Printed in the United States of America

10 9 8 7 6 5 4 3 2 1

Distributed by Kensington Publishing Corp.
Submit Orders to:
Customer Service
400 Hahn Road
Westminster, MD 21157-4627
Phone: 1-800-733-3000
Fax: 1-800-659-2436

ACKNOWLEDGMENTS

Grateful is the only word I can use to describe the way I feel at this very moment in writing my acknowledgments. First and foremost, I must always thank my Heavenly Father. He is the one who gave me the gift of writing, a very vivid imagination full of creativity, as well as the dedication to complete my third novel in the past three years. I am overwhelmed with gratitude to be on this journey, and I am truly indebted to be able to touch a small part of the hearts and lives of those that come in contact with my books. Thank you, God, for choosing me and trusting me with this.

Then, it goes without saying that I must thank everyone with Urban Books, from Carl Weber, Martha Weber, Jasmine Weber, Karen, and anyone else behind the scenes. I thank you all from the bottom of my heart for working with me and your patience and dedication in getting my novels to where they need to be. You have all become like a family to me, and I would not want to work with any other publishing company. I especially thank my editor for this book, Diane Taber-Markiewicz. I appreciate your words of encouragement and your commitment to making this novel its best.

Then, as always, a heartfelt thanks goes to my family, friends, and each and every one of my new book friends. I can only hope that I have once again created a quality read that captures your hearts, minds, souls, and imaginations. I do this solely for you, so with that, I simply say thank you!

CHAPTER 1

MYA

Falling in love was starting to become such an un-orthodox thing. Growing up, I always dreamed that my high school sweetheart, Michael, and I would marry right after graduating from college. I would have had my dream destination wedding, saying *I Do* to the only man I'd ever truly loved as our feet kissed the sand of the Virgin Islands. We would have had a weeklong, luxury honeymoon fit perfectly for a king and queen as we made love under the moonlit stars every . . . single . . . night. Then afterward, we would have lived in a mansion-like home, living our best lives in our dream careers while also partnering in a joint business, all while traveling the world and whatnot for at least a couple of years. And finally, we would have settled down and had a baby boy named Michael Junior and a baby girl named Miriam. We would have had the perfect life and love as one of Atlanta's elite black power couples and families, all complete with a white picket fence and a dog named Max.

That was the way I thought things were supposed to be. At least, that was until I caught him behind the school's football field with his pants down in the back seat of his black Mustang and the high school's tramp, Tasha McMillan, sitting her bare-naked ass on top of his lap. I felt like I'd had an out-of-body experience that night as I smashed his foggy, sex-stained window with a brick while trying to climb through and strangle the bitch to death. The three of us ended up in the tussle of our lives until, out of nowhere, red and blue lights came flashing all around us, and officers threw each one of us to the ground, slapping handcuffs around our wrists. It took me forever to live down the humiliation of that night and the rejection I'd felt from the one person I thought would always be in my corner. Losing him had almost been unbearable for me. Yet, over time, I simply got over it; however, never forgetting. And as for Michael, all I'd gotten was an *"I'm sorry. I never meant for you to find out this way,"* as I remembered standing there looking like a deranged, lovesick girl while my heart shattered into a million little pieces.

After Michael decided against pressing any charges, he and Tasha, of course, had driven off into the sunset together as if I'd never existed. Later, I heard through a few of the neighborhood gossips that they later married each other and completed their family with a total of five children. Needless to say, I found out that after the fifth child, they'd divorced when Tasha caught him on top of his desk with his secretary. Karma was a real bitch for sure, and that was exactly the payback I felt she deserved for stealing the one and only person who I'd ever loved and desired to have a future with.

I guess one could say I actually dodged a bullet with Michael's low-down, dirty, lying, cheating ass, but honestly, although I was well past it all, love still hadn't been the same in my eyes ever since. True enough, I had a couple of relationships that lasted a year or more, and one even almost three. But they'd always somehow fizzled out either from hectic work-life schedules or simply losing interest in each other altogether. But no one at all had made my heart skip several beats the way Michael

Washington had, not even the man that was on top of me at the moment, affectionately known as my number two.

Here I lay, eyes shut tight, body slippery from the dripping moisture between my body and this half-man, half-creature that was dicking me down and about to break my headboard in two. For anyone on the outside looking in, they would have sworn that we were experiencing the most magical and sensational moment that could possibly be shared by two individuals—true soul-tying, satisfying intimacy—yet still, in my mind, something was missing. The love I once shared with Michael Washington was missing.

Here this man was, thrusting all his pleasure and pain in and out of me in a rhythmic, slow-winding motion type of way. He was so deep inside of my body that I could almost swear I felt his manhood in the pit of my belly, but honestly, that was it. He had no idea what I was truly feeling inside of my mind, inside of my heart, or, more so, inside of my soul. What I really wanted, needed, and longed for ever since my senior year of high school could only be summed up in one word. *Love.* Instead, however, he'd mistaken the tears that were beginning to flow from my eyes as a sweet expression of my gratification instead of what they truly were—simple reminders of what I didn't have with Michael and hadn't experienced with any other man. My number two and I were so close at that very moment but still couldn't have been further away from one another.

All at once, my mind traveled back to the very day that I'd come in contact with him. It was an average day for me, like any other day, except for having to go and get an oil change at my dealership directly after work. There I was, all dressed in my attorney attire: a black suit with a pencil skirt that fit my curves in all the right places, a white button-down blouse, and red bottom heels. I remembered, too, that I'd just gotten my hair done the day before, and my long, loose curls were still perfectly flowy and bouncy. I suspected that I could do some work while there because it normally took them at least an hour before my car was ready. So, with that in mind, I took my roller bag in, found a quiet space in the corner of the waiting room, and got to work. But then, after maybe ten minutes of being there, this god-like creature with all his muscles on display dressed in gray joggers and a wife beater came striding in. Being drawn to him was a mere understatement. My pussy got drenched in a matter of seconds, and I wanted to pounce on the man the second I laid eyes on him. The crazy thing about it was he was everything I was normally *not* attracted to. Although I liked his height and, of course, his physique, at that time, he had long dreads and wasn't dressed in a tailor-made suit, which was my usual. In other words, he had more of a roughneck nature about him instead of the clean-cut, well-manicured type of man that I was attracted to. Yet, I was still intrigued.

Not being the type of woman to approach a man, since men had always approached me, I waited, just knowing that he would try to initiate some type of conversation. But there was nothing. I'd even gotten up a few times to walk past him to allow him to see all my ass walk away, but nothing. We'd even made eye contact at times; I was sure to soften the muscles in my face and smile at him, but still, nothing. It wasn't until I saw the worker hand him his keys and he was about to leave that I decided to make some type of move. I gathered up all my things and acted as if I was leaving at the same time, and then it happened. Making it to the door at the exact same moment, he said, "Hey, ma," and opened the door for me.

At first, I wasn't totally sure if the *Hey, ma* was in reference to my age because I was sure I had a couple of years over him, but I quickly learned that was simply his nature. Once outside, I made up something quick in my head and asked if he knew where I could get some good barbeque. Immediately, I recalled the way he took his toothpick from his mouth and licked his lips before telling me the name of the spot. I said thanks, gave a little smirk, and told him I owed him one just to give a hint of interest, and boy, did he make sure I made good on my promise. After exchanging numbers, that night he stopped by and made certain I repaid him with not one, not two, or even three, but four orgasms for my little barbeque request. Needless to say, we'd been repaying one another in some of the best sexual gratification two could have since that day.

Now, at present, I tried to grip my legs around his waist as tight as I possibly could. I sank my nails into his back and pressed my face next to his while inhaling his scent of Versace Dylan Blue cologne and sweat all mixed together. Yet, there was still nothing. I was giving this man all of me, simply wanting to feel his love, but once again, what was happening could only be defined in three letters. S-E-X. And to tell the truth, I was beginning to be far beyond that. I'd had my share of wild, fun nights with no expectations of anything after twenty-four hours together. But now, I was at a point in my life where I needed far more than just good sex.

Well, wait a minute, let me take that back. With my number two, Kevin, it was more like *incredible, mind-blowing, on-a-natural-high* type of sex that left my legs trembling after multiple back-to-back orgasms. Yet now I needed that along with the feeling of being head over heels, completely in love. I wanted that special someone where our minds and souls connected on another level with one another—not just our bodies, and to be honest, Kevin just didn't offer that. I mean, when it came down to physical looks and his sexual know-how, he was a woman's dream. But beyond that, he didn't offer anything else. He and I never conversed about anything that truly mattered—religion, politics, our backgrounds, or even future dreams and aspirations. Our relationship, if that was what it could be known as, was based solely off what we shared in the bedroom . . . or kitchen, or car, or wherever else we found ourselves indulging.

It wasn't his fault, either. He'd told me from the day we met that he didn't want anything serious. He said that because he wasn't exactly where he wanted to be in life in order to settle down, he was just having fun. Initially, I was more than cool with it because I respected his honesty. Not to mention, the man was drop-dead fine. But that was all of two years ago, and nothing had changed the way I hoped it would. Plus, I was beginning to realize that I needed *substance* along with a good—no *fantastic*—dick-me-down session. I surely didn't want to let all of this go, but I also wasn't sure how much longer I could keep this up either.

As I drifted further in thought, I could feel it was almost time. His thrusting became faster, breathing and panting heavier—until . . . until . . .

"Kevin, stop . . . wait. Do you hear that?"

"No, baby. Hear what?" His strokes never stopped.

"That. Someone's knocking at my door!"

"So what? Let them knock. They'll go away."

"No, it's almost one in the morning, and I wasn't expecting anyone. I have to see who this is."

"Damn, woman. Right now?"

I sensed his instant displeasure with me as I pushed his body off mine, grabbed my silk robe, and wrapped it around me as I headed to the door. I had no clue who it could be, but they'd better have a damn good reason for banging on my door this time of the night.

The closer I got, the louder the banging was. I started to panic as I took *hot sauce* out of the closet next to the front door. Yeah, my Aunt Deidra and Beyoncé taught me well—always have protection nearby for anything or anyone unexpected. Standing there, my heart practically felt like it was about to jump completely out of my chest at any second, and I almost yelled for Kevin. At least, that was until I remembered the time some chick and a couple of her friends had followed him to my house. Part of me wondered if it was the same bold heffa that he promised me he was done with. If it was, I knew exactly what I was going to do this time around, so I decided to handle things on my own.

I tried to be as quiet as possible as I debated on whether I wanted to yank the door open or ask who it was first. Then I stood on my tippy toes to look out of the peephole and confirm my prior suspicions. But to my surprise, I laid eyes on some old lady dressed in her flowered nightgown, robe, bonnet, and pink house shoes.

Who in the hell? I thought to myself. She had to have the wrong house, so I left my bat in the corner behind the door and opened it, prepared to tell her just that.

"I'm sorry, ma'am, but you—"

"Where the hell is he?" she yelled with a strong, deep, and forceful tone.

I looked at this woman like she was crazy, knowing good and well *she* couldn't possibly be looking for Kevin. In an attempt to quiet her down so she wouldn't wake up the rest of the damn neighborhood, I spoke softly.

"Ma'am, can you please lower your—"

"I'm not lowering a damn thing until you tell me where Tyrone is, and I know he's in there. He thinks he's going to run his tail over here with you every other night while he leaves his damn kids with me. Oh, hell no, I don't think so. And *you*. Lady, you should be ashamed of your

old self messing with a little twenty-five-year-old boy that
can barely take care of himself or his kids. Hell, the boy
doesn't even have a job, let alone a pot to piss in. So, what
do you want with him anyway? You know what? Don't
even answer that because I just know it's something
ungodly. But I'll tell you one thing. Keep messing with
him, and I promise, I'm going to send him and those kids
right on over here with your ass."

"Exactly how old are you, anyway, honey?" she had the
nerve to ask in the middle of all her ranting while looking me up and down and barging her large-framed body
into my home and glancing around. If I hadn't been at a
total loss for words, I would have been cussing by now,
but this was what I got for giving my number to the little
boy who worked at the gas station I frequent every morning. I only had him around because of the way he boosted
my ego. He had a way of making me feel young and vibrant. He was my number four—my just in case one, two,
or three didn't work out—but now I knew for sure I had
to cut him loose. Thank goodness I had only been intimate with him once. Or was it twice? Anyway, it seemed
it was enough to get him hooked to where both he and
his grandmother came showing up at my home unexpect-
edly.

The large old lady continued yelling at me and calling
out for Tyrone, until Kevin came from the bedroom in
the back with a towel wrapped around his waist. Her
loudness stopped all at once, and I could have sworn I
heard her sucking her teeth while she studied his muscular, dark-skinned physique that was still glistening with
small beads of sweat. The old biddy looked mesmerized,
to say the least, like she hadn't seen a man's body in the
last twenty or thirty years as we both watched his towel
hang on for dear life.

"Can we help you, ma'am?" Kevin asked in his baritone
voice.

"Uh, uh, no, sir," she said quickly while straightening up her whole act. "I thought my . . . you know what . . . never mind. I'm so sorry I disturbed you all."

Just that second, we watched her walk out without another word. Then, without having a chance to gather my thoughts, Kevin looked at me with a million questions but still didn't say a thing. He simply walked up close, loosened my robe, and let it fall to the floor. Then he dropped his towel and picked me up. Right away, he finished right there against the wall what we had started in the bedroom, and just that quick, I had forgotten all about love and substance, Michael and Tasha, or whatever other squibble-squabble I was thinking about in the back of my mind before Granny showed up. I needed a release after that chaos, and he was definitely the one to give it to me.

So, once again, love would have to wait. But I had already made up my mind—not for long. I wanted what I wanted, even if I had to make the sacrifice of being alone until it found me. With that in mind, I held on tight to his body and enjoyed the ride for what might be my last time with my number two.

CHAPTER 2

MYA

The second I hopped into my white Range Rover and threw all of my belongings into the passenger seat, I glanced at the display on my dashboard to see exactly how much time I had to get through the morning traffic. A difference in even five minutes would tell me whether I could glide my way through on cruise control or weave in and out like a bat out of hell. Luckily, it was one of those mornings when I had enough time to cruise and possibly even stop by Starbucks for my caffeine fix. As exhausted as I felt from last night's activities, sugar and caffeine were definitely a must. Not to mention, I was positive that my day would more than likely include some very eventful and dramatic storytelling by my best friend and co-worker, Alize. She and her children's father, Anthony, always had some type of shenanigans going on that I had to brace myself for and be prepared whether I wanted to hear it or not.

As I made my way to the heavenly yet ungodly taste of the cinnamon roll Frappuccino, I connected my cell phone to my truck and turned on my Pandora station. It was right at the beginning of Jazmine Sullivan's "Girl Like Me," and I couldn't help but sing my heart out as her lyrics reminded me once again of my breakup with Michael all those years ago. Like she said, I would have given whatever he asked, but chicks like Tasha McMillan kept winning.

You must've wanted somethin' different. Still don't know what I was missin'. What you asked I would've given. It ain't right how these hoes be winnin'. Why they be winnin'? No hope for a girl like me. How come they be winnin'? And I ain't wanna be, but you gon' make a ho out of me.

I knew deep down that it was probably immature of me to feel the way I did, and Alize always told me that I was too old to still be *whining,* as she put it, over someone from high school. And truth be told, maybe she was right. But I still blamed him for my having to deal with four separate men to make one good one. I blamed him for the fact that I wasn't a wife by now. And I especially blamed him for not being my happily ever after. So, if immaturity was the end result of all of that, then so be it, immature I was.

Thirty minutes later, I was pulling up to my office at New Horizons Family Law. After studying law in college, I became a divorce attorney for one of the major law firms here in Atlanta. How ironic was it that here I was in search of my happily ever after while assisting others in the demise of theirs? But it was the profession I'd chosen, so a girl had to do what she had to do.

Walking in, I went through my whole morning routine of saying hello to Milton, the firm's doorman and security guard, chatting with Diane, the office's front desk assistant, stopping by the café to toss my lunch in the refrigerator, and finally heading to the second floor where my office and Alize's desk was. I hadn't set my frappé down or made it behind my desk before Alize and her four children entered the office like a whole tsunami.

"Sit down right there on the floor, y'all, and cut out all the noise. Champagne, Hennessy, Moet, and Moscato, did you hear what I said? Quiet down," she yelled, drowning out their chattering and crying and fussing with one another.

"Alize, what are the children doing here again? I thought we talked about this before, and I clearly said that this couldn't be an all-the-time type of thing."

"I'm sorry, Mya, but I had no other choice," she explained as she pulled each child over to her and slapped a palm of Vaseline on their faces. "It's all Anthony's fault."

I walked over to close the door to my office just in case any of the other partners came strolling down to the second floor. They had a habit of making their way down there sometime during the day, and I was sure it was only to see all of Alize's curves stuffed in her fashionable, trendy, and very sexy daily attire. However, I couldn't take a chance on them seeing the children there yet again. Although I knew that they respected me as an attorney, I wasn't exactly sure that they had that same respect for Alize, my executive assistant and friend. She was a bit rough around the edges, to say the least. She stood about five-foot-six and had a very curvaceous body, with her breasts, hips, and buttocks being well-defined and everything else falling in all the right places. In fact, there was no way anyone who didn't know her would think that she had four small children. Her skin was a dark, buttery and silky brown complexion. Her natural coils were beautifully voluminous and bold, but no one would ever know it from the various wigs she wore, which this week seemed to be the long and straight platinum blonde one. And her eyes, which in my opinion were her prettiest feature, were big, bold, and very intriguing. They appeared to be as innocent as a child's laughter. Well, that is when they weren't all weighed down with heavy and lengthy false lashes. She had a small, pudgy type of nose and full, plump lips that rounded out her face.

I always told her that she didn't need all the extra and that her natural beauty was more than enough, but she was simply the type of woman who loved her lashes, long nails, and lace front wigs with homemade baby hairs, and no one was going to tell her any different—especially not me, who was more of a plain Jane. Besides, her outward appearance was all a part of her big and bold personality that she tried so hard to portray. However, I knew the real Alize behind all the glitz and glam.

She and I met when I first graduated from college and moved to Atlanta. We were customer service reps for a company that we both despised. She was a bit over the top, and I really didn't see us being anything more than coworkers, but somehow, we had grown to be the closest of friends. In fact, I promised her that when I got my own firm, she would definitely come and work for me. So, it was a no-brainer when the previous administrative assistant left and the position became available. And in return, she promised that I would have an ongoing discount at the clothing store she dreamt of opening one day.

Slowly but surely, I came to find out that my friend was soft and extremely sensitive underneath the fabulous exterior. And what I loved most was that she had a heart as pure as gold. Alize would have no qualms about giving me or anyone the shirt off her back, and I absolutely loved that about her.

My only wish was that her trifling, good-for-nothing baby daddy could finally see the diamond in the rough that he had in my friend. I hated feeling the way I did about Anthony because she loved him with all of her heart, but I simply didn't like him and felt she could do ten times better. They'd been together for seven years, and she still had nothing at all to show for it. He hadn't been able to keep a steady nine-to-five job. He didn't help her pay any of the bills in her Section 8 home, which he shouldn't have been residing in in the first place. He always reeked of marijuana and wore jailhouse braids that were so juvenile to me. I'd always felt that when a grown man became a certain age, he should grow out of certain fashions and be more clean-cut. But, outside of the looks and all, I just wanted him to help her more with the children so she didn't have to feel like a single mother even with a man in the house.

"All right, so what did Anthony do this time?" I questioned while making myself comfortable to hear the next episode of the *Alize and Anthony Show*.

"Girl, can you believe this man had the nerve to stroll in my house at two in the morning, drunk, and just tried to crawl up in my bed without any explanation? I laid there for a second, pissed, of course, waiting for him to say something. But in a matter of minutes, he started snoring, and I heard his cell phone buzzing. Do you know some female had the nerve to text him asking if he'd made it home safely?"

"Um, maybe we should finish talking about this when the kids are gone."

"Naw, we are good because they might be young, but my babies are smart, and they know how good for nothing their daddy is, too. Anyway, I pushed his drunk behind out of my bed onto the floor. He woke right up, trying to figure out what was going on, but I wasn't asking him anything about the text just to hear a bunch of lies. Instead, I pushed him all the way to the front door and told him to get the hell out of my house and don't come back unless he was coming to pick up his belongings."

Other than the playful noises from the babies, there was total silence in the room after that. Alize stared at me long and hard. "So, what do you have to say, Mya? Because I know you're thinking something."

"No, no, I don't have anything at all to say," I said, trying not to look her way because I was sure that she knew I was lying.

"Yes, you do. That's why you can't look at me right now," she said, standing there with her hands on her hips and giving me a stern look that damn near made me feel like one of the children in the room. "Mya, I know you're thinking that me and Anthony go through this all the time and that I'm just going to take him right back. But this time, you're wrong. I'm sick of this, and I really think it's time to call it quits."

"Well, girl, look. I can't say that I would blame you if you did. I mean, you should be tired of going through this week after week with him, and honestly, I don't think it's at all healthy for the kids. You deserve so much more than what he's been giving you, and as the old saying goes, honey, you can do bad all by yourself."

I saw the huge puddles of water beginning to form in her big eyes, and as I went over to hug her, we heard a knock at the door. Walking over to the desk, I grabbed some tissue from her tissue box before seeing who was there. We didn't need anyone in the building to get into our personal business. To my surprise, though, I wish I'd never opened it and wanted to slam the door shut the second I saw his pathetic ass standing there. He looked exactly like she'd said—like he'd been drunk and was now getting over a hangover. Still appearing as if he hadn't even thought about showering, because I could tell he must have been wearing the same wrinkled clothing from last night, he hesitated to speak.

"Um, hey, Mya, is Alize available?" he said, barely able to look at me in my eyes.

"She's here," was all I could say as I pushed the door open wide, and before I knew it, the two older kids hopped up, running toward him, shouting, "Daddy!"

"Hey, Zae," he quietly said to her with sad, puppy dog eyes.

I watched intensely to see if she would speak and what she would say, but I was in complete shock when there was nothing. She only stood there with her arms crossed, not even looking in his direction. A second later, he walked closer to her.

"Baby, I'm so sorry," he spoke softly, pleading over her and throwing his arms around her like I'd witnessed him do a million times before. "Please forgive me, Zae. Please. I messed up, but I promise it will never happen again."

At that point, I almost wished I had a bucket of popcorn in front of me because this was usually the time when all the dramatics would come in. Instead, I could see Alize was trying her hardest to keep her guard up. She only handed him the keys to her car before saying in a very straightforward way with no emotion, "The kids need to get to daycare before they charge me extra, and I get off at exactly five. Please don't be late. Then, at that time, we can discuss which direction we should go from here."

There was no 'I forgive you, baby,' no cursing him out or acting a fool the way he was used to, no hug or kiss good-bye or anything. Alize was very matter-of-fact in her words and tone, and I couldn't have been prouder of her. In fact, I wanted to give her applause with a standing ovation. But instead, I simply gave her an imaginary high-five and said, *Yes, bitch,* in the back of my head.

CHAPTER 3

ALIZE

The office had been pretty serene for a couple of hours once Anthony and the children left, mainly because I had been in my feelings regarding our situation and because I was sure that whatever Mya wanted to say, she'd decided against unless she wanted to feel my wrath. Although she was my closest friend, I was in no mood for her to talk bad about my man the way she usually did; especially since I wasn't altogether sure what I was going to do about us. But mostly because she was in no position to talk about or judge my relationship with my children's father. Good or bad, I'd been with him for the past seven years, while she'd been juggling four different men for two. I loved my friend dearly but hated the way that she could come off extremely judgmental when people didn't live up to her high standards.

I kept trying to think of ways to ease the tension in the room, but before I had a chance to break the ice, in walked Leslie Tolliver from the fourth floor.

"Hi, ladies. How are y'all doing today?" she asked in a Southern drawl while walking right in, in her loud and boisterous way and looking at me up and down from head to toe. Anyone who had been in the building for at least the last four years knew that we really didn't like one another. For one, everyone knew that she was always trying to compete with me, whether it was the way I dressed, my hair, or even my nails. She always wanted to outdo me, but little did she realize, she couldn't outdo the originator of it. And the second reason was her interaction with my man.

It all happened way back when Anthony came to pick me up from work. She was being a little too talkative and flirty with him, in my opinion. So, in the nicest way possible, which frankly wasn't nice at all, I asked her to address me and me only, and not Anthony. She happened to mumble some stuff under her breath like what she had to say to him was none of my business, and the next thing I knew, I'd snatched her wig off her head, punched her in the face, and we were rolling and tussling on the ground like two teenage high schoolers fighting on the playground. Since that day, we'd both played nice with one another just to keep our jobs, but I was sure I'd gotten my point across, and she knew exactly how far *not* to go when it came to Anthony.

"How can we help you, Leslie?" I said, stone-faced and without all the fake pleasantries.

"Well, I really only stopped down here to speak and see how y'all's weekend was. Mine? Oh, my goodness ladies, it was so fantastic. I went out with this new guy that I met a few weeks ago. He's so amazingly handsome and charming. I still can't believe I actually met someone like him online. Anyway, he took me to the new five-star restaurant over in Buckhead for cocktails and appetizers. It's called Aveline. Have you heard of it or been there before, Mya?" she asked, completely bypassing me as if I wasn't familiar with any five-star establishments.

What got me most, though, was that she was talking like we really cared about her weekend or who she'd met. My words started to form on my lips to say that we didn't give a damn one bit, but of course, my very diplomatic boss and friend entertained her. "Yes, Leslie. Um, I went with a friend the week that they opened. It's very nice and attractive inside."

"Yeah, that's what I thought too, Mya. I loved it and can't wait to go again. Oh, and I'm sure your children's father will be able to take you there one day too, Alize." She grinned, waving over to me. I wanted desperately to just slap that smug grin from her face, but Mya was eyeing me in a way to say just let it go.

"Speaking of your children's father," she continued without hesitation. "I saw that he came by this morning to get your kids. Are you guys still together? When are the two of you getting married? Because, if you don't mind me saying it, it seems like you all have been playing house for quite some time now, haven't you?"

All right, that was it for me. I had held my peace long enough. "You know what, Leslie—"

"Um, Leslie, I'm sorry, but I have a lot that I need to go over with Alize. We have a very important meeting with a client this afternoon, and I need to debrief her. Do you mind if we finish this conversation later?"

"Oh, no, not at all. I need to get back to my floor anyway, but it was nice chatting with you two, and maybe the three of us can go to Aveline for drinks after work one day. Anyway, have a good day, ladies. Toodles!" She kicked her foot back and left like she'd really done something.

"Why did you stop me, Mya? You know she was asking for exactly what was coming her way." I scowled while closing the door to our office.

"I know, which is the very reason I stepped in. You can't always let Leslie get to you the way she does. I believe that's the only reason she does it in the first place, because she can see it bothers you so much."

"That's not the reason, Mya, and we know it. She's still salty that I whooped her tail for flirting with Anthony all those years ago, so she continually tries to find any way that she can to get up under my skin."

"And, if you know this, then why do you let it happen? Girl, just smile and go about your merry way. Showing her how unbothered you are by her stunts will piss her off more than you think."

"Yeah, that's the polite and ladylike way to go about it, but you and I both know that's just not my style. One day she's going to catch me on the wrong day when you're not around to protect her, and I'm going to have her ass on that ground once again."

We both looked at each other and burst out laughing at the thought of what happened back then. Although I didn't see anything at all funny at the time that it happened, it was surely something we joked about and got a good laugh about now. Quickly, I realized that Leslie coming down here was a good thing because she was just the ice we needed to break the tension between Mya and me. Before the silence settled in the room once again, I continued in on Leslie.

"Why do you think she comes down here all the time anyway? I mean, there's plenty of other people in the office that she could bother. And those people may just like her, unlike us."

"I don't know. I have a feeling that she might feel more comfortable with us because, you know, the obvious. Besides Milton, the three of us are the only African American women in the building, and she can probably relate to us better. Plus, I don't think she has much family here in Atlanta. When she first started, I remembered her telling me about an aunt and a couple of cousins, but they weren't all that close."

"Wow, you almost make me feel a little sorry for the woman. I can't imagine living in a state where I don't have anyone close at all."

"Yeah, it's like we all work together day in and day out, and we know the *work* persona of one another. But honestly, we don't truly know what each of us might be experiencing outside of these walls. Except for me and you, that is." She got up and handed me a manilla folder she'd been working on. "Can you make me three sets of these documents, please?"

"Sure." I got up to go to the copier but kept talking. "So, you never shared with me how your weekend was."

"Girl, it was nothing eventful, trust me. Friday, after we left, I grabbed some takeout and relaxed for the evening. Saturday, I deep cleaned my home, did the laundry, went grocery shopping, and then hung out with my mother and two aunts that evening. However, that didn't last long because the whole conversation all evening was, '*When is Mya going to find a good and decent man to marry?*' And finally, last night, I saw my number two, and I guess you could say everything was cool until my number four's grandmother came knocking on the door."

"Girl, what? His grandmother?" I said with my mouth hanging wide open, no longer focusing on the copier.

"Zae, the woman was dressed in her housecoat and slippers, all right. She basically came looking for him while in the process calling me old and wondering what I was doing dealing with someone so young who didn't own anything or have a J-O-B, for that matter. Then she had the nerve to say that she was going to send him and his children to live with me."

"Oh, no." I covered my chest in disbelief. "And where was Kevin in all of this? Did he have anything to say?"

"Now, you know that man doesn't care about anything but getting his rocks off, and that's it. So no, he didn't have anything to say."

"Wow, and you said it was nothing eventful. Girl, please. Your life could be on someone's movie screen," I said, finishing up the copies and stapling them together before handing them back to her.

"Thanks. But, Zae, I don't think that I can do this anymore."

"What's that?"

"Deal with all these men just to make *the perfect man*. I mean, I'm thirty-seven and no closer to getting married than I was ten years ago. Something's got to give already."

"Chile, marriage is nothing to rush into, and I think it's a little overrated anyway. Me and Anthony always say that if you're happy, that's all that matters . . . with or without a ring."

"Well, that's easy for you to say when you have your live-in common-law husband right there with you. You don't have to choose from man after man every other night."

"Having a live-in or *common-law* husband, as you put it, is not all it's cracked up to be either. Hell, you saw that this morning for yourself. You don't go through any unnecessary drama with the same person over and over again. But you, on the other hand, have the freedom of seeing who you want, if you want, and when you want. I don't think it gets any better than that."

"I do. Girl, I just want that one man who gets me in every single way. That man that is my provider, protector, my confidant, my lover, my business partner . . . my best friend. And I don't think I'm asking for too much."

"In some ways, you are, and some you're not. It doesn't seem like the men these days desire love and commitment the way we do or the type of marriages our parents had. We're living in a whole different age and time. But then again, if there's a man who wants what you want, he's never going to come your way with all that you have going on. Maybe you should just take a little time to yourself and not focus so much on your one, two, three, or four. Then, I'm sure before you know it, God will send the right man into your life, if he's not already there."

"I don't know. Every time I think about leaving each one of them alone, I feel like I'm just going to end up being some lonely, depressed, sexless and horny forty-year-old woman with nothing but a rose sex toy at home to keep her happy. And I need more than that, Zae. I want something solid, real, and healthy. I'm ready for a husband and family. Aren't you? You and Anthony have been together seven whole years and have four beautiful children together. Aren't you ready to be his wife and not just his girlfriend and children's mother?"

"Of course I am, Mya. I want Anthony to make me his wife one day more than anything, but he has to do it in his time. I damn sure don't want to pressure the man into spending the rest of his life with me."

"So, are you telling me that in the meantime, he gets a roof over his head, he doesn't have to pay any bills, he can lay up with you and make child after child, all with no commitment?"

"Well, you sure sound like you have it all figured out, huh," I shot at her, feeling somewhat attacked.

"No, please, don't take it the wrong way. All I'm trying to say is we should both want more in a man and in our relationships. We should both desire to be someone's wife with a covenant and a commitment, not just their part-time lover or roommate. We are both beautiful, strong, educated women who should have someone catering to us the way we cater to them. At least that's what I want, and to be honest, I want mine to happen now or never."

"I hear you, girl. But first of all, what do you know about a covenant? When is the last time you've been to anyone's church, Mya Anderson?"

"Look, I read from time to time or catch a sermon here or there on YouTube. I know a little."

"All right then, what are you going to do about it, *Ms. Now or Never*? Are you finally ready to let the quadruplets go and wait on God to send you something real, or do you think the perfect guy might possibly be one in the deck?"

She giggled a little at my depiction of the four men in my life before responding. "Well, Tyrone would be easy to let go. There's no way I can ever see him again after his grandmother's shenanigans last night. Besides, I knew he was too young for me in the very beginning. I don't have time to teach a grown man how to be a man. Then my number three, Will, he might be fairly easy to let go as well because he's just too . . . I don't know . . . church boyish for me. I really can't see myself being with him long term either."

"Church boyish? What the hell?" I interrupted and laughed out loud at her comment. "Girl, now he might be the very one you need. Weren't you the one just talking about God and a covenant a second ago, and now you're saying someone is too church boyish?"

"Yeah, but he's a bit boring too. Everything we talk about turns out to be a sermon or spiritual lesson with him. It's like he never lets his guard down to just relax and be . . . human. Hell, he's so holy and sanctified that we've never once been intimate with each other or at least come close to kissing. Girl, the man even gives me church hugs when he sees me."

"So, what's wrong with that?"

"Zae, he wants to wait until marriage for intimacy and intercourse."

"And again, what is wrong with that? At least you'll know that you were his one and only."

"Okay, sure, it sounds great in theory, but can I really go without something that I get on a regular basis right now? Especially trying to go from someone spectacular in the bedroom to someone who might be mediocre at best. I mean, like I said, the man has barely even hugged or kissed me or made my damn nipples stand at attention. Am I really supposed to expect him to suddenly be this sexual god on our wedding night? I just don't want to get with him and end up cheating on the man because my needs aren't being met, all right?"

Trying to contain my laughter, I moved right along. "Okay, so that takes care of two of them, and I'll even dare to say three of them, because you know I can't stand Charles. He shouldn't even be in the running."

"Zae, Charles is my number one and the *only one* I would consider a real relationship with, out of all four men. We've been together the longest, a little over two years now. He has the financial means to take care of me, and the time we have been intimate was cool. His sex, I would say, was decent."

"Cool and decent, huh? Really? So, you're going to accept cool and decent over your sexual god, Kevin?"

"That's not what I'm saying, but I don't think that I would have the desire to cheat on him. Anyway, why do you dislike him so much? What has he ever done to you, Alize?"

"It's not so much what he's done to me. It's how I watch him treat you. Plus, he's just so cocky and arrogant. Then there's the fact that I can't stand how he looks at me, like I'm so much less than him or something. And have I mentioned the way he practically bosses you around? Girl, I'd much rather you be with Kevin if you're going to choose one of them. At least he is fine, and you know you'll be sexually satisfied with him."

"Yes, that's very true, but Kevin and I just aren't on the same page. He keeps saying that he doesn't want a relationship right now and he's focusing solely on establishing his business."

"All right, he doesn't want a relationship, yet he's over there giving you the business every other night? I see."

"Trust me, if he thought differently, I would probably be with him in a heartbeat, but just like you said, who wants to pressure someone into being with them? But, as for Charles, I just think that you don't know him the way I do. It's a little true that he can be a little arrogant, but that's only because the man is an Alpha male with money, power, and prestige. He's basically entitled to be that way. And I'll apologize on his behalf if you think he looks at you as less than. I'm sure that's not his intention at all. You two just need to get to know one another a lot better, that's it."

"I think I already know more than enough to know about him. But, Mya, if he's so perfect, and seeing that you've been with him the longest, then what's been the need for number two, three, or four? Why not just date him exclusively?"

"Honestly, I don't know. Something is just missing with me and him. I mean, when we're together, we have a wonderful time. We can talk about a little of anything and everything. He's established, well-off, and in some ways ambitious. All the things that I want in a mate. But still, sometimes, things seem a little off, and he seems—"

"Shallow? Conniving? Disrespectful? Superficial?" I cut her off. "I think any of those words would work."

"No, none of those describe the real him, Alize. I was going to say he just seems . . . not ready."

I rolled my eyes at her while she gazed off into never-never land while still talking about the man. My friend may have thought I'd been mistaken when it came to Charles, but I was positive that I knew his type very well. Plus, I usually got the most eerie and uncomfortable feeling whenever he came around. Then, when it came to Kevin, I felt that he could say a million times he was focused on his business and didn't want a relationship, but being a man that fine told me otherwise. I figured that if anything, he just didn't want a relationship with *her* and in fact, was more than likely involved with someone else already. I didn't know much about Will, however, to think one way or the other about him because she simply didn't give him the time of day. I only hoped she wouldn't live to regret her choices because I was sure some other woman would eventually snatch up his very saved, sanctified, and boring self. And Tyrone was simply a non-factor from day one. I wasn't sure what void he was filling in her life and hoped she was being sincere in calling it quits with him.

A few minutes later, there was another knock at our door, and I prayed that Leslie hadn't made her way back down to the second floor. Opening the door, however, I saw nothing but dark-skinned legs in Khaki-colored shorts and a bouquet of at least a hundred roses covering someone's face.

"Hello. I have a delivery for Ms. Mya Anderson," the gentleman said in a deep but pleasant tone.

"Oh, my goodness." Mya hopped up from her desk. "Are you sure all of these are for me?"

"They sure are." The handsome gentleman with pearly white teeth smiled as he peeked around the roses. "Looks like someone has quite an admirer, and I can definitely see why."

Mya blushed from ear to ear as he handed the flowers to her. "Oh, let me grab you something for your trouble."

"Nope, no need at all, beautiful. The tip has already been taken care of by the sender. So, you ladies have a wonderful rest of the day and enjoy your roses. Oh, and if by chance this guy somehow messes up, give me a call," he said, still smiling while handing her his card, which she took graciously. As soon as he left, though, Mya threw his card on her desk and went right in.

"Zae, who could these be from? Wait, silly me, they have to have come from Charles. Only he would do something so romantic and extravagant. And besides, no one else I'm dealing with could possibly afford these but him."

"Well, I don't see a card anywhere, so whoever sent them wanted to keep you guessing."

"I don't have to guess, Zae. When you're connected to someone the way Charles and I are, it's second nature. He's probably waiting next to his phone for me to call and thank him."

I watched her blush and carry on like a teenage girl in love, and honestly, it was sickening. I hated Charles for more reasons than one, and I couldn't wait for my best friend to finally see his true colors.

CHAPTER 4

MYA

I pulled out my cell phone to FaceTime Charles to thank him for the wonderful gesture. He must have been waiting for my call because he answered on the very first ring.

"Hi, sweetie," I said to him while grinning from ear to ear, almost unable to keep my composure.

"Hey, Mya. I was actually just thinking about you and going to give you a call."

"I'm sure you were, and trust me, I couldn't call you fast enough either. Baby, they are absolutely beautiful."

"What's absolutely beautiful?" he questioned with a puzzled look written across his face, like he had no idea what I was talking about.

"The bouquet of one hundred red roses that you sent, silly," I said, trying to pick them up and hold my phone at the same time for him to see them. "I love them and can't wait to show you how much."

"Oh, okay. Well, uh, maybe you can show me how much this evening. That's kind of what I needed to talk to you about. I have a dinner date with an associate and his wife, so I'll need you to join me."

"Um, sure, of course, but actually, that wasn't the kind of *show you how much* I was referring to."

"I know, and I'm sorry, sweetie, but this is a very important dinner meeting, and I can't have any mishaps whatsoever. So, what do you have on right now?"

"Oh, just some simple white slacks and a black blouse. But I have some jewelry here in the office that I can dress it up with."

"No, that won't do. Why don't you run home after work and throw on the little black dress I bought you with the black heels? Then come back to the office, and I'll pick you up from there because the restaurant is closer to where you work."

"Charles, that's a lot of going back and forth that I really don't feel like doing. Trust me, I think what I have on already will be just fine."

"No, it won't, Mya, so please don't debate me on this and don't mess this night up for me, all right. Just be the woman on my arm and sit beside me at the table, try not to overeat or say anything out of the way. As a matter of fact, you don't have to say much at all. Just be your beautiful self. Nothing more, nothing less."

"Wow, are you sure you'll even need me there?"

"C'mon now, Mya, don't be that way. You know what I mean."

"All right. Of course, Charles," I said, not quite feeling as jovial and vibrant as I had when I first called.

"Anyway, I'll be by your office around six or six-thirty. All right?"

"Sure, okay."

We disconnected, and immediately, I could feel Alize staring at me almost the same way I had watched her earlier with Anthony.

"What, Alize?" I asked with a heavy sigh.

"I haven't said a word," she said, holding her arms up as if she were completely innocent. "I mean, if you like a man telling you what to wear and what not to eat or what not to say, then that's your choice. If you like it, I love it."

"Look, I told you that you just don't understand Charles. Like he said, this is a very important meeting, and I'm sure that he's under a lot of pressure. That's why he's talking and behaving the way he is. That's all."

"Oh, I see. So, being under pressure gives him permission to act like a real jerk. And by the way, he didn't sound very convincing that he's the one that sent those roses either. But I'm going to zip my mouth and stay out of it."

"Please do. Why don't you do just that, all right?"

We both went into our separate corners before either of us said anything further that we would regret later. Then, maybe all of ten minutes later, my cell phone began to ring with the one person's name I wasn't expecting to hear from scrolling across the front of it.

"It's Will," I said aloud, breaking our quick little silent treatment.

"Okay, are you going to answer or just sit there looking at the phone?"

"I don't know. I wonder what he could want."

"Well, you won't find out unless you answer," she answered back sarcastically while tapping her fingers on her desk.

Although I really didn't want to talk to him, I went ahead and picked up before my voicemail caught it. I was super curious as to what he wanted because he'd never called me during my hours of work.

"Hi, Will." I tried to sound upbeat but was positive my dryness probably still came through.

"Hey there, pretty lady. How are you doing today?"

"I'm good, but a little surprised to hear from you. You normally don't call while I'm working."

"I know, but I couldn't wait until later to hear your voice. Plus, you should have gotten quite a surprise this afternoon."

"A surprise? From you?" I questioned what he was referring to.

"Yep, from yours truly."

"The only thing I got were . . . oh my goodness . . . you weren't the one that sent the flowers, were you?" I asked, with Alize gawking at me.

"I sure am. All one hundred. Do you like them?"

"Um, um . . . yes, of course. They're beautiful." My heart sank that they hadn't actually come from Charles like I had thought.

"I know you probably think that I went a little bit overboard, but a little over three months ago was our first date. So, I thought it was only befitting that I got one hundred roses—a rose for each day."

"Will, I can't begin to tell you how thoughtful that was. I truly appreciate it."

"Uh, is everything all right? You don't quite sound like yourself."

"Oh, sure, everything is fine. Just pretty busy with work, that's all."

"Yeah, I understand, so I'll hurry up and let you go. But before I do, how would you like to join me for dinner this evening?"

"Dinner? Tonight? You mean to tell me that you don't have some kind of church service to attend?" I said jokingly but was dead serious.

"No, Mya, not tonight. Bible study is tomorrow evening, and I do hope you'll join me for that one day. But tonight, I would love to just be in your beautiful presence."

"I'm so sorry, Will, but I have a ton of work that I need to catch up on. Maybe we can try for another night."

"Um, sure, that's fine. Just try not to work too hard, all right? I'll talk to you later."

We hung up, and there was Alize, standing there with her arms folded across her chest, staring at me as if she were about to reprimand one of her children.

"What?"

"A ton of work, Mya? Maybe some other night? You don't like him and never plan on seeing him, so why didn't you just tell the man the truth?"

"Oh, like I was supposed to come right out and say, *'Hey, you're a little too spiritual for me and quite boring. I don't think we should see one another anymore.'* Was I really supposed to say that after he sent me a hundred damn roses?"

"If that's the honest-to-God truth, then yes. It would be much better than him waiting around until you finally decide to be straightforward with him or until he finally decides to give up entirely. And speaking of roses, why didn't your *lover man* come clean and tell you he *wasn't* the one that sent them? You know what? Don't answer. I'll tell you why. Because he's a good-for-nothing, low-down creep that gets off on telling his women what to do. Who would expect a man like that to be honest?"

"Alize, that's enough, okay." I found myself raising my voice at her. "You don't want me saying a bunch of negative things about Anthony, so don't go saying negative things about Charles, someone that you really don't know."

"Okay," she said with a ton of attitude still in her tone and her face all frowned up.

"Okay?"

"Okay." She tried to lighten up a bit.

But no matter how frustrated she made me, she was actually kind of right about a couple of things. Maybe I should have told Will the truth—that I never planned on dating him or that I couldn't see a future with him. Maybe I owed him that much. Then, I couldn't help but wonder how he could afford to do something so lavish as a hundred roses. Outside of his sanitation position, which I was sure probably didn't pay that much, I wasn't aware of any other sources of income. To top things off was Charles. Why hadn't he told me the truth instead of allowing me to believe that he was the one who sent the roses? Part of me wanted to cancel dinner with him entirely for lying in my face. But truth be told, I didn't want to go home alone tonight to nothing but takeout dinner, a bottle of wine, and my rose. I almost wanted to bounce my concerns off my best friend, but it seemed that we continued to bump heads every other hour during the day, so I figured I'd just leave well enough alone.

CHAPTER 5

ALIZE

Mya had left a little over an hour ago to rush home and get ready for her dinner date. I still hated the fact that she was going, but one thing I'd learned about my friend was that once she got something wrapped around her mind, it was hard to shift her in the opposite direction. So, I knew that no matter how I'd pointed out Charles's flaws and shortcomings, she would never see it the way I did unless he did something drastically wrong, and even then, I wasn't sure if she would leave him alone.

She was so infatuated with the man that it almost seemed like a repeat of her relationship with Michael she'd described to me long ago. The way she painted a picture of him made him out to be a real jerk in my eyes, too, but in hers, he could do no wrong, and now Charles was surely his twin flame. I supposed that maybe that was simply the type of guy that she was attracted to, the same way Anthony was mine. We both liked the bad boy type, even if they weren't what we truly needed in our lives.

After packing my belongings, I decided to go down to the front door and wait for Anthony to get there. I had still been racking my brain, trying to figure out what I was going to do about our situation—whether or not I would give him yet another chance or if this was truly the final straw. No matter what Mya or anyone else thought, I loved him, and when things were good, they were incredibly good. But now, it was beginning to seem like the bad was occurring more and more often and outweighing any good we once shared. In fact, the only thing that had kept him around as of late were the children. My babies loved and adored their father because, to tell the truth, that's the one thing he'd gotten right. We'd had some beautiful children together, and he took so much pride and joy in parenting them. It was being a good, faithful, and committed partner and mate that he needed to work on.

Making my way to the front door, I gave a huge sigh of relief when I saw Leslie a few steps ahead of me and about to exit. There was no way I could deal with any of her sarcastic comments or remarks, plus I didn't want her bumping into Anthony again when he arrived to pick me up. I slowed my pace down to give her enough time to get into her car and drive off completely. However, once I'd made it to the front door, I still saw her car sitting there along with a black SUV that had pulled up on the side of her. Standing in the corner of the doorway so that I couldn't be visibly seen, I peered out the glass door, watching them. Charles seemed quite friendly with her. A little too friendly, in my opinion. So, I cracked the door with my foot to get an earful of what they were saying.

"I know you're not getting ready to leave without giving me a way to contact you," he said, all cocky and arrogant in his usual tone.

"But I thought you just said you were picking someone up for a dinner date. You're not trying to be a playa, are you?" She swung the long black tresses from her wig off her face in a very flirtatious way.

"See, you weren't paying attention. I said I'm here to pick up an associate for a dinner *meeting,* not date.

Besides, what does that have to do with us getting to know one another better?"

"I guess it sounds harmless enough." She giggled while handing him her business card and then getting into her car.

You low-down, dirty bastard. Just wait until my friend finds out you're trying to screw her coworker while passing her off as just your associate, I thought to myself. I was blazing hot with his ass and wished I could have stayed there to tell Mya exactly what he'd just done, but the next thing I knew, Leslie pulled off, and Anthony pulled up. The second that I stepped out of the door, Charles looked at me as if he'd been caught red-handed, and I stared right back at him in a way to let him know he had. I'd seen everything. I had to find the best way to tell Mya, though, because I knew that even if I had the three of them in the exact same room, she'd find a way to make up an excuse for his ass.

I had to admit, though, that the man was fine. In fact, he was better than fine and extremely well put together. But I couldn't help but wonder how attractive he would appear without all his money. It was his money that bought the nice, tailored suits that he wore. The money that kept his hair and beard all trimmed up and perfect. The money that purchased the expensive jewelry, classic shoes, and luxury cars. And I was sure that without the money, he was probably nothing more than a broken-down version of himself. And whether it came from Mya's lips or not, I knew in my gut that's what she was attracted to the most. Although she tried hard not to come off as shallow, her taste was quite expensive. She liked what she liked, including men. I just hoped this one didn't come back to bite her on the butt.

I almost got in the car and greeted Anthony with a kiss like I would normally, but I quickly remembered him strolling into my house in the wee hours of the morning and the text he received from the unknown female. Instead, I got in, and there was dead silence until he spoke.

"Hey, baby." He touched my hand and began massaging it.

"Hi," was all I gave back to him while slowly sliding my hand from underneath his. "Where are my children?"

"*Our* kids are at my mother's house. I thought we could use the time alone on the ride home to talk," he said, pulling the car out of the parking lot.

This was the very feeling I didn't want to come over me, but it did. I'd been strong all day by not calling him or responding to his numerous calls or texts. Yet as soon as I got in the car and saw his face while taking a whiff of his scent and hearing his voice, I practically turned into damn putty in his hands.

"Talk about what, Anthony?" I asked with a shaky and trembling voice and puddles of tears building in my eyes. "Until you wanna come clean with where you were until two in the morning or who the heffa was that texted you, then we have nothing to talk about.

He didn't say one single word back to me. He simply pulled the car over into the nearest lot, got out, and came around to the passenger side. Then he opened the door, pulled me out, put his arms around me, and held me as tight as he could.

"I'm sorry, Zae. I'm so sorry," he spoke softly in my ear. "I had a little too much to drink with the fellas and I stayed out later than I should. But I'm sorry, and I promise it will never happen again."

He may have been sorry, but I wasn't accepting any apologies until he gave me the answers I was truly looking for. With as much force as I could, I pushed his body off mine and began pounding his chest with my fists.

"Who was the female that texted you, Anthony? Who was she? Did you fuck her?"

"Baby, no, no," he yelled while trying to grab my hands. And then, before I knew it, he put me in a bear hug. "Calm down, Alize. Please calm down. I don't even know the chick, all right? She was someone that was flirting with me at the club. I chopped it up with her, but that was it. But then, she grabbed my phone and put her number in it and called herself so that she would have my number. But I don't even know her like that, and I definitely didn't fuck her. I wouldn't do that to you, Zae. You gotta believe me, baby. I love you, and you and the kids are my whole life."

I pushed him off once again and stood there pouting with my arms folded because I didn't know what to believe. My brain kept telling me not to be stupid, but my heart and my pussy needed the love and affection of my man. He must have sensed it, too, because the next thing I knew, he grabbed my face with both of his hands and threw his tongue down my throat, kissing me as tenderly but as passionately as he could. With both of our hearts beating a million miles a second, we hopped into the back seat of the car, he slid his pants down, and I climbed my round, plump ass right on top of him. I was so drenched as his manhood slid inside of me, and then, right there, he showed me just how sorry he was. As he thrust his thick inches of wood inside the warmth of my pussy and held my breasts in the palm of his hands, visions of the past seven years flashed through my mind. Anthony hadn't always been perfect, but somehow, he was still perfect for me.

"I love you, Alize," he moaned repeatedly as all of him caressed all of me.

"I love you too, baby. Lord, Anthony, I love you too."

At that very moment, I felt his release, and mine came a second after. It was what we both wanted and needed, and I'd decided then that I wasn't going to allow some random chick to destroy what we had.

CHAPTER 6

MYA

As I glanced at myself in the mirror one last time, I had to confess that I really didn't like the black dress Charles bought me. That was the very reason I had thrown it way back in my closet after only wearing it one time. But hearing how important this dinner meeting was to him tonight, I figured I'd just go along with it once more. After getting dressed, I dabbed some Jimmy Choo I Want Choo perfume on the inside of my wrists, a little behind my ears and then both kneecaps, and grabbed my pumps to run out the door.

The whole ride back to my job, I kept thinking about Charles and my relationship with him. With my whole mission of being a wife, now or never, I started to wonder if I really could date him exclusively. Like I'd told Alize earlier, letting go of Tyrone and Will would be easy. But Kevin and Charles were both a whole different matter. There was something about my number two that my number one just didn't have. Everything about Kevin was intentional yet effortless, and I craved him in ways that I didn't with Charles. It wasn't simply in a sexual manner either. Kevin's whole nature and being excited me in ways that I couldn't explain. I wasn't sure that I was completely ready to let that type of feeling go in hopes of settling down with Charles. But then Charles was the exact male version of me. We both basically had our shit together when it came to our finances and careers. But honestly, that was pretty much it, and I wasn't sure if that was enough. I compared and debated the two men some more before finally arriving back to the job and pulling up aside Charles's black truck. Then I got out and immediately saw him get out to open his passenger side door for me.

"Well, you aren't going to hug me or anything?" I questioned.

"Baby, can we bypass all of that right now? We're already running a little behind. I thought I was going to have to leave without you."

"Are you serious?" I asked once we were both inside, just knowing that he had to be joking. "You really would have left after having me go all the way home to change clothes? I mean, when I only did this for you."

"Mya, I told you that this meeting is important, and I'm not going to stroll in late just because you're fixated on your looks."

"I'm fixated on my looks? Charles, I went home to change because I was trying to acknowledge your request for the evening. Remember? Sit quietly beside you and look pretty. Isn't that what you asked of me?"

He shot me a dirty look for throwing his own words in his face but didn't say anything in return. Instead, he changed the subject altogether.

"And, what's up with your secretary, by the way?" he asked as if his lips were itching and he couldn't wait to bring her up.

"Alize? My *friend*? What do you mean what's up with her?"

"I feel like maybe you've said something negative about me to her. She's always giving me dirty looks like she hates my guts or something."

"Don't you think you're being a little paranoid, Charles? Besides, what would I have negative to say about you?"

"I don't know what it is then, but she has it out for me," he said, stopping at a red light and then looking over at me. "Why do you hang out with her anyway? She seems like she's from the other side of the tracks and not someone that you should even be compatible with," he let out before the light turned green.

"Charles, Alize is my closest friend here in Atlanta, all right. She has a beautiful heart, and she's one of the sweetest people I know. Maybe the two of you just need the opportunity to get to know one another better," I threw out there while looking at the polish on my nails.

"No, thank you . . . and if you ever plan on becoming my wife, I don't want you hanging out with her either. So, you may as well start searching for another secretary."

"Well, no future husband of mine is going to tell me who I can or cannot be friends with. And furthermore, there has yet to be a ring placed on my finger, so that search isn't quite necessary, now, is it?" I asked, waving my hand in front of his face.

"And there never will be as long as you hang out with her. Mya, all I'm saying is birds of a feather flock together. And no decent, well-to-do man is going to put up with you hanging out with her kind—including me," he pushed my hand aside and then pulled into valet parking at the restaurant.

I was so bothered by his words and overall attitude that I almost called off this whole dinner date-slash-meeting tonight. And I probably would have done so had I driven my own car.

As he got out and came around to open my door, I thought to myself how I would have more than enough time to mull over my whole relationship with him while sitting there being silent. I had never really seen this side of Charles, and honestly, I didn't like it one bit. The way I was feeling at that moment, it seemed like Alize might just get her wish, and Kevin just might move up to the number one and only spot.

We walked inside, and Charles informed the maître d' that we had reservations with another couple. His guests had already arrived, and as soon as he laid eyes on them at the table, he took my arm inside of his as if we were the perfect happy couple.

"All right, there they are, Mya. Just remember what I said. Let me do all the talking, okay?"

"Whatever you say, dear," I responded very sarcastically while rolling my eyes to the back of my head.

We reached the table, and suddenly, he turned into a totally different man than who I'd ridden there with. In fact, all at once, he was the charming and charismatic man that I'd known for the past couple of years. It was odd and completely insane how he just turned it on and off so quickly.

The couple instantly stood up.

"Mr. and Mrs. Tate, it's such a pleasure to see you. Uh, this is my *fiancée*, Mya. And sweetheart, this is the wonderful couple that I've been telling you about," he said as everyone began shaking hands. I, however, couldn't believe the horse manure that came from his mouth. *Fiancée?* I thought. I could have sworn he'd just said in his truck there would be no way he'd marry me because of my association with my ghetto friend, and now, in a matter of seconds, I'm his fiancée. I simply cracked a fake smile before taking a seat.

"That's a lovely dress, Mya," Mrs. Tate said, taking her seat across the table from me.

"Oh, thank you. It was a gift from my wonderful and thoughtful fiancé. He's always getting me gifts like this,"

I said, laying it on thick because I was sure it pissed him off that I was talking too much.

"Always getting gifts, huh, Charles?" Mr. Tate questioned. "Maybe that just means that you must have quite a bit to apologize for," he joked, and he and his wife started to laugh.

"No, it's more so because gifts are just this beautiful lady's love language, and I try to do what I can to keep her happy. That's just the kind of man I am."

I don't think that any of us believed the words coming from his mouth at that point, and we all gave him a look that said so. He seemed so fake and insincere, and I was utterly shocked that after knowing him all this time, I'd never seen this side of him before.

Right at that moment, I searched my mind for any traces of red flags that would have led to that point, and other than his overall feelings regarding Alize, there was nothing. I even went back to the very beginning when we met to see if I had missed any signs, but nothing stood out in my mind.

As my thoughts trickled back to that very day, I recalled how we were both in court trying our separate cases and had a recess at the exact same time. I wasn't paying attention, and neither was he, resulting in us bumping into one another and my Frappuccino spilling all over me. I remember him apologizing a million times over and over and then begging me to allow him to take me to dinner to make it up to me. Something inside told me to decline because I wasn't fond of dating other attorneys simply from knowing how hectic both of our schedules could be.

However, Charles was extremely easy on the eyes. He was handsome, dressed nicely, and very well-spoken when he opened his mouth. And then, once we went to dinner, I found many other qualities that I liked in him. Not to mention, from that very first night, he wined and dined me every chance he could. In the first six months or so, we went to fine restaurants, Broadway shows, operas, comedy shows, and even took a trip to Aruba. But after that, things slowly started to die down a bit. I figured it was nothing more than our schedules, just like I was afraid of, but I tried to hang in there. We still talked often and occasionally saw one another when time permitted. He would even send me *just thinking of you* gifts from time to time, which was why I'd assumed it was him that sent the roses. Nothing about this man seemed off or inappropriate until tonight.

But then, as I thought some more, I started to think that maybe it was only because I hadn't wanted to see this side of him. From day one, I'd thought so highly of him because of what he possessed and who he portrayed himself to be that I was blinded from the truth. The truth had probably been staring me directly in the face the whole time. But now, after talking down about Alize along with his behavior towards me tonight, it had opened my eyes clearly to who he really was, and I was beginning to rethink everything.

Before it was time for them to get right down to business, Mr. Tate and his wife started to ask questions that I knew didn't sit well with Charles at all. They both wanted to know how long we'd been together, how we'd met, exactly when we were getting married, and what we felt was going to keep us together and away from divorce. I laughed inside, watching him squirm as he tried to answer each and every question *without* me. Since he wanted me to sit there and look cute without saying a word at all, that's exactly what I'd done. I sat there smiling and nodding my head in agreement with whatever came from his mouth.

Then, after a few more minutes of the Tates joking, prodding, and even giving relationship advice to Charles and me while I continued to watch him portray this whole phony persona, we finally ordered some drinks and hors d'oeuvres before they got to what they'd come there for. I thought I would have been bothered by Charles's request to be mute the entire time, but little did he know, I was perfectly fine sitting there, quietly in my own little world, not saying a word. At least, that was until I glanced over my shoulder and saw the one person I had never imagined seeing, especially not with another woman.

Kevin? I questioned myself as my eyes zoomed in on him. Immediately, my stomach started to become queasy and unsettled, and I thought I had to be seeing things. This man was just all up inside of me last night, tossing, flipping, sucking, and fucking me like crazy and like I was the only woman on the face of the earth. And now here he was in front of me with another woman. I watched him slowly and carefully as if I were watching a movie on a big screen. He pulled out this woman's chair for her to be seated before he sat and then placed her napkin in her lap before doing the same with his. He was so noble and gentleman-like that I almost couldn't believe my eyes. He was dressed in a navy blue Armani suit that I wasn't even aware he owned. His shoes were exotic loafers, and he wore a pair of Gucci glasses that made him look refined and distinguished. *This* Kevin was far from the thuggish, jailbird-looking man that I knew who always came to my house in the wee hours of the morning in a pair of gray sweats and a t-shirt to dick me down. I practically felt as if I was being punked, as these two men were total opposites of what they'd presented to me this entire time.

Then there was *her*. She was actually beautiful, soft, and feminine as I watched her throw her long, dark tresses of hair over her shoulder when she laughed. In fact, she was so alluring that as I gazed at her, feelings of admiration, jealousy, and especially a little hate all mixed up together came over me. Who was she, and what the hell was she doing with *my man* as if he belonged to her? The ratchet side of me wanted to switch my round, plump ass that he loved so much right over there and ask him what the hell was going on, who was that bitch, and why he was all up in between my legs every other night if he had her. However, the classier and realistic side of me knew there was no way I could do that without making myself look like a complete fool.

"Sweetie, would you like for me to order for you?" Charles asked as he squeezed my hand underneath the table and gave a very stern look, reprimanding me without saying anything. I knew then that I must have been way too focused on Kevin, but still, I didn't care. I hurried to respond so that I could get right back to the matter at hand.

"Uh, that's fine honey, you know what I like," was all that I said, moving my eyes and attention right away back to them.

Thankfully, his back was to me, so he couldn't see me watching or, better yet, gawking. But I had to keep looking and turning away, and then looking again so that her eyes wouldn't eventually connect with mine. Then, there it was again—that smile that made her whole face light up, and I couldn't help but wonder the things he was saying or, more so, why he hadn't said them to me to make my face light up that way. Before I knew it, I stared with my mouth wide open in amazement and wonder at him taking his hand and brushing her frazzled strands of hair away from her face and then brushing his lips against hers as he kissed her softly. *Fuck*, I said to myself. Those kisses belonged to me, dammit, me, and at once, my eyes began to blur from the teardrops that were starting to invade them.

"Is everything all right, Mya?" I heard a voice ask but couldn't snap out of my daze enough to answer. Until she called again. "Mya, are you okay?"

"Huh?" I looked around, and all three of them were staring directly at me with concerned expressions. Well, more so, Mr. and Mrs. Tate did. Charles looked more like he could kill me in the blink of an eye.

"Um, yes, I'm fine. I don't know what came over me," I said, trying to think fast on my feet. "All of a sudden, I felt a little nauseous," I continued, not totally lying.

"Well, why don't you go to the lady's room and splash some water on your face?" Charles demanded more than asking.

"Sure, I think I'll do that," I answered back quickly after seeing Kevin's companion get up and head in that same direction.

"How about I go with you and make sure everything's all right," Mrs. Tate offered.

"Um, no, please, that won't be necessary. I feel like I've disturbed things enough already. I'll just go and gather myself, and I'll be right back."

I walked as quickly as I could to catch the unknown woman before she came out. I hadn't clearly thought about what I would say or do once I got inside. All I knew was that I wasn't going to let her walk away without finding out exactly who she was and what her relationship was with Kevin.

Once I made it inside, I glanced under each of the stalls to see if anyone else was there with us. When I noticed that the coast was clear, I began to formulate in my mind what I planned to say to this woman, but everything I came up with was sure to make me sound like a real maniac. Then, a second later, she came out of the stall and headed over to the sink. I pretended as if I were just washing my hands as well.

"That's a beautiful dress you have on," I said, looking at her in the mirror while trying to spark conversation to at least hear the sound of her voice and see what her demeanor would be like.

"Oh, thank you. Yours is pretty as well." She smiled back.

Part of me had hoped she would be a little stuck up or snooty, but I could easily tell by her thank you that snooty was far from her natural character. She was sweet, and honestly, I hated it.

"Thanks," I returned before asking what I really wanted to know. "Um, is the gentleman's name you're with Derrick?"

"Oh, no, it's not." I watched her grab a paper towel and start to pat her hands dry.

"Oh, okay, I'm sorry. He just looks exactly like a guy that I grew up with named Derrick. I could have sworn that was him. But I guess everyone has a twin in the world, huh?"

"Yeah, I guess so," she replied before getting ready to head out of the door. And that's when I saw it lying there on the sink. Once again, my eyes had to be deceiving me and playing tricks on me because it surely couldn't be what I thought.

"Um, miss, you left your ring here on the sink." I picked it up, not truly wanting to give it to her.

"Oh my goodness, thank you so much," she said in relief while grabbing her chest. "My fiancé just proposed to me right before coming here, and I guess I'm not used to wearing it yet. He would have killed me had I lost it."

"Your *fiancé*?" It slipped out before I realized it as my knees became weak and began to buckle. I'd heard that same word way too much tonight, and it was really starting to get to me.

"Yeah, we've been together for a couple of years now, and he finally popped the question. I still can't believe it either. It's like all my dreams are coming true. Anyway, have a great night, and thanks again," she said happily before strolling out in pure bliss.

"Yeah, all her dreams are coming true while I'm having a damn nightmare play out right in front of me," I spoke out loud, and two ladies that entered peered at me strangely for standing there talking to myself. I was in complete disbelief and felt like I'd been hit with a ton of bricks. There was no way that Kevin would do this to me, I thought. And then my mind wondered if that was the reason his dick felt extra good last night—because he planned on it being our last time. Well, it wasn't going to be, especially not if I had anything to do with it. I truly hated the idea of crushing this woman's hopes and dreams, but it was going to be over my dead body that I was simply going to hand Kevin over to her without a word about the matter.

After a few more minutes of contemplating, I walked out, passing by their table and making sure mine and Kevin's eyes met so that he'd know I'd seen him there. However, he only stared at me as if he'd done nothing wrong and even had the nerve to give me a slight wink without her noticing. I was angry, furious, and to some degree aroused by the entire situation. All I wanted was to go home, call him over, and ride his manhood until he loved me and not her.

CHAPTER 7

ALIZE

After our quick escapade in the car, Anthony and I picked up the kids, and our little family arrived home safe and sound for the evening. I hurried to get the kids settled in so that I could take a quick shower and maybe go for round two after putting them to bed. Anthony, however, had already beaten me to the punch. The second we got there, he had a trail of his clothing leading to the shower, and instantly, I heard him singing his heart out. I couldn't help but think to myself that this was the way things were supposed to be—happy, peaceful, and loving one another without all the drama we'd gone through earlier, last night, or any time before that.

As a matter of fact, I felt that this was what Mya was referring to when asking if I wanted to be a wife. For the longest time, it really hadn't mattered to me one way or the other because I knew Anthony was mine and I was his without the piece of paper or all the legalities. But seeing that text on his phone made me realize that there was a real possibility of us not being a family. It had me thinking about everything differently, and Mya was right. Seven years had been way too long for us to continue to play house, especially with four children involved. I wanted all of us to have the same last name. I wanted and deserved a title worth more than just *baby momma.* I wanted what my parents had. I *wanted* to be his wife and him to be my husband, *with* the paperwork to solidify it. So, with that in mind, I planned on talking to him before the end of the night, and he would have to give me some type of definite answer about where our future stood. If not, I was starting to think there was going to be a strong possibility we would need to go our separate ways.

Moments later, I heard the water in the bathroom shut off while he continued to sing. Hearing him so happy made me happy inside to the point that I sang along with him. As I left the children to watch Tabitha Brown's Tab Time, I headed to the kitchen to go ahead and start dinner. That way, after I showered and put the children to bed, I would have Anthony's full and undivided attention. However, it seemed that I was in for a huge surprise myself when, all of ten minutes later, he strolled in fully dressed.

"Hey, baby, I'm going to run by Antoine's house for a bit. I'll be back later tonight," he said, walking over to me at the sink with his keys jingling and then kissing me on the cheek.

"Anthony, um, I was hoping that me, you, and the kids could have a family dinner together tonight, and then after putting them to bed, we could have some *us* time," I said in a sweet and gentle tone so that I wouldn't come off too aggressive. Embracing my soft-girl era was actually something I'd learned from Mya.

"Oh, I see. You want some more of big daddy's good loving, huh?" He played behind me while dancing and rubbing his wood against my backside.

I chuckled a bit on the inside but tried my best not to let him see it because I needed him to take me seriously in the end. Pushing him away, I turned to face him, hoping he could see the sincerity in my eyes with what I was about to say. "Look, it has nothing to do with sex, all right. You and I need to talk."

"Damn, really, Zae? Talk about what now? We just got home after making some of the best, most passionate, and wildest love in the car. What's happened from that point until now? I thought we were all good."

"So, what did you think? A quick sex session was going to make everything all good between us? Do you really think that's all it takes?" The real Alize was beginning to come out of me instead of all the soft and gentle shit I'd seen with Mya.

"Listen, I just thought that you accepted my apology and that we could get past last night. Was I wrong?"

"No, Ant, you weren't wrong. I did accept your apology, and I'm going to let that go, but this is about something way deeper than last night." I walked away from him with my head down so that our eyes wouldn't connect.

"*Way deeper*? Wait a minute, what's up? Are you trying to tell me you're pregnant again or something? Man, please don't tell me that, Zae. I mean, I would love to have another baby with you, but sweetie, we can barely afford the four we have now."

"Maybe that's because I'm the only one working," I mumbled under my breath.

"What did you say?"

"Look, I'm not pregnant, all right?" I threw my hands up in the air.

"Are you sure? I mean, maybe I should run to the drugstore and get a pregnancy test just to be on the safe side. You know how fertile you are, and it seems you always end up pregnant when we least expect it."

"Anthony, I said I'm not pregnant, okay?" My voice started to rise, so I tried my best to soften up a bit. "Baby, I . . . I . . . I want to get married, Anthony. I wanna be your wife."

A dead and deafening silence came over the entire kitchen as he stood there with his hands on his forehead and a look on his face as if I said someone had died.

"Whoa, married?" He took a few steps back as if he were unbalanced. "I thought we had already talked about that, Alize. I thought that we agreed that we didn't need some piece of paper to define our relationship."

"Well, I did used to feel that way, but I don't any longer. I've been thinking, and I've realized that marriage is way more than just a piece of paper, Anthony. It's a covenant before God, and if something happens to either one of us, there are certain rights and privileges that we'll have as a husband and wife and not just a baby momma or baby daddy."

"Oh, okay," he said, pointing his finger at me as if something had suddenly dawned on him. "I see what it is now. It's all starting to make sense to me. All this talk about marriage, a covenant, and rights and privileges isn't coming from you, Zae. This is all coming from that nosy busybody, can't-get-her-own-husband boss of yours, isn't it? Yeah, I should have known that sooner or later she was going to start filling your head up with some type of garbage. I mean, she's never liked me, and I see the way she looks at me every time I come up to the job, including this morning. She thinks you can do better than me, doesn't she? That's what all this talk is about. She's telling you that if I don't marry you, then you should leave me, isn't she, Zae? Is that what you're going to do? Leave me?"

I didn't say anything in response to his question. After hearing one of the kids crying, I felt that was the perfect excuse to exit. "I think I hear Moet or Moscato crying. Let's just finish this later."

"No, no." He grabbed my arm to stop me before I was able to leave. "We're not going to finish anything later. You're going to tell me right here and now if you plan on leaving me if I don't want to get married right now."

"Well, I don't want to, but I'm not sure how much longer I can do this."

"Wow. All right, then. Why don't I just save you the trouble and help you figure it out?"

"What the hell is that supposed to mean?"

"I can show you better than I can tell you."

The next thing I knew, I watched him storm out of the kitchen and head straight to our bedroom. I trailed right behind him, knowing good and well that he wasn't about to do what I thought. Once we reached the threshold of what had always been our little sanctuary, my eyes practically stalked him. Instantly, he went from the closet to the dresser and then our master bathroom, throwing item after item into his duffle bag.

"Where do you think you're going, Anthony?" I finally spoke up. But still, he didn't say anything. Instead, he continued to move at a swift pace until he gathered everything he wanted.

"I'll be back, Zae . . . either when you change your mind about this nonsense or to get the rest of my things. One or the other," was all he said before kissing my forehead and walking to the front door.

"Don't you dare leave here, Anthony," I yelled. "How are you just going to leave me with four children by myself? And don't forget, it's *my* car you're trying to take," I shot at him, trying to send a quick reminder that he had no means of transportation and everything he had actually belonged to me.

It didn't stop him, though. Before walking out, he simply threw the keys to the car on the couch and said, "We'll work out arrangements with the kids once I get settled."

I knew once I saw the door close behind him that I'd made a huge mistake. So much of me wanted to run out and beg him to stay, but my pride simply wouldn't let me. Maybe he was right. Maybe I had listened to Mya too much with this whole marriage thing. Anthony and I had always been on the same page and said that if things weren't broken, then there was nothing to fix. And now, because I'd pushed the envelope, here I was, left without the love of my life, four children by myself, and not knowing what to do. I was so torn that as I laid my back against the front door, I slid down to the floor and buried my head in my legs as tears began to rush down my face.

Then, before I knew it, I felt a small hand patting me on my back. It was my oldest child, Champagne. "It's going to be okay, Mommy."

Immediately, I grabbed her and held her as close to me as I could. Knowing she didn't have a true idea of what was happening between her father and me and that she was only imitating what she'd seen me do when they cried, I simply agreed with her.

"Yes, baby, you're right. Everything is going to be just fine. I promise."

CHAPTER 8

MYA

Slamming the door to Charles's truck, I was relieved to finally make it to my car and head home for the night and that I no longer had to suffer in silence watching him and his phony representation of the perfect man with the Tates. And more so that I could, at last, be alone to try and reach out to Kevin.

Despite Charles's anger with me, I had assumed that the night had indeed paid off business-wise. They both seemed fairly pleased with him, no matter how fake he appeared to me. However, other than the goodbyes at the table and requesting the check from the waiter, I hadn't heard one single peep out of Charles since. He hadn't said a word to me on the car ride back to my job, and honestly, for me, it hadn't mattered one bit. He was the very least of my worries, and after all this time, I'd truly discovered that he was simply not the one for me, and there was no real future for us. Sitting quietly at the table allowed me to think about what Alize said along with his sudden behavior. He was a jerk, and there was no way I could see myself being with someone like him, no matter how much money and prestige he had.

Kevin, on the other hand, still hadn't escaped my thoughts, which was why the very second I closed my car door, I began to dial his number before even starting my car.

"Voicemail? Really? Answer the phone, dammit."

I dialed a few more times back-to-back, only to get the same result. It was like he'd turned his phone off completely, which frustrated me even more. All I could visualize was him making love to her the way he had with me for all this time. The entire situation playing out in my mind also brought back to my memory when I'd caught Michael with Tasha. It all made me wonder what it was about me that made me good enough to be the other woman and never the prize. Did it all boil down to the type of men I was choosing in my life, or was I the one lacking something?

Personally, I honestly felt like I had it all together and had all that a man would desire. I believed I was attractive. I was financially stable with a good career. I was versatile enough to be the head in a boardroom, the homegirl at a ballgame, and even the freak behind closed doors. Yet, even with all of that, it hadn't panned out good enough for the men I dealt with to make me their number one. But then I thought how maybe I was the one settling. When Charles dated me without wanting anything more, I should have let him go instead of hoping things would change. When Kevin told me from the start that he didn't want anything serious, I should have kept going instead of thinking he would eventually change his mind. The second I'd known I wasn't fully into Will as he was with me, I should have walked away. And Tyrone, well, he was one that I should never have started with in the first place. But where would that have left me but single and on the hunt for the perfect man? If he even existed.

As I started my car, my mind was like a whirlwind of thoughts of all the men in my life—from Michael to Kevin to Charles to Will to Tyrone. All the men held something that I desired, but who was the one good enough to be my now and forever or never was the question.

I must have been thinking too much because the second I pulled out of the parking lot, my phone lit up, and the name Tyrone displayed on the car's dashboard. I really wasn't in the mood and didn't have much to say to him, but a small part of me was curious and needed to hear what he had to say about his grandmother's shenanigans of stopping by my home.

"Hello?"

"Hey, Ms. Anderson. How are you?" he asked, and I could tell he was smiling from ear to ear. I wasn't sure why, but hearing his voice had actually put a smile on my face. I was also tickled inside by the way he always called me Ms. Anderson instead of Mya. It might have been a little weird, but to me, it was cute and rather endearing.

"Hey, Tyrone. I'm good, and how are you?" I asked in return before getting to what I really wanted to know.

"I would be better if I could be in the presence of a beautiful woman such as yourself tonight."

"Is that right? You really know how to flatter a woman, huh?" I said sarcastically while rolling my eyes in the back of my head,

"I try, I try . . . but it's easy with someone like you. I'm only saying what's true."

"Thank you, Tyrone. I really appreciate it, but how about we get right down to business?" I said with my attorney side coming out of me at full speed.

"What's that?" he questioned innocently.

"So, you know that your grandmother came to my house last night . . . um, in her robe and house shoes."

"She did?" his voice cracked, and all of a sudden, I could hear his embarrassment. "Uh, yeah, my granny can be a little bit extra, Ms. Anderson, but trust me, she doesn't mean any harm."

"Tyrone, whether she meant harm or not, she just can't show up at my home in the middle of the night, yelling at the top of her lungs and basically telling me I'm too old to deal with you. The woman even threatened to drop you and your kids off to live with me," I said, carefully remembering not to say a word about Kevin.

He didn't say anything to my words, however, and I assumed it was only because he really didn't have a clue what to say.

"I'm sorry, Ms. Anderson. I'll have a talk with her, and I promise she won't be doing that again."

"Let's hope not."

"But, in the meantime, would you like some company tonight?"

I heard the question the second it was asked, but it took me some time to answer. Being in the arms and affection of a man at that very moment would have been perfect if it was a completely different man. But, then part of me—that part in between my legs—wanted to at least allow him to come over and do that one thing I liked so much before sending him on his way and never dealing with him again. That was my mood, but I quickly decided against it. Not even a little horniness could have made me entertain Tyrone at that moment.

"Look, how about we do a raincheck on that? It's been a long day, and I have to be up early in the morning for work."

"Are you sure, Ms. Anderson? I can do that thing you like so much, put you to sleep, and then leave. I'll even let myself out and lock the door behind me."

I couldn't help but laugh that the youngster thought he had it like that, but then again, maybe I was to blame for him feeling that way. Of course, the couple of times we'd been intimate were cool, but he was truly no Kevin in the least bit. Not to mention the fact that I had to *teach* him that thing I liked so much, and I simply wasn't trying to give any lessons tonight. The way I felt, I needed someone who could come right in and handle their business from the start.

"It's very tempting, Tyrone, but it's late. I'm tired, and like I said, I need to get up early tomorrow. But I'll give you a call some other time, okay," I said, knowing good and well that I was lying through my teeth.

"All right, I guess. Well, have a good night, Ms. Anderson."

"You too," I answered, happy to get off the phone with him because a second later, I was pushing my garage door opener and pulling inside. Walking into my home, I kicked off my heels, slid off my dress, and let it fall to the floor as I went straight to my master suite to run some bath water. The entire time, I kept my cell phone in my hand, continually trying to call Kevin but still only getting his voicemail.

"How could you do this to me, Kevin? How could you ask someone else to marry you?" I spoke out loud to myself. My mind was all over the place when it came to him.

I refused to believe that he'd *cheated* on me all this time and picked another woman to spend his future with. It was unfair, to say the least, and he owed me some type of explanation. However, until I heard back from him, I decided to take matters into my own hands and release some stress. Throwing my cell phone on my bed, I took off my panties and bra, grabbed my rose toy, and headed towards the bathroom. Before I could truly relax for the evening, I had to get the monkey off my back and release the built-up tension from the evening. I started to run the water while filling it with bubble bath and oils just the way I liked it. While allowing it to fill up completely, I ran to the kitchen to get a bottle of wine and a glass and then picked up a scented candle from my living room table on the way back.

Once I returned, I tested the water to make sure it was perfect before sliding right inside and letting it consume every inch of me. Then, before I went any further, I lit my candle and poured myself a huge glass of the bubbly Prosecco. A second later, my head was laid back and eyes rolled into the back of my head as I allowed my rose to begin to work its magic. Vivid visions of Kevin and our escapade from last night, as well as over the years, started to run through my mind. I reminisced on him kissing me, sucking my breasts, throwing my legs over his shoulders, and placing all of him inside of me, practically playing my body like it was a flute. It was insane how in tune my body was with his. I could literally feel his lips begin to kiss and suck between my legs as I slowly but surely became closer and closer to my release.

At least that was, until I was suddenly taken by surprise when my cellphone began to play his special ringtone from my bedroom. I couldn't believe my ears and almost felt it was too good to be true. I just knew in the back of my mind that he would be celebrating with her for the rest of the night. But I also knew from the look in his eyes as I walked past their table, along with the wink he'd given me, that there was no way he could stay away from me either. At once, I threw my battery-operated gratification into the water and raced to the real thing. Hopping out of the tub, I didn't even bother to wipe off the water and bubbles that were gathered between the crevices of my body. In fact, I almost broke my neck from slipping a couple of times from my wet feet, yet nothing was going to stop me from making my way to him. My heart and pussy danced to the rhythm of the ringtone as I thought about being next to him again.

"I knew you would call, baby. I knew there was no way you could stay away from this pussy for long."

Finally getting to my bed, I picked up my phone as my life depended on it and answered in between a few heavy breaths and panting. However, the second I picked it up, the ringing stopped, and I saw a text message begin to come through.

Mya, are you awake? I need to see you.

My fingers trembled as I tried to respond as quickly as I could. His words were so vague, and different scenarios quickly shot through my mind. Did he want to see me to tell me about this sudden proposal to his now fiancée? Did he want to tell me it was over and he could never see me again? Or did he want to make love to me one last time to make sure that what he was doing was best? Either way, I needed to see him just as much and hear his voice for myself. And I was sure that after I gave him the pleasure of his life and rode his dick until he rolled over and slept like a brand-new baby, that he would have second thoughts about ever leaving me.

Yes, I'm awake, baby, and yes, you can see me.

Open the door.

I thought about putting my robe on but quickly decided against it. Instead, Kevin was going to get all these bare tits and ass staring him dead in the face, and I'd already started to imagine what he was going to do with it. Steadily, I walked to the door with no such urgency at all, hoping to have him panting and wagging his tongue like a dog in heat. Then, once I got there, I opened it gradually, permitting him to see only bits and pieces of my uncovered, still partially wet skin.

"Something told me I'd see you again tonight," I said with a half-smile and half-devilish look on my face.

"Really? And something told me that you were a sneaky-ass, low-down, conniving-ass bitch when you walked into that bathroom will all your fake-ass chitter chatter. Did you really think I didn't see straight through that bullshit . . . *or* the look you gave my husband when you walked past our table? Grinning all up in my damn face and congratulating me and then thinking you were about to fuck my husband tonight. Just look at your naked, pathetic ass standing there, butt-ass naked, craving a hard dick but can't get your own man to save your soul. What kind of woman are you?"

I'd heard every single word from her lips, but still couldn't believe my ears, or my eyes for that matter. There she stood, right in front of me with pain, hurt, and anguish written all over her face, far from the joy and happiness I'd seen in it earlier. I was at a complete loss for words and couldn't figure out what to say or do. Before trying to speak, however, I grabbed a blanket from my couch and started to try to cover my body.

"Um, um, look, I'm sure that the words 'I'm sorry' wouldn't matter much to you right now, but I truly am sorry for all of this. I—"

"You're damn right, you're sorry," she cut me off. "A sorry-ass excuse of a black woman is what you are. But listen, I didn't come by here for your pitiful-ass apologies, okay? I came by here to tell you one thing and one thing only. Stay the fuck away from my husband. Don't call him, don't text him, don't even think about his ass or his big-ass dick, because if I find out that you had anything at all to do with him, trust and believe that there will be hell to pay for the both of you. Now, have your ass a good night, Mya. Bitch," she said, walking off and right to his truck. As she opened the passenger side door, I caught a glimpse of his eyes peering back at me.

"What the fuck!" I screamed after shutting my door and dropping to my knees to the floor in tears. Maybe it was true that Kevin and I weren't actually *together* and that he was about to marry her. But that still didn't stop the pain I'd felt in my heart at that very moment. I was embarrassed that this unknown woman had seen my whole naked body. I was ashamed that she knew I wanted to have sex with him after congratulating her on the proposal. I was confused about why he'd brought her to my home to confront me. And more importantly, hurt and devastated from knowing that it was over and I would no longer see him again. Curling up on the floor, I lay there in a fetal position with my blanket wrapped around me while crying my heart out. First Charles and then Kevin—my number one and two. The two men I believed I needed and thought I would end up spending my life with at least one. Both were gone from my world in one night.

Wanting the pain to disappear and needing a man's arms around me to feel safe and protected, I crawled to my bedroom, where I'd left my cell phone. Then I picked it up and dialed his number, already knowing I was probably making a huge mistake, but it was what it was. He answered on the first ring.

"Hey, Ms. Anderson," he said, and I could hear his smile once again.

"Hey, Tyrone," I said, hesitating and almost changing my mind. "Um, I was hoping that if it's not too late, I could go ahead and take you up on that rain check tonight. I could really use some company right now."

"Nothing but a word, Ms. Anderson. I'll be there within the next fifteen minutes or so."

"Make it ten, Tyrone. Please."

CHAPTER 9

ALIZE

"Champagne and Hennessy, stop it, babies. Please don't start fighting with each other. I need you two to behave like big girls while I get your two little sisters out of the car, okay?" I said to them while struggling with Moet and Moscato, my purse, lunch bag, and other work-related items.

Any other morning, I would have had Anthony help me with the kids and everything. But since he'd left after our argument about marriage, I hadn't heard one peep out of him until today. And even then, that was simply a mere text message saying that he would come by the job to get the kids sometime this morning. I knew right away that Mya would have a fit about them being here yet again, which was why I decided to get to work a little earlier than normal. I hoped to get them in and out without her or anyone else in the building seeing them.

Luckily for me, Diane hadn't made it in yet, although Milton was already at his usual post. It didn't matter much about him, though, because he adored the girls and always loved seeing them, so I knew he wouldn't say anything. In fact, I had always thought of Milton as a big brother or father figure in my life, more than just the security guard at work. He had always been there for me in the past anytime I needed something, whether

I was having car trouble, low on cash, or just needing a listening ear. I could always depend on Milton, just like now as I tried stumbling and fumbling with four children and all our things to the building.

"How about I help you with that, Ms. Alize?" he said, walking out onto the parking lot. "Hey girls, how's Uncle Milton's babies this morning?"

"Hey, Milton. Thank you so much. I guess I'm kind of struggling this morning."

"Oh, it's all right, Ms. Alize. We all need a little help from time to time," he said, smiling and taking my bags and things from my hands while picking up Champagne as I dealt with the other three.

"You're here quite early this morning, aren't you?" he asked while holding the door open for us.

"Yeah, I'm hoping the girls' father will pick them up before Mya sees them here."

"Oh, I see. Yeah, she is a stickler about that, but hopefully we can have them out before she arrives. But, if you don't mind me asking, is everything all right?"

"Uh, sure. Why would you ask?"

"I don't mean any disrespect, Ms. Alize, but you don't quite seem like your normal self. I usually look forward to seeing your attire for the day. It's normally much more flamboyant than today," he finished, finally dropping me and my things and the kids off to the office.

"I just have some things going on right now, but I promise not to let you down tomorrow," I said while trying to force a smile instead of shedding a tear.

"Okay, good. We don't want Ms. Leslie to think she's got you beat," he joked, trying to make me smile. "And, Ms. Alize, if you need anything at all for you or the kids, I'm always here for you," he finished.

He left before I was able to put up any rebuttals because Milton knew I didn't like any handouts. However, today, there was no way I was going to put up any fights. Besides my spirit being broken, I was basically in survival mode with Anthony gone. So, if it meant bringing the kids to work, taking handouts from Milton, or anything else until things returned to normal, then I had to do what I had to do. And I'd decided that I wasn't going to stress myself about Mya finding the children there either. If I couldn't get them out before she arrived, then there was nothing I could do about that. Besides, part of me still felt like most of this was partially her fault anyway, so she owed me a little grace and compassion right now.

"Okay, girls, sit right here on the floor and play until your father gets here, and no fighting, all right," I instructed them after Milton left and I'd laid a blanket out on the floor.

"Where's Daddy, Mommy?" Champagne asked immediately. She had always been my inquisitive and outspoken child. I wished I could tell her exactly where he was and that he'd be there soon, but the truth was I had no idea. I didn't know where he went right after leaving the house. I had no clue where he'd laid his head last night or who he was with. I didn't know how he planned on picking them up from me since I had the car. And most of all, I wasn't sure if and when he would ever return home. That was if he even still considered our house his home.

"Um, Daddy will be here soon, sweetie. Don't worry, all right?" I tried assuring her as well as myself. Although I acted big, bad, and tough like I wouldn't care if he wasn't home with us, not knowing his whereabouts had been driving me crazy. Not to mention the fact that I didn't know what he was thinking, and I *always* knew Anthony's thoughts better than he did himself. Was he really that upset that I'd given him an ultimatum about marriage? Was that actually enough to destroy our whole relationship and family?

I turned my back to the children as I walked over to my desk, not wanting them to see me cry. Anthony and I had had many arguments and fallouts in the past, but nothing of this magnitude—nothing that would have made him leave home, but now that he had, I was beginning to get scared.

Sitting there, I tried to think of the best way to ask him to come back home without seeming like I was giving up or throwing in the towel on the whole marriage theory. I still wanted to be a wife, *his wife*, more than anything. But I needed him to want it too.

While debating back and forth on the right words to say, I suddenly heard a text message come through my cell phone. Picking it up, my eyes took in the words.

I'm here. Bring the kids outside.

Staring at the six words on the cell phone screen, I couldn't help but wonder where his mind and heart were. There were no sweet pet names or emojis, no warmth or gentleness, and especially no love shown within them. He was very matter-of-fact in what he wanted, which instantly made me angry. I wanted to go right down there and curse him out with everything inside of me, but I also knew that would only push him further away. So, instead, I decided to dig deep into myself for my soft and grown woman attributes again and handle this much differently than I would any other time.

Hurrying to gather the kids together, I walked them outside, ready to practically beg Anthony for forgiveness, until I stepped out of the door and saw *them*. There he was, standing on the outside of her black Chevy Equinox with a damaged back end with a Newport dangling from his lips, while she sat inside on the passenger side watching me. Immediately getting pissed, I held onto my children so that they wouldn't run to him. Then, before I knew it, I started yelling at the top of my lungs.

"Really, Anthony? Really? You left me and your children to run straight to this raggedy bitch?" I screamed, not caring that my children, Milton, or anyone else was watching, for that matter.

"Just give me the kids so I can go, Zae, and I'll drop them back off here later."

"No, no, to hell with that. My kids are not going to be anywhere near that crazy broad. Hell, you barely want your own damn son around her, and she's his mother."

"Girl, stop playing and give me the kids." His voice started to rise.

"I mean, Monique, though, Anthony?" I questioned while feeling tears build up in my eyes. "Of all people? I would have rather you cheated with the chick from the club other than your sorry-ass baby momma. Is this what it is now? All because I asked you to finally make me your wife?" I pleaded, hoping he could make sense of things for me.

"Naw, this is what it is because you're listening to that boss of yours and giving me a fuckin' ultimatum. Like I said before, I'll ask you to marry me in my time only, not yours, your momma's, your boss's, or anyone else's. My time, my way . . . *if* I ever ask at all."

"All right, Anthony, then cool. Well, since you feel that way, then we don't have anything else to say to each other. So you and your baby momma can go ahead and leave, and I'll take my kids to the sitter's myself. Oh, and I'll throw your shit in some trash bags and leave it on the porch. You can come by the house this evening and pick them up."

I tried to get the kids to turn around and head back into the building with me, but Champagne and Hennessy had started crying and screaming for their daddy in the middle of all the chaos.

Then, out of nowhere, I felt Anthony grab me by the arm. "Zae, I swear, if you touch my things, I'll—"

"You'll what, Anthony? What? You're going to put your hands on me now? Especially while I'm holding your children. Is that where we are now?"

He didn't get a chance to answer because by that time, Milton had come out of the building and given him a look that said he needed to leave. And without another word, he did just that. He let me go, jumped back inside of the car, and sped out of the parking lot as quickly as he could. And all I could remember was Monique throwing up the deuces at me as they left.

There I stood, stuck in place and unable to move while drowning in a pool of tears from my eyes as well as my kids. They were still screaming for their father, and although I hated what he'd done, deep down inside, I was screaming for him too. I didn't want him with her; I didn't want him gone from the house. And most of all, I wished I could take back our whole conversation from the day before and go back to that very feeling we'd shared after making love inside the car.

Then, out of nowhere, I felt Milton's large, masculine arms surround me. He didn't reprimand me for my behavior, and he didn't even suggest that I leave Anthony for good. He simply held me and my children tight, making us feel loved, protected, and secure while telling me everything would be all right. As I laid my head on his chest, I prayed that was true.

All of thirty minutes after the whole incident with Anthony, Mya and other employees in the building started to arrive at work. I was thankful that none of them had witnessed what happened and more so grateful that after seeing the children, no one had anything to say, including Mya. After sharing with her what went down between me and Anthony, she hadn't come down hard on me at all. In fact, she'd gone as far as to make a small play area in our office for them to spend the day in the building with us because, honestly, I had nowhere else for them to go. The sitter hadn't been answering her phone, and although Anthony had been texting repeatedly after he left, I refused to answer him. As a matter of fact, I barely looked at them.

Having the children in the office, however, must have brightened the day for everyone because people from other floors had been stopping by all morning, bringing them snacks and such. Diane had even let Champagne sit at the front desk with her for a bit and help answer the phones. I was so grateful to God and my village for helping me through this, and finally, my nerves started to settle a bit, and I could breathe a sigh of relief.

"I still can't believe that he showed up here with his son's mother, knowing how much the two of you hate each other," Mya said while Champagne was somewhere in the building with Milton or Diane. Hennessy played quietly by herself, and both the twins were fast asleep. It must have seemed like the best time, if any, to finally have a conversation about it.

"I can't believe it either, Mya. He's gone on and on for years about how much he couldn't stand the girl and wished he never had a child with her, but now, the first time he decides to leave the house, he runs straight to her. It doesn't make sense to me unless he's been involved with her all this time," I said, feeling tears trying to make their way into my eyes, but I refused to continually cry over Anthony.

"Now, do you honestly believe that, Alize? I think he only ran to her because he didn't have anywhere else to go."

"No, that's where you're wrong. He did have somewhere else to go. He could have come back home with his family right where he belongs." The tears started to creep down my face, whether I wanted them to or not. Mya then came over and sat on the edge of my desk while rubbing my back.

"Everything's going to be all right, Zae."

There was that damn statement again. *Everything is going to be all right.* I was tired of hearing it because, in all actuality, how did anyone really know that to be true? Better yet, how did they even know I still wanted everything to be all right between Anthony and me? His actions this morning by showing up to *my* job to pick *our* children up while being with *her* spoke volumes to me. And if this was how he wanted it, then so be it. Two could very well play this game.

"You're exactly right, Mya. Everything is going to be all right because I've decided that my focus is no longer going to be on my children's father. I want what I want, and I still want to be someone's wife. I deserve that much. And if Anthony doesn't want to make me his, then I'm positive there's a wonderful man out there somewhere who does."

CHAPTER 10

MYA

I looked at my friend and heard the words coming from her mouth, and wished I could be in total agreement with her. However, I couldn't help but be a tad bit skeptical in regard to her theory. I mean, here I was, single, educated, financially stable, with no children or baby fathers, ambitious, and I believed attractive, and had yet to get a proposal. And there she was, although beautiful inside and out, she had limited education, was not so financially well off, and had four children and a crazy-ass deadbeat for a baby father. Not to mention, I'd never heard her have any realistic goals or aspirations outside of catering to and taking care of Anthony. Yet she was positive that this wonderful man was going to fall from the sky and sweep her off her feet and take care of her and her children. I simply didn't have it in me to shoot her dreams down and make her believe that Anthony was probably as good as it was going to get for her in the *man* category.

"Well, you know that I'm with you no matter what you decide."

"Thanks. But enough about me and Anthony. I don't want to talk about him, let alone think about him anymore today. So, how was your dinner date yesterday evening with *Mr. Wonderful*?" she asked. Instantly, my stomach began to turn flips just at the thought of Charles.

"Girl, *Mr. Wonderful* is now *Mr. Could Drop Dead* for all I care."

"Oh, no, no, ma'am. I know that didn't just come from your mouth," she said, completely shocked.

"Alize, the entire night was horrible," I said, watching her face. "And stop sitting there looking like I told you so."

"Listen, those are your words, not mine . . . but I did tell you so, Mya."

"Anyway." I rolled my eyes at her. "It was bad from the time he picked me up all the way until he dropped me back off to my car. He was nothing like the man I've known all this time. It was like I was dealing with a totally different person . . . one that was a complete jerk."

She sat there quietly with the same expression and kept listening to every detail about my terrible evening with Charles. I told her about the Tates, the food, and more about Charles's fakeness while deciding if I should mention anything about Kevin and the whole incident with his fiancée. Finally, after all of that, she interrupted.

"Mya, did you honestly not see this in the man? After all the time you've been with him, was last night truthfully the first night he came across as a jerk?"

"I don't know, Alize. I mean, maybe I didn't want to see it in him, but trust me, I was far from blinded by it last night. My eyes were definitely opened wide, and I didn't like what I saw at all."

"I hear you. So, does that mean you're officially done with him altogether?"

"Yeah, I think it's official," I hesitated to say.

"Okay, but why do I feel like there's something you're not telling me?"

My eyes suddenly caught a glimpse of Hennessy, who had fallen fast asleep with her sisters. Instead of answering Alize, I went to cover her up with a blanket.

"Mya, I know you hear me talking to you. What is it that you're not saying?" she asked again, but this time, my cell phone alerted me that I'd had a text message come in.

Good morning, Ms. Anderson. I hope you enjoyed our time together last night.

Taking a deep inhale, my eyes read the words, and immediately, I thought about how typical that was for a youngster like Tyrone. Kevin or Charles would have never said they *hoped* I enjoyed our time together because they would have already known I had. That alone showed Tyrone's immaturity as well as his insecurities, which immediately explained why I should have followed my first instinct. I never should have let him come by, no matter how vulnerable I was. He should have been the last one that I chose for the attention and affection of a man that I needed last night, and now I was regretting it and kicking myself in the rear for it. That was the very reason I'd decided not to respond to the text and, better yet, not to ever call him again.

"Um, excuse me, Mya Anderson, but I'm waiting for a response," Alize said while coming up to me and snatching my phone out of my hand.

"Okay, okay. As much as I don't want to relive it, I guess I have no choice but to tell you all the dirty little details."

"Dirty details? Relive what? What happened?" I could tell her curiosity was getting the best of her.

"It's Kevin, all right. He was there . . . at the restaurant last night . . . with another woman."

"What?" Her mouth stood wide open for a few moments. "So, he does have a girlfriend, huh?"

"How about more of a fiancée?"

"A fiancée?" she repeated, shocked even more. "Are you serious?"

"Very serious," I confirmed, walking over and sitting down on the edge of her desk. "She and I ended up in the lady's room at the same time and exchanged some pleasantries, and that's when she told me they were celebrating their proposal."

"Oh, no, I'm so sorry, Mya. I know how much you liked Kevin."

"But . . ." I said, feeling as if there was one coming.

"Um, there's no *but*," she tried to say innocently but then continued, "although you had to already know that he was involved with someone. I mean, the way you've always described him, I automatically assumed there was a woman in the picture somewhere. Mya, a man like that usually has several women begging for his attention."

"I hear you, all right, but he told me that he wasn't in a position right now to be in a committed relationship, and I believed it. Yet now he's all of a sudden engaged."

"You mean you chose to believe it because of how amazing the sex was."

"Alize, this is the very reason I almost didn't tell you. It's like you're determined to say I told you so."

"That's not it, Mya, but we have to call it what it is. Half of these men's red flags have been there the entire time, but you simply chose to ignore them. Whether it was for loneliness, good sex, the desire to be committed, or whatever the case may be, the truth was always present. And well, if that's saying I told you so, then so be it."

"Wow, you almost act as if Anthony has no red flags when we both know he has a ton of them."

She looked at me and didn't say anything, and instantly, I felt horrible. "I'm sorry, Zae. I didn't mean that the way it sounded."

"Yes, you did, Mya. You always mean it that way when it comes to him. And listen, I know that Anthony isn't the perfect man in your eyes, all right? But he was perfect for me, and that means more than anything."

From that statement alone, as well as the look on her face, I knew it was time to shut up. We both became quiet and went to our desks to do some work instead of talking about the men in our lives. That had always been the good thing about us. We knew when to back off from each other and just let things be.

Everything had pretty much been peaceful from that point on, too. The children had woken up, and Alize had given them snacks and things, and now they were all playing amongst themselves. That was what I appreciated most about my friend and coworker. She was a wonderful mother to four beautiful children and did whatever she needed to do to take care of them.

"Hi, ladies," Leslie exclaimed as she walked in, loud and boisterous as ever.

"Hi, Leslie," Alize and I said in a dry, harmonious tone.

I couldn't help but notice her attire and the fact that she'd had Alize beat for the day. With all that was going on with Anthony when I arrived, I hadn't paid much attention to her clothing. But now, put up against Leslie, she was nowhere near her trendy self. In fact, she looked like she was dressed for a funeral.

"What's going on, Leslie?" I asked, wondering what she would go on and on about today.

"Nothing much, Mya. I just saw Alize's oldest walking around the building with Milton and thought I would come down and see all the children. Just look at them. They're getting so big and so adorable . . . and looking more and more like their handsome father, I see," she said as I saw Alize cut her eyes at her.

"Yes, and their beautiful mother," I said, trying to ease the blow of her comment.

"Anyway, I also wanted to come down and tell you all about the most amazing guy I met."

"Leslie, didn't you tell us about him yesterday? The one you met online and went to the new restaurant with?"

"Girl, no, this is someone new that I just met yesterday when leaving work. He's so nice-looking and charming and charismatic. I still can't believe I simply met him on a whim. We talked all last night after he made it home from a dinner meeting . . . maybe 'til like two this morning. And I'm not even one to stay up late at all because a girl does need her beauty rest. But there was something about him that made him worth it. We laughed and joked and talked about things that mattered, like our hopes and dreams. He is just perfect. Do you know that the man already sent me a couple dozen roses earlier here to the job? It's like I met my Prince Charming, and he's literally sweeping me off my feet."

"Maybe he should sweep you off your feet back to your floor," Alize said under her breath. However, Leslie was still too caught up in her bliss to hear her. We both listened to her go on and on about her new beau, and it practically made me think of when I first met Charles. He was sweet and charming and charismatic, exactly like this man she spoke of. I almost wanted to warn her and tell her that she needed to get to know him a lot better before falling head over heels in love. She surely didn't want to be in my shoes and end up discovering a couple of years later that he was nothing like the man that she thought he was. However, time and a lot of wisdom taught me to mind my own business when it comes to friends and matters of the heart. That was the one reason I only went so far with sharing my opinions with Alize when it came to her and Anthony. Finally, I found an opportunity to sneak in between her words.

"Leslie, he sounds wonderful, but I hope you take your time with him. These men can sometimes put on a very convincing façade before their true colors start to come out."

"I know what you mean, Mya, but something tells me that this particular man is different. In fact, I think I could have met the one."

"The one?" Alize repeated before water came flying out of her mouth as she started laughing. Leslie only rolled her eyes and continued with her thoughts, completely ignoring my friend.

"Anyway, Mya, I appreciate your concern, but like I said, something is different about this man. I really believe he's a good one and that he's just the one for me.

"Well, I hope it works out for you, Leslie."

"I'll definitely keep you posted. Anyway, I better get back upstairs. He just might give me a call on his break, and I don't want to miss hearing his voice. Toodles, ladies. See you later."

CHAPTER 11

ALIZE

Leslie finally leaving couldn't come soon enough for me. I didn't care one bit about her sad sob story of not having family and friends in Atlanta, either. She irritated me like no other, and there was absolutely nothing that was going to make me feel sorry for her or suddenly become her best friend. The one person I did feel sorry for, however, was Mya. Watching her reaction as Leslie went on and on over her new guy, I didn't have it inside of me to tell her that she was referring to Charles. Speaking of him, I couldn't believe the audacity he had to have my friend suffering through that horrible evening with him, only to go home and chop it up with Leslie all night. Then, on top of that, to send her a bouquet after lying to Mya about sending her flowers yesterday confirmed how much of a real creep he was. Instantly, I prayed in the back of my mind that she was completely serious about being done with the man. If not, I might just have to let it all slip out on who Leslie's new boo was.

"Can you believe she's met a couple of perfect men in a matter of days that are practically treating her like a queen, and we can't meet anyone?"

"We? Chile, speak for yourself. I'm not the one out here trying to meet these lame-ass jokers, and besides, who said that any of these men she's coming across are perfect? You and I both know how everyone, men and women, show their representative in the very beginning. Hell, that's exactly how Anthony got me. When we first met, he was charming and Mr. Wonderful too. But it was only a matter of time before the real Anthony started to show his true colors."

"Well, either way, I still feel like *I'm* the one that's doing something wrong. There has to be a way to meet a good and decent man."

"There is. How about finally acknowledging the good one that you have in your life already?"

"Who? You mean Will?" she asked, knowing good and well who I was talking about.

"Yes, Will. From everything you've told me, he seems like a really good guy with standards and morals. Don't be one of those women who won't give the nice guy the time of day because you're too busy chasing after the bad ones. Or there is another option, too."

"What's that?"

"Stop looking and let him find you."

"Yeah, but how long is that going to take?"

"Mya, it's not like you're going to your grave tomorrow. Give it some time and take some time for yourself. That's exactly what I plan to do now that it seems like Anthony has made his choice. And when I do decide to start dating, I'll have all my shit together for the perfect man to come and hunt me down."

"Seems like you have it all figured out," she mumbled, and I could see she was still thinking about everything that I said.

"Not quite, but I know what I'm going to put up with and what I'm not, and I don't plan to settle," I said firmly, speaking more to myself than her as I watched yet another text from Anthony come across my cell phone.

Zae, can we please talk?

Talk about what, Anthony? I think you said everything you needed to say when you showed up to my job with Monique.

Listen, you know I don't care about that bitch. I only did that shit to piss you off all right.

Don't go calling her a bitch now. And I'm sorry to tell you, but you didn't succeed. At this point, you and your son's mother can have each other and have a wonderful life together. Bye!

I turned my phone over facedown and focused my attention back on Mya.

"You know what? You should try that new dating show on social media."

"What show? What are you talking about?"

"Girl, sometimes when I have trouble sleeping, I log onto my social media and watch this new dating show called *For Singles Only*. A local radio host here in Atlanta gets on live and basically hooks people up on social media. She asks questions like what type of person you're looking for, their age range, whether or not you can accept if they have children, and right down to how much money they need to make. Girl, when I say it's crazy, believe me, it's crazy."

"Are you serious? But how do they meet you?"

"You give them your Facebook or Instagram name, and if they're interested, they can message you in your DMs."

"I don't know, Zae. I mean, it sounds interesting, but it also sounds like I'll be putting myself on display like a piece of meat."

"Mya, girl, take the fork out of your butt. It's all about having fun and meeting people. And you'll be the one in control in the end anyway. You'll decide who you want to call or who to ignore. It's just that simple."

"If you say so, Alize. But, since things are pretty slow around here today, do you think that you could hold down the fort for me if I got out of here a couple of hours earlier? I have a ton of errands that I need to take care of."

"Oh, Mya, go. I have everything under control here. I'll just see you tomorrow."

"Okay, good, and please, if you see Leslie again before the day ends, please play nice, all right?"

"Always," I said while displaying a slight, innocent smile because Mya had to know that I would never play nice with that woman. In fact, ever since she strolled in earlier, I had been trying to think of a way for Mya to suddenly find out just who her new companion was.

Shortly after Mya left, Milton came up to our office carrying Champagne in his arms. She must have worn herself out with him and Diane all morning and afternoon because now she was fast asleep.

"You got yourself a handful with this one right here, Ms. Alize," he said, placing her next to her little sisters in their makeshift play and sleep area.

"Yeah, I know, and the scary thing about it is she's just like me when I was her age."

"Oh, boy, watch out now," he said as we both started to laugh at the thought. "So, how are you doing? Are you feeling a little bit better than this morning?"

"Yeah, I guess so," I answered, trying not to show how bothered I truly was.

"That's good to know, Ms. Alize. Just keep your head up, all right? Things will get better," he encouraged, but little did he know that was much easier said than done. He turned his back to walk out of the door, until I called his name.

"Milton, do you mind if I ask you a question?"

"Of course not, Ms. Alize. What's on your mind?"

"Why does it take men so long to finally settle down and get married?"

He sort of chuckled a bit before his lips parted to answer. "If you want the simple and most honest answer, it's because we're stupid."

"What?" I was confused.

"Ms. Alize, have a seat." He pulled my chair from behind my desk for me and then took a seat himself on the edge of the desk. "You know, I used to have a beautiful woman in my life, just like yourself, Ms. Alize. Oh, boy, I was completely in love with her. Faye was my everything, and at that time, I couldn't imagine life without her."

"Really," I said, listening intensely because he and I had never talked on this level before, and I could only imagine what he was about to share with me.

"Yep. But the problem was that back then, I was just like your children's father, Anthony. I was so much more focused on the wrong things in life, only thinking about myself and never thinking about marriage and family or our future together the way she did. I was only coasting through the relationship and basically having fun. Anyway, it became a point in our relationship that Faye wanted the exact same things you're probably wanting from Mr. Anthony right now—to be married, have a stable household and family life, and to grow our future together. But Ms. Alize, we as men are just downright stupid. I mean, there's no better way to put it. We don't think the same way women do, and unfortunately, we don't make the best choices either," he said, slightly lowering his head with his eyes low as if he were ashamed of his past choices.

"So, what happened with you and Faye?" I asked eagerly with my ears at attention like a child listening toa their favorite storytime and longing for some sense of hope for me and Anthony.

"Uh, we stayed together for quite a while and even had a beautiful daughter together. But still, I was too stubborn, Ms. Alize, and thought I would be missing out on something by settling down with her. And it's not to say that I was cheating or even had a desire to cheat. I just didn't want to give up my so-called freedom."

"Wow, so, I guess things didn't work out, huh?" My heart snk at the thought of my and Anthony's fate.

"No, they didn't. Faye ended up meeting someone that was ready and willing to give her the life that I hadn't the entire time that she was with me. And well, now she's happy and complete, and this young fool of a man simply turned into an old fool . . . single and lonely."

"Milton, I'm so sorry. That sounds so sad."

"Oh, hush, girl. Don't feel sorry for this ol' man. I could very well have made some different choices, just like Mr. Anthony could. But telling you about my past wasn't for me to go down memory lane or simply to answer your question. I told you all of that, Ms. Alize, hoping that you will also have the confidence as a woman to do what you need for you and your children and what will ultimately make you happy in the end. And don't worry about Mr. Anthony choosing you to be his wife. The right man will make you his wife with no questions asked. And either Mr. Anthony is going to get himself together and be the man he needs to be for you and these babies or end up a lonely ol' fool like me."

"Milton, what about your daughter? Do you see her often?"

"I speak with her from time to time because she's my flesh and blood. But although she was too young to really understand what was happening with me and her mother, all she can remember is her mother's tears, and she knew I was the cause of them. In fact, she treats her stepfather more like her real father. I assume because he was the first man to always make her mother smile in her eyes."

"She's an adult now, though. Can't you explain to her how you are with me right now that you were young back then and didn't know any better?"

"I could, and believe me, I have. And although she understands, that's still no excuse."

"But I think that's so wrong. I mean, we all make mistakes when we're young and dumb. She shouldn't hold that against you forever."

"Listen, what you need to be worried about are those four little ones right there," he said, pointing to the children. "You have to do what you can to give them the best life possible, with or without Mr. Anthony."

"Milton, is that your way of telling me that I need to leave Anthony?" I asked, standing up and folding my arms while waiting to hear his response.

"Ms. Alize, that is my way of telling you to trust your gut and follow your heart. Don't be desperate like these other women around here, and just know that you are worthy to be a wife and not just someone's baby momma. Now, the direction you go will have to be all up to you."

"I appreciate that, Milton. I'm always being told how I need to *make* Anthony make me his wife, as if I can't do any better than him."

"Let me guess . . . Mya?" he asked, and I nodded my head in response. "Look, I know that you and Ms. Mya are each other's best friends, and I love her just as much as I do you. But stop listening to folks who don't have their own business in order. She can't tell you anything about your relationship when she's running around out here with this one and that one."

My mouth dropped wide open at the fact that he knew anything about Mya's one, two, three, or four. "Milton, how—"

"Just trust me, I know." He cut me off. "I've had a couple of run-ins with that arrogant one that has come here a couple of times. I don't know why she even deals with him, but to each her own. And then I've seen her letting that young boy that used to work at the gas station around the corner fill her head up. He was like, 'Hey, Ms. Anderson, you look so beautiful today . . . but that's every day,' and she was sucking up every single word. But then, I know from her attitude in the mornings when she's more than likely seen the man she really wants. When she comes in in the morning, all talkative, chatty, and smiling from ear to ear, I know she's seen him the night before. And when she's quiet, reserved, and heads straight to her office without so much as a hello, then she hasn't."

"Oh, wow, Milton. I guess I didn't realize how observant you were. I'm a bit scared to ask what you've observed about me."

"Ms. Alize, don't worry. You're pretty consistent, and what I love most is that you are who you are . . . from the way you dress, your hair, nails, eyelashes, and everything. But you better not come in here dressed like you're headed to someone's funeral again the way you are today. It's not your style or personality, and more importantly, it might make that Leslie chick on the third floor think that she has you beat, and she doesn't, because you know she tries her best to compete with you."

I bellowed over with laughter at how Milton knew everyone in this entire office building like a book.

"Anyway, it's been a pleasure conversing with you, ma'am, but I should be getting back downstairs to my post."

"Okay. And Milton, thank you for everything. I love you so much," I said, going over to him and giving him the biggest hug that I could, one from a daughter to a father, which was what I knew he needed most.

The minute he left, I went back over to my desk and noticed at least three missed phone calls and ten new text messages from Anthony. The last one read, Alize, please, I'm begging you to hear me out and let me come home tonight. Again, no one is worried about Monique. I only did what I did this morning to make you upset, but I want you and I want our children. Please.

His words seemed sincere, but truth be told, Anthony and I had been here before. He'd never taken things as far as to run to his son's mother or throw her in my face. But here he was yet again, having to beg to get back in my good graces and come back home. I was becoming so sick of the back and forth, and after listening to Milton, I knew it was time for me to decide permanently what to do. Either I was going to allow my children's father back into our lives or finally get the strength and courage to leave this situation for good. The problem was, my mind and my gut were leaning toward the latter. However, this damn heart of mine wanted to give him another chance.

CHAPTER 12

MYA

As I hopped into my car to head home, I couldn't help but think about my conversation with Alize from the day, particularly the part about not looking anymore and letting the man find me. I started to wonder if that was actually the direction I was headed in and, if so, was that even possible for me? It seemed like, one by one, the different men in my life were quickly showing me that they weren't the ones I needed to be with, but a part of me still didn't want to let any of them go. Honestly, I believed it all boiled down to the fact that I didn't want to be alone, but truth be told, it probably wouldn't be any different than how I felt right at the very moment. Even with the four of them circulating in and out of my life, a major part of me still felt alone. So much so that I was thinking about calling the one person I never would have imagined reaching out to. Without another thought, I spoke to my device that was connected to my car and instructed it to dial out. It was odd to me how quickly he answered.

"Well, this is a pleasant surprise. How are you doing today, beautiful?"

"I'm good, Will, and how are you?"

"I'm decent. I'll be a whole a lot better once the clock strikes five, though."

"I'm sure," I said, trying to think of the next thing to say to keep the conversation flowing smoothly because it seemed as if he was simply following my lead. I usually liked it more when a man took charge, but frankly, I understood what he was doing. I had shot him down numerous times already, so I was positive he didn't want to just put himself out there again. "Um, I wanted to thank you again for the roses yesterday. They really were beautiful."

"You're more than welcome, Mya. I just wanted to do something special for you."

"Why, Will?"

"Why? What do you mean why?" He sounded completely confused.

"I guess I'm just wondering, after all this time of us getting to know one another, why do you still try so hard with me? I mean, if I'm being totally honest with you as well as myself, I haven't really invested as much time into you or what we're doing as I possibly could. Yet, you've still stuck around without disrespecting or disregarding me. So, why?"

"Do you not feel that you're deserving of that much? Mya, you're a beautiful, extremely intelligent, charismatic woman. I really want to take my time getting to know you inside and out. And if that means dealing with a hectic schedule here and there, then so be it. I'm a man and can handle that. And if the time comes where I start to feel like I'm putting far more into this than you, or God tells me that this isn't the route I should take, then, and only then, I'll back off."

"I see," I said, smiling and perfectly satisfied with his response. "So, what are your plans for the evening? I was hoping that maybe I could take you up on that dinner offer from yesterday."

"Well, that would be great if it was any other time, but I have Bible study tonight."

I had to admit that I was a little bit stunned and taken aback by his response. I was absolutely sure that he went to his Bible study week in and week out, and now he couldn't miss one in order to finally take me out to dinner like he'd been begging for weeks. It practically had me at a loss for words.

"Oh, okay. Well, maybe we can reschedule for another time," I said, trying not to sound too disappointed. However, I immediately started to think what my plans would be once I arrived home, other than a bottle of wine and catching up on my ratchet television programs or a good book. *Oh, what a life,* I thought to myself, hoping that this was not how every night would end up being like if and when I became completely manless. Until the most unexpected question came.

"Would you like to join me?"

"J-j-join you?" I stuttered. "For your Bible study?"

"Of course. Why not?"

Immediately, all the reasons for *why not* came rushing through my head. I couldn't remember the last time I'd stepped foot into anyone's church. Did I have anything appropriate enough to wear to the house of God that wasn't way too form-fitting or showing a ton of skin? Would all eyes be on me, with everyone knowing I was a true and complete sinner? And could I take my line of thinking and mental images far away from fucking Kevin as I had been thinking all day in order to direct my attention to God and only God?

"Um, to be honest, Will, I must say that you've kind of caught me off guard. I'm not sure that I have anything to wear."

"You can just throw on whatever. It's not like it's Sunday morning worship service, so anything will do.

And besides, church is come as you are. No one will judge you, Mya."

"Okay, I guess. But I won't have to say anything, will I?"

"No, Mya." He chuckled at me. "They might, however, ask all first-time visitors to stand to be acknowledged, but that's it. You won't have to say anything at all . . . unless you want to."

I took a second or two to mull over his request. All I wanted was a nice relaxing dinner date with no expectations, simply to get me out of the house and take my mind away from Kevin. And now, somehow, I'd been suckered almost into attending a mid-week church service. I couldn't help but wonder what exactly this meant. Going to church with someone was a huge deal in my eyes, right up there with meeting someone's family for the first time. And more importantly, I knew deep down that I was still far too much into my carnal life to be sitting in church. I was afraid I would set the pew on fire as soon as I sat down. But, while trying to turn over a whole new leaf, I went ahead and accepted.

"Um, sure, Will. Why not? Bible study sounds good. I mean, we can't have too much God in our lives, right?"

"Right," he said with a slight chuckle under his breath. "But really, this is great. It starts at seven thirty, so how about I pick you up around seven?"

"Better yet, why don't I just meet you there? I can text you or something when I arrive if you don't mind," I suggested, mainly because I wanted to have the option to leave any time I wanted to.

"Uh, okay, if that will work better for you. Then sure, I'll see you there."

We hung up, and immediately, I wondered what the hell I had gotten myself into. Or maybe this was the perfect time to stop using the word *hell* or any other form of profanity. Anyway, I pushed my foot to the pedal to pick up speed through the traffic and hurry to get home. I didn't care what Will said about this not being a Sunday worship service. This was going to be my first time entering the house of God since I was practically a child attending with my parents, and God was not going to see me stepping in there like a typical heathen. Tonight, I was going to be the angel He created.

"All right, God, I'm asking You in advance to please forgive me for all my sins and don't strike the building down as soon as I walk in."

A few minutes later, after making it home, I jumped in the shower and then rushed to my closet to find the whitest, most angelic and churchiest dress that I could find.

"No, that won't do. Nope, too tight. This won't do either . . . my back would be out, and I wouldn't have a bra on. Ugh! C'mon, Mya, there has to be something in here," I yelled at myself while pulling out piece after piece that reminded me of how unholy I truly was. And then I finally found it. It was a plain white dress, not too form-fitting or too loose, but just right. I knew that once I put on the right undergarments, it would be perfect. Then I searched my closet for some sandals to match it, and I even found a white, modest-looking hat that should make me fit right in.

Thirty minutes later, I was pulling up to the address that Will had given me. I texted him before actually getting out of my car, and he answered in a matter of seconds.

Hi, Will. I'm here.

Cool, I'll meet you at the front door.

Instead of the sandals that I initially planned on wearing, I'd decided on some white heels, and now I was quickly regretting that decision. The main parking lot of the church was full, which made me have to park in the overflow lot, which just happened to be grass and dirt. After walking extremely slowly, I was able to wobble my way over to the main entrance. My eyes began to survey the area where many of the parishioners had gathered while trying to make their way in. Then, instantly, I saw Will standing there, basically looking like Mr. Church himself. He had on some dark denim jeans that looked so starched up that they could practically stand on their own. Up top, he wore a white button-down shirt and navy blue blazer with a white and blue handkerchief in the pocket. And although he summed his whole look up with some low-top Nike sneakers, he still appeared more religious than probably the pastor himself.

I hated to think it, but nothing about him actually turned me on or made me overly excited to see him. In fact, at that very moment, I had to search my memory and think back to when I met him and why I'd even given him my number. I remembered it being such a beautiful fall day out that I'd decided to do some work inside of Starbucks instead of in the office. It was almost like a relaxing self-care day for me instead of working because I was doing all the things that I loved.

I'd gotten up and gone to get a full-body massage. I went to get my hair done and then a manicure and pedicure, and then ended up at Starbucks. As I sat there quietly in my zone, Will approached and asked if he could borrow some of my sugar. His request had come out so awkward and weird that it was almost kind of cute. Anyway, I invited him to have a seat at my table in the overly crowded dining area, and we enjoyed one another's company. It was so innocent and sweet that I completely overlooked this whole church thing with him. When he first explained that he was a Christian and had certain standards and beliefs, I didn't feel one way or the other by it. At least, that was until he explained that one of his beliefs was no sex before marriage. That was the one thing that had basically thrown me for a loop and made me rethink any kind of relationship with him at all.

"Mya, hey. Wow, look at you. You're looking quite, um, *Mothers' Board-ish*. I thought I told you that it was only Bible study and that you could dress more casually."

"I heard what you said, Will, but I just didn't want to seem out of place . . . the way I do right now."

"Look, it's okay. Maybe just take off the hat, and hopefully no one else will notice the rest of your outfit." He laughed.

I thought that maybe I would blend right in with the crowd but that was far from the truth. Everyone else had on jeans or sneakers, with some women in leggings or joggers and some men even in baseball caps, while I stood out like a sore thumb in this white dress. I at least hoped we would sit far in the back of the sanctuary so that I wouldn't be so noticeable. However, just as I thought, Will escorted me right to the very front for us to sit in the second row.

"Will, do you think we should really sit this close to the front?"

"Why not? This is where I normally sit."

Before I was able to give any type of rebuttal, a tall, slender woman walked over with a big smile across her face and extending her arms for a hug.

"Hey, brother Will, I see you brought a guest with you this evening."

"Yes, yes, this is my friend, Mya. Mya, this is Sister Doris."

"Sister Mya, it's such a pleasure to meet you, and look how beautiful you are in all your white. We're so glad you could come and join us for Bible study tonight and hope that this won't be your last time."

"Um, it's a pleasure to meet you too . . . uh, Sister Doris. I'm glad to be here as well," I answered, trying to fit right in with the church lingo and all, although I wasn't so sure about being called *Sister Mya*. I almost felt like I was immediately ordained a nun or something.

We sat on the pew, and the choir entered. All at once, the whole church got quiet and gave their undivided attention. It was like we were at a mid-week concert or something because before I knew it, the bass player, drummer, and organist were playing their hearts and souls out while the choir sang. Everybody jumped up on their feet and was dancing and grooving to the nonsecular song that was coming across as extremely secular. Being a woman who lacked any rhythm whatsoever, I simply swayed left to right while trying to clap my hands on the right beat.

Clearly, I had been missing out on the whole Black church experience. I even cut my eyes at Will a couple of times. He was grooving right along with everyone else. I had to admit that it was all very entertaining, and I was truly enjoying myself so far. Then, after the faster-paced song, they slowed it down a bit with a mid-tempo tune that I believe was called "I Told the Storm." I'd heard it on the radio several times before, but it had never resonated with me like it had at that very moment.

As they were finishing up, the minister finally came out to teach. He'd given a few good evenings and hellos and said how good it was seeing everybody out, but you could tell that he was ready to get right into his teaching for the evening. This was honestly the part that I'd dreaded because anytime I'd been in church before, my mind would start to wander to things that it shouldn't. However, I tried to remain focused. Before he started, he asked everyone to join hands for prayer.

Will's hand was strong and warm as he gripped mine. I almost began to imagine what it would feel like to have his hands on me in other places.

"Stop it, Mya, just stop it," I whispered to myself softly once the prayer concluded.

"What's wrong? Is everything all right?" Will leaned over and asked.

"Yeah, everything is fine," I confirmed sheepishly while trying not to embarrass myself any more than I felt I had.

Then, after the prayer, the minister told us to turn our Bibles to Matthew 6:33. Of course, I hadn't come with a Bible, so Will allowed me to look on with him. I was surprised that I'd actually heard the particular passage before, yet honestly, I'd never truly applied it in my life. *What if I sought after God first with everything inside of me? Would He really give me all that my heart truly desired, including a husband and family?* I wondered. I started to think how maybe I should try to take God for His word. It wasn't like I would be losing out on anything.

The more I began contemplating giving up all these men for a true relationship with God, I felt my phone vibrating inside of my purse. Luckily for me, I had turned the ringer off. Although I wanted to see who it could have been that was calling, I didn't want to be inappropriate by pulling out my phone in church, so I let it go to voicemail until it started again. Whoever it was was seriously trying to get in touch with me.

Looking around, I noticed how some people were using their phones to read their Bibles on them, so if Will asked, that's what I planned to tell him. Slowly, I dug my hand inside and pulled out my phone. I could have pissed my pants when I saw Kevin's face and his name scrolling on the front of it. Was it actually him or his fiancée again? I couldn't help but think.

"Um, Will, I need to run to the ladies' room," I whispered quietly. "Do you think that's okay?"

"Oh, sure," he whispered back. "It's right in the back of the church by where we came in."

"Thanks." I got up in my all white, trying to be discreet, yet knowing all eyes were on me. However, I didn't care one bit because there was one thing on my mind and one thing only: Kevin's dick.

Instead of going inside of the bathroom, where I saw other women in and out, I stood in the front of the church.

"Please be Kevin . . . please be Kevin . . . please be Kevin," I spoke to myself after calling his number back.

"Hey," was all he said nonchalantly, like he hadn't brought his whole fiancée to my house to threaten me if I had any more dealings with him.

"Hey," was all I decided to answer back, putting the ball back in his court.

"Are you home? I wanna see you."

Was he serious right now? Did he fuckin' forget about everything? I mean, everything. Yet, there I was, falling for it and throwing on my sexy little girl voice to answer.

"I'm not right now, Kevin, but I should be in about an hour or so," I said, following his lead and acting as if nothing had happened, mostly because part of me still wanted to be with him physically, while the other part just wanted to see how far he would take things.

"Good. I need some of your head right now. You know you're the only woman that knows how to handle my dick."

I listened to his words, and no matter how wrong it was to be on the steps of the church having the type of thoughts scrolling through my mind, I took them in. In fact, they almost made me feel proud in a way that *I* was the *only* woman that could control his dick and not her.

"Kevin, I have to ask. What about—"

"Listen, don't worry about all that. I've handled it. I'll see you in an hour, and make sure you come to the door with no clothes on."

He hung up, and my nipples were at attention from the mere thought of having him inside of me again. Then I laughed at the fact that he wanted me to come to the door unclothed like I already had, only for his fiancée to see me butt-ass naked.

Quickly coming out of my sinful thoughts, I remembered where I was and tried to think of the best way to tell Will that I needed to leave. I didn't have to go back in and walk down that aisle to the front, however, because a second later, he peeked his head out of the door.

"There you are. I was looking for you. I hope everything is all right," he said, seeming concerned.

"Um, actually, I'm going to have to leave earlier than I would like. I'm sorry, Will."

"Oh, it's okay."

"Yeah. I was really enjoying everything, but now Alize needs my help, and I need to go to her. I mean, she is my best friend and all."

"Mya, you don't have to explain. Go and help Alize, and I will be here. And you can join me again for Bible study anytime. It happens every Wednesday night, and I would love for you to come again . . . just without the white dress next time."We both laughed, and Will gave me a big hug, yet it was nothing like the hug I anticipated when Kevin walked through the door. In fact, my girlfriend was turning flips inside of my panties from the excitement I felt.

Once Will went back inside of the church, I wobbled my way as quickly as I could back to my car. A small part of me felt horrible for lying to Will and more so for lying in front of the church, but then my mind went to the one statement I'd always heard people say whenever they sinned. God knows my heart. I also believed that He knew I just wasn't the Christian that Will was. So, with that in mind, I figured it was time I called it quits with him, whether I wanted to or not. Besides, maybe Sister Doris would be a much better fit for him.

CHAPTER 13

ALIZE

Everyone else in the building had left for the day at their normal time, but I decided to stick around and try to get some extra work done. With all that had been going on between Anthony and me, I wanted to keep my mind focused on things other than our relationship. Plus, I just didn't want to go home alone again. Besides, I had brought the kids more than enough snacks to eat and toys to play with, so we were all good.

As I prepared documentation for Mya's next couple of meetings, I couldn't seem to take my mind away from all the things that Milton had said and which way I should go with my children's father. It had been seven whole years of being with him, and I honestly couldn't see any growth on his side. He was still very much content with not working a real job, smoking marijuana, playing video games all day, and hanging out with his friends. True enough, those things were fun and exciting when we first started, but now I was in a whole different mindset. I wanted a real family and a bigger home with a white picket fence that wasn't under Section 8. One day, I wanted to leave this administrative position and start my own business. And as much as I had been preaching to Mya about building her relationship with God, I finally want to establish my own with the man above. But I didn't believe I could do all of that with Anthony laying up under me like a deadbeat and me flipping all the bills.

I needed more, and maybe it was time for me to be that strong woman Milton had encouraged me to be, just like Faye.

A few minutes later, I heard footsteps heading my way, and then my eyes glanced over at the clock. It was Milton's usual time to lock up.

"Hey, young lady." He peeked in. "How late are you and the babies going to be here?"

"Uh, I don't know. Maybe another hour or so."

"Okay, I can hang around until then."

"No, Milton, you don't have to do that. We're fine. If you just want to make sure the other offices are locked, I'll lock this door and the front door when I leave."

"Are you sure about that? I don't feel so comfortable leaving you and four little children here alone," he said and stared at me.

"Milton, trust me. We'll be fine. Just lock up the other offices, and I'll take care of everything else from here."

"All right, if you say so. But, Ms. Alize, I want you to call me if you need anything at all. I'm only fifteen minutes or so away," he said, pointing his finger at me like he was someone's grandfather.

"Okay, can you do me one favor, though? Can you keep an eye on them while I pull my car in the rear parking lot? It will be a lot easier for me when I leave, and that way, no one will see one car sitting by itself in the lot."

"Okay."

I ran downstairs in record time, changed lots, and hurried back inside, all without breaking a sweat. Milton then kissed the kiddos, hugged me, and left for the day. However, it seemed he must have forgotten something or just didn't feel right about leaving because only ten minutes later, I heard footsteps again. I waited to hear his voice or see him peek back inside of the office, but there was nothing. Knowing good and well that my mind wasn't playing tricks on me, I got up and looked out of the office. I started to hear voices but still did not see any faces. From what I could tell, it sounded like a man and a woman, but I had no idea who it was. In fact, all I'd seen were their shadows going toward the stairs.

Although I'd watched a million scary movies in my life and knew I shouldn't follow the unknown, I went toward the voices anyway.

"Champagne, watch after your sisters, okay? Mommy will be right back," I told her before tip-toeing up the stairs until I was closer to the voices. They were on the third floor, and as I peered in the direction of the sound, I saw Leslie and Charles inside her supervisor's office. "What the hell are you up to, Leslie?" I whispered to myself.

"Was it really necessary to walk up three flights of stairs?" he asked her.

"Yes, Charles. I told you that our security guard shuts down the elevator every evening."

"All right, and you're sure no one else is in the building? Because I thought I saw a light on toward the office downstairs."

"Did you see any cars outside in the parking lot? Trust me, there's no one here. It's way past everyone's time to be here. And anyway, you probably just saw the light from one of the other attorney's offices. Mya Anderson. Her rattlebrain administrative assistant probably forgot to shut them off."

"Rattlebrain? Bitch, who are you calling a rattlebrain?" I said to myself, wishing I could say it directly to her.

"Mya Anderson? I think I've heard that name before," he had the nerve to say.

"I'm sure you probably have. Although I'm not quite fond of her or her assistant, I must admit that she's one of the most popular attorneys in the Atlanta area. Anyway, I think we should hurry up and get out of here. Let me just grab the petty cash from my drawer."

Petty cash? I thought.

"How much do you have?"

"This is about seven hundred here. Will that work?"

"Yeah, that should be good."

"And what did you need this for again?"

"Uh, I'm in between business deals right now, and I need to handle something. You know how it is, right? The life of an entrepreneur," he said.

"I understand. Just please make sure you give it back because I've never done anything like this before."

"Anything like what?"

"Given money to a man or taken money from my boss's petty cash."

"Oh, I see. Well, just look at it as an investment, but don't worry, I should be able to get this back to you in a couple of days, tops."

She flicked off the light the second I ran back downstairs to my office. I couldn't believe she was giving money to that creep. Especially a creep that claimed to have it all together. "The life of an entrepreneur, my ass. You should feel real pathetic getting money from a woman you just met," I said softly. And then to hear from Leslie the part about her not liking me or Mya when Mya was always the one that looked out for her when it came to me. She had proved to me in that very moment how low down and clueless she really was, and I debated on when I would share it with Mya because I knew her feelings would be hurt.

A few minutes later, I heard them creep back downstairs and heard the glass front door shut. Then I looked out the window and saw his truck pull off the lot. I had gotten more than an earful from Leslie and Charles that I hadn't even wanted. So much so that I knew it was time for me to pack up my things and the kids to finally head home.

After making it down the stairs and getting the children settled into the car, I tried starting my ignition, but to my surprise, it wouldn't start. "C'mon now, don't do this to me," I said, turning the key a couple more times. Then, on top of the car not starting, both of the twins started to scream at the top of their lungs, I'm sure from being hungry for dinner, and someone in the back seat didn't smell so good.

"C'mon, God, please let this car start," I begged the Man up above. I didn't know a thing about cars since Anthony always took care of any repairs, and I honestly didn't have the extra cash to spare to have it looked at. My heart began to race a million times per second as I tried to think of what to do. I thought about calling Milton, but I didn't want to continue to bother him with my problems. Then I figured I would unpack everybody and go back into the building until I could think of what to do. However, I suddenly saw Anthony's number pop up. *To hell with not speaking to him*, I thought to myself. I went ahead and answered.

"Hello."

"Zae, what's wrong? Why do you sound like that?"

I burst into tears before I could answer, and my words came out broken in between my crying. "It's . . . the . . . car. It . . . won't . . . start. The . . . girls . . . are screaming. It's . . . just . . . us . . . here and the children here. Everyone else . . . is gone . . . and . . . I . . . don't know . . . what to do."

"Okay, just calm down, baby, and hang on. I'm headed that way."

"Anthony, please don't bring that woman back to my job. I can't take that right now."

"Zae, I'm with my brother. I've been trying to tell you all day that I only did that to make you upset. So, just hang tight, and I'll be there in a sec, okay."

He hung up, and all at once, my tears dried. Immediately, I thought about how, although I felt Anthony lacked in some areas, he was still good in others. And how he was also still the man that held my heart in his hands. I tried calming all the girls down, who were all agitated at that point, until their father arrived ten minutes later. Just like magic, the minute they saw his face, it was like everything was good in their world. How could I ever think of taking that away from them? What kind of mother would I be to leave their father knowing how much they needed him?

He pulled me out of the car and hugged me tightly for a few minutes before doing anything else. Then he kissed all the children and dried their tears. Without saying one single word, I knew without a doubt that we meant the world to him and were his first priority.

"All right, pop the hood for me, baby."

I did as told and sat in the car, watching him do his thing with his brother. They took out a couple of tools here and there and then told me to start her up. In a matter of twenty minutes tops, my car was like brand new.

I hopped out and threw my arms around his neck. "Anthony, I can't thank you enough for coming to our rescue."

"Baby, you don't have to thank me. This is what I'm here for," he said as his lips headed toward mine, but then he opted to kiss my cheek. "Um, anyway, is it all right if I still come by and pick up the rest of my things from the house? I'm going to stay with my brother for a little while."

"No, that's not all right," I said, gazing at him, and he looked back, completely confused. "It's not all right because I'd rather you come back home."

He didn't say anything for a minute or so other than a smile coming across his face. "Zae, but what about—"

"Can we talk about that some other time? I'm just ready to go home . . . all of us."

CHAPTER 14

MYA

Racing home, I kept my eyes on the time more than the traffic. I knew that if I took a few shortcuts here and there, I would have enough time to shower again and be ready for Kevin once I arrived home. It still had me dumbfounded and a little appalled that he didn't at least attempt to explain what happened last night or anything about his new fiancée. All it boiled down to was that he needed a quick fix, and he called me as usual. And, like always, here I was dropping everything to be with him.

"Mya, why do you keep doing this? Why on earth do you keep allowing this man to have his way with you, yet he's asked a whole other woman to be his wife?" I asked myself aloud. I honestly felt a little silly about it but reminded myself that it wasn't like I wasn't getting something out of it, either.

Then I thought about my whole mission and everything that Alize said. I had to admit that she was right. How did I expect God to send my forever when I continued to have men like Kevin around? Bordering on feeling a sense of conviction, I was about to dial Kevin's number when the last number I'd expected to see came flashing across the screen. I nearly sent it straight to my voicemail, but my curiosity was at an all-time high. I had to know what he could possibly want.

"Hello," I answered with a slight hint of an attitude in my tone.

"Hello, Mya. So, are we going to talk about last night or what?"

"What exactly is there to discuss, Charles? I feel like you gave me an assignment, and I did precisely what you wanted me to do. That was it."

"Really? Is that all that you believed happened? Mya, you weren't paying attention to the conversation at all. You made a complete spectacle of yourself by claiming that you weren't feeling well, and you embarrassed the hell out of me in front of two very important clients. So, at bare minimum, I think I deserve some type of an apology before things can go any further between us."

Before things can go any further? I thought. He had to be kidding me, but after witnessing the man I'd seen last night, I knew he wasn't.

"If you really think I owe you an apology, Charles, then you're far more delusional than I actually thought. I did you a favor by going and playing along with your whole charade of being your, what was it again, fiancée? I sat through some boring-ass conversation all evening while trying to grin and bear it, and then you didn't even have the decency to acknowledge me once we got in your car. And to make matters worse, you allowed me, as a woman, to get out of your car and then drove off without making sure I was okay and didn't even bother calling to make sure I made it home safely. Yet, you think I owe you an apology."

"You know what? You're really pushing it, Mya, and if I didn't know you the way I did, I would say you were starting to take on characteristics like that ghetto-ass assistant of yours. I already told you last night that even if I did want to ask you to marry me, it would never happen with you behaving like this or while you're still connected to her."

"Well, from what I'd seen yesterday and observing right now, that just might be a good thing," I said, not giving a damn how it came out or how I sounded. I didn't know what had come over this man because his attitude and language were far beyond how he'd ever conducted himself with me.

But seeing that he was the last of my concerns since I had much better things on my mind, like Kevin, I decided to cut the conversation short at that point and more than likely for good. "Look, Charles, I can't do this with you right now. I'm about to go and handle something important."

"Something important, huh? So, when are we going to finish talking about this?"

"I don't know. Maybe tomorrow if I'm free. I'll check my schedule."

"Wow, you can't be serious. And just to think I was about to waste seven hundred bucks on you tonight."

"Well, Charles, I'm sorry, but I gotta go. Like I said, we'll possibly chat tomorrow. Or maybe never." I hung up, and five seconds later, I was pressing the button on my garage door opener. Whatever judgment I was beginning to feel before my call with Charles, I no longer felt. In fact, I needed a release more than ever after that call, and Kevin was the perfect person to give it to me, fiancée or not.

After hopping in the shower, I oiled my body with various oils and scented sprays to be just the way Kevin always liked me to be. Not to mention, I wanted to taste absolutely scrumptious to him. Then, I slipped on my robe and headed for the kitchen to pour myself a glass of wine. After that, I decided to flip through some channels in my sitting room while waiting for him to arrive.

When I first left work, I had no idea that I would have been in contact with or had any communication with any of these men, especially after yesterday. But here they all were, still very much a part of my life, and I needed to figure out which one I was going to keep around.

Kevin, of course, would be the likeliest one, but we had the little problem of that fiancée of his. Then there was Charles. After yesterday and today, I wasn't sure if he would ever go back to being the man known as my number one—the man I truly adored. And then Will. I'd realized that I actually liked some qualities about him. I loved how he wasn't shy or afraid to show his love for God. And he remained a pure gentleman, even after I lied and told him that I had to leave. I just wished I could deal with how dedicated and committed to his religion he truly was.

I started to wonder, if I did make him the only one in my life, what would that mean for me? Would he expect me to be as devoted as him? Would I damn near have to be on the Mothers' Board, dressed in all white, like he joked earlier? The theory of it all was cool, but I wasn't positive I could ever be that type of Christian. Especially not since I was practically in heat waiting for Kevin.

"Where the hell are you? I thought you would have been here by now," I questioned while going back into the kitchen to pour myself another glass. "And I would surely need to give up all of my casual drinking if I chose Will," I thought aloud.

As I headed back to the couch, the doorbell rang, and finally, I felt a sense of excitement and relief all wrapped in one. However, it threw me off that he'd used the bell. Any other time, he would simply text and tell me to open the door, so this was strange. Immediately, I wondered if this was his fiancée again, but then I recalled that I actually spoke to him outside of the church. Trying not to let my fears and inhibitions get the best of me, I downed another swallow of wine and finally went to the door. I put on a smile before opening it, and then it immediately went away.

"Uh, hey, Mya," Will said, standing there, trying his best not to look at me from head to toe in my silk robe, but I caught him catching glances. "Uh, I'm sorry to just pop up on you like this, but um, you left this on the church pew," he said with my white hat in his hand. "I was going to leave it in your mailbox because I figured you were with Alize. . . ." He left his statement hanging as if he wanted an answer to why I was home in my robe.

"Um, thank you. I . . . I . . . I . . ." I started to try to speak until, just like that, Kevin's truck entered my driveway. I could have pissed my panties when he got out in his gray sweats and a wife beater showing basically every muscle in his body, including the one I was still craving to put my mouth on. At a loss for words, I watched Kevin walk directly past Will like he didn't mean shit as he slightly acknowledged him.

"What's up, man?"

"Uh, hey, what's up?" Will managed to get out while staring at me as if I were some everyday ho.

"Will, I—"

"Mya, listen, it's okay. You don't owe me any explanation. Like I said, I shouldn't have just popped up at your house like this. I'm sorry. You take care of yourself, all right."

He walked away, and I literally felt like the worst person on earth as I closed the door, until I turned around and laid eyes on Kevin standing there, stripped of his clothing and his manhood at full attention, ready for me. Although my heart wanted to run to Will and offer a million apologies, I didn't want to turn down what was staring me dead in the face.

I walked over to him without asking about the fiancée, why he was late, or anything. None of that mattered at that time and moment. I simply pushed him down on the couch, straddled my legs around him, and put my tongue in his mouth.

"Damn," was all he said as he kissed me back, and all at once, the only thing that mattered was me and him—not his fiancée, not Charles, not Tyrone and his grandmother, and not even Will. Just me and him, like I wanted it to be.

At that moment, I realized that I didn't need the other men in my life and that Kevin could very well be my now and forever, if there wasn't the little factor of his fiancée.

As he flipped me over onto my back on the couch and his mouth made its way to my treasure, I moaned in pure enjoyment and satisfaction. With both of my hands gripping his head, I begged him not to stop, and he fully obliged my request, until I said the one thing that managed to change the whole trajectory of the entire night.

"I love you, Kevin."

CHAPTER 15

MYA

"All I did was tell him I loved him, Alize. What's so bad about that?" I asked her after she'd finally made it to work and I was able to spill all the details about my dealings with Will and Kevin the day prior.

"Wait a minute. Before we get to that, can you please tell me about this outfit that you wore to the man's Bible study again?" She burst out laughing as if I were in some type of comedy show.

After giving her a look of irritation, I noticed how good of a mood she was in, grinning and cheesing from ear to ear and damn near glowing. I also saw that she hadn't brought the kids in with her and that she was back to her usual style of dress. All of that told me that something was going on that I didn't know about, but I decided to wait before asking her so that I could finish venting all my frustrations.

"Look, I'm trying to be serious, all right? I think I've lost Kevin for good, and this is really bothering me."

"Girl, I'm sorry, but are you for real?" she asked, looking at me like I was crazy.

"What?"

"Mya, what do you mean, *what*? Just listen to yourself. *You think you've lost Kevin for good*? Honey, you were never *with* the man. It was only sex. And hello? The man has a whole fiancée. That's why he doesn't want to be all *in love* with you, because he's in love with someone else."

"All right, all right, I hear you, and part of me already knows that. But I can't help but wonder why he continually comes back to me if there are no feelings involved. I mean, he's the one that called me yesterday, Alize. I was minding my own business at Bible study with Will, and then he called."

"Girl, listen. Kevin is the type that's going to come back as long as you allow him to. That's it. And the only feelings he has are for his soon-to-be wife, and even then, I'm a little skeptical about that, seeing that he keeps running back to you and who knows who else. And as for you *minding your own business*, you should have continued doing that and stayed at that Bible study with Will. Don't you know that was just the devil trying to distract by having the one man you want the most call you as soon as you're in church? He was a distraction, a hindrance. That's all. And the one person I feel sorry for the most is Will. Not only did you leave him hanging high and dry at the church, but to find that you only went home to be entertained by another man? That was just awful, Mya, and I'm sure heartbreaking. He probably thinks you're some type of ho."

"Well, damn, Zae, tell me how you really feel. Don't you think that I already feel bad enough? And now here you go, making it worse."

"I'm sorry, okay? That wasn't my intention at all. I was only putting myself in his shoes, and I can only imagine how things looked to him."

"Yeah, I'm sure you're right. And honestly, I practically felt like a ho, too, with the way Kevin just walked right past him and inside with me standing there in my robe. It was horrible, Zae, and I don't know how to make it up to him."

"*How to make it up to him*? By leaving him alone, that's how."

"What do you mean leave him alone?"

"Exactly what I said. Mya. You don't want the man. You didn't want him when you met him, and you surely don't see a future with him now, so stop wasting his time and blocking another woman's blessing that won't find him too *churchy* and will see a relationship with him."

"I never said I didn't want him, okay? I only said that he was a bit too churchy and hasn't quite grown on me yet. But I did see some things that I liked yesterday, so who knows what the future holds."

"Girl, stop lying to me and yourself, all right? We both know that your future doesn't hold Will in it, so please just set him free. And while you're at it, you might as well set Kevin free, set the young one free, and please, please, please set that good-for-nothing Charles free."

She said his name, and it dawned on me that I hadn't mentioned the fact that he'd contacted me yesterday, too. I really didn't want to mention much about Charles to her, especially after the not-so-pleasant things he had to say about her, but I knew there was no way of keeping it from her. Alize always had a way of getting things out of me, so I decided to bite the bullet.

"By the way, speaking of Charles, I heard from him yesterday too."

"What? You can't be serious. What the hell did he have to say? And please, Mya, please don't tell me you're keeping that jerk around."

"No, no, I'm not. I mean, at least I don't think I am. Anyway, he went on and on about me owing him an apology for the other night. Can you believe that? *I* owed *him* an apology, he said, for embarrassing him in front of his clients. Then I think that once he saw he wasn't about to get one, he threw out some mess that he was about to *waste* seven hundred dollars on me for the evening. *Seven hundred*, Zae, like I really cared. I started to tell him that I can make that in an hour or less, but I was so focused on Kevin that I just ended the call with him."

"Never to call him back, I hope. Mya, look, I know you're an adult, and who you choose to be with is your decision, but I really think you should find someone brand new who wants the same things that you want. Or better yet, sit still and be alone for a while and wait until he finds you."

"I don't know. Maybe you're right," I said, getting up from the edge of her desk and heading over to mine, "but honestly, it's the alone part that scares me the most."

"Listen, I'm sure it does. Hell, just a day or so without Anthony had me scared out of my mind. But if we truly want our now and forever or never like you said, then we just have to suck it up and swallow that *alone* pill until we get what we truly want and deserve."

I'd heard everything that had just come from her mouth, but I was stuck way back at the "just a day or so without Anthony."

"Um, wait a minute. Can we rewind that just a bit? What exactly do you mean 'just a day or so'? See, I knew something was up with all that grinning and laughing you were doing earlier and not running in here super late with the kids trailing right behind you. So, you let him come back, huh?" I asked, staring at her and waiting for a response.

CHAPTER 16

ALIZE

It took me a few minutes before answering her. After hearing how distraught she was about her evening last night, I almost regretted saying anything about how amazing mine had been in my household. However, I knew that she wasn't about to give this a rest.

"Yes, Mya. I let him back, all right?"

"Zae, listen, if Anthony truly makes you happy and you're fine with you all's situation, then who am I to say anything? I just hate seeing you come in here time and time again bawling your eyes out over something he's done."

"Look, of course me and Anthony have our ups and downs, Mya. Every relationship does. But I've been with the man for the past seven years, and he's the father of my four children. It's not so easy to just walk away from all of that. And I don't want to leave and then end up being alone like—"

"Like me?" I interrupted her comment. "But weren't you the one just telling me to take some time alone?"

"I did, and I meant every word, but things are different for me and him."

She didn't say much of anything after that. I knew that she probably thought I was being a complete hypocrite, but what she refused to see was things *were* different for me and her. Extremely. She could easily move on to the next man she found attractive and educated and run off into the sunset with him. But who was I running off into the sunset with, with four small children trailing right behind me? And it wasn't to say that I didn't think I could find someone else outside of Anthony, but I came as a complete package. Whoever I did end up with, if Anthony went back to his same old ways, would have to accept that.

Suddenly thinking about him and his old ways, I remembered what I'd done after he went to sleep last night. After getting home, I decided to cook a home-cooked meal that we sat at the table and ate. I'd even put Moet and Moscato in their little seats so that no one would be left out. I'd made some Salisbury steaks, potatoes au gratin, a nice chef salad, and topped it all off with some red and purple Kool-Aid mixed. It was Anthony's favorite meal, and I felt like it was the least I could do for rushing to us to fix the car. We'd laughed and talked about his brother and the fact that I was going to put his things in trash bags, and I even shared with him what I'd seen between Leslie and Charles. I was very careful, though, not to say anything about his son's mother, Monique, or marriage. I knew that had I brought up either subject, our wonderful evening would have gone down the drain.

He did, however, weigh in on the matter with Mya, Charles, and Leslie. He felt that as a good friend, I needed to tell her everything I knew, but something inside still wouldn't let me. It all boiled down to not wanting to hurt Mya. Plus, I continued to pray that she would leave him alone and Charles would simply be Leslie's problem from here on out.

After dinner, I gave all the children their baths and settled them in for the night. Then, it was finally time for me and Anthony. He'd already showered and was lying across the bed, fat, full, and happy. When I walked in and was about to shower, he stopped me dead in my tracks and began to hug and kiss me. I begged and pleaded for him to stop so that I could clean up, but his response, as usual, was, "I like it when you're all natural." Needless to say, our evening ended in some of the most passionate and raunchiest lovemaking we'd ever had. But although he went straight to sleep like a brand-new baby, I still felt a little unsettled in my mind and spirit. I couldn't stop wondering what made him run right to Monique, whether or not he'd cheated on me with her before, and now, since he was back, if he was done with her. In fact, unless I scheduled his visits with his son, he shouldn't have any need to call her himself. With that in mind, I peeked over on his side of the bed and saw his cell phone lying face down on the nightside. Instead of taking the time to go through his texts to see his communication with her, I decided to share his location with my phone. That way, everywhere he went today, I would know, including if he went to her house. True enough, I knew it was wrong, but if I was going to continue with our relationship, I had to do something to put my spirit as ease.

While it appeared as if Mya was getting caught up on some work, I decided to check his whereabouts. It gave me a spot that was actually not too far from the job. Then, as my eyes zoomed in a little closer, I realized that I knew exactly where he was because we had been there a couple of times in the past before. This creep was at the damn abortion clinic. My complexion may have been dark as the midnight sky, but I wondered if Mya could tell how red hot I was at that very moment. Instead of letting her in on what I'd done, though, I decided to go outside and call the creep.

"Mya, I'll be right back, okay? I need some air."

"Sure thing," she said, never looking up from the documents on her desk.

Then I switched my ass as fast as I could downstairs to the front parking lot. I hadn't even spoken to a couple of people that I passed by in the hallway until I'd gotten to Milton. He grabbed my arm after noticing how much of a hurry I was in.

"Whoa, whoa, Ms. Alize. Where are you running off huffing and puffing like that?"

"I just need to make a quick phone call, that's all, Milton," I said, not looking him dead in the eyes because I was sure he would see the water building inside of them. Instead of leaving me to myself, he stepped outside with me.

"Ms. Alize, now you know I can tell when something's got you all in a frenzy. Now, I'm not trying to overstep or pry, but what's going on? Is everything all right?"

My legs wouldn't stop moving, and before I knew it, I covered my face before he could see me cry. Then, I felt his arms surround me.

"Come here, come here, it's okay. Everything is going to be all right."

I wanted to tell him so desperately, but the words just wouldn't seem to come from my mouth.

"Whatever it is, I got you, and just remember, you are strong enough to handle this, and this too shall pass."

All at once, his words from before came back to me. I wanted to be that strong woman just like Faye was. And now, since I knew that there was no changing Anthony, this relationship was no longer serving its purpose, and it was time for me to walk away. And even though deep down in my heart, I didn't want that, I knew it had to happen. Pulling away from Milton, I tried to pat my eyes dry.

"Are you okay, Ms. Alize?"

I simply nodded my head before forcing words to come out, "I will be. It's time, Milton."

"All right, I am here for you one hundred percent."

We stood there in complete silence for a few minutes until I decided I'd calmed down enough and wiped my eyes before going back in. At that point, it was no longer necessary for me to call him and say anything. My actions were going to speak much, much louder than my words ever could.

"Milton?" I said as he opened the door for me. "Can we please keep this all between you and me? I don't want Mya to know what's going on."

"Hey, you never have to worry about me saying anything to anyone. What's shared between you and me will always remain between you and me."

CHAPTER 17

MYA

Catching a glance of Alize as she came back inside, I kind of noticed that she was no longer her happy, jovial self as when she'd first gotten to work. My suspicions told me that it most likely had to do with Anthony, as usual, but I decided not to pressure her into telling me what was going on. Knowing my friend the way I did, I was sure that I would find out sooner than later.

The office remained quiet after that. At least, that was until Leslie made her daily appearance.

"Hey ladies," she said, all happy and chipper.

"Hi, Leslie," I replied all by myself, with Alize never looking up to acknowledge her.

"I just stopped down here to tell you that you guys left your lights on and the door to your office unlocked after hours yesterday."

"Oh, we did? I left a little early yesterday, so I thought Alize would handle that." I looked over at her, a little puzzled.

"I did handle it, Mya. I was here pretty late yesterday . Me and the girls. It was well after hours. You know, when the elevators are shut down, and you have to walk up the stairs to the floors. It's amazing what you see and hear once everyone is gone for the day, isn't that right, Leslie?" she said, looking her square in the eyes. I had no clue what was going on between the two women, but whatever it was was enough to make Leslie not outstay her welcome.

"I see. Well, it's about that time to head out, so I will see you ladies tomorrow. I have a hot date tonight with my Mr. Wonderful."

"Good for you. Just be sure to take enough cash to cover the bill. You know, we can never have enough petty cash," Alize said.

Leslie high-tailed it out of there quickly after that without another word, and I couldn't help but look at my friend in shock.

"Zae, what the hell was that all about with you and Leslie?"

"Girl, it doesn't matter, all right? I'm just tired of her coming down here all high and mighty. Someone has to put her in her place from time to time."

"Well, you sure did that. But enough about her. Are you okay? You seem a little different ever since you went outside."

"I'm fine," was all she said, so I took that as my sign that she still wasn't ready to share.

"All right. Well, I'm about to head out if that's okay with you."

"Yeah, that's cool. I'll be leaving as soon as Anthony gets here."

I had assumed that whatever had her in such a negative disposition had to do with Anthony, but since he was still picking her up, I figured that maybe I was wrong.

"Okay, well, just be sure to turn out the lights and lock the door," I said with a slight chuckle, hoping to brighten her spirits, but she hadn't cracked a smile.

She simply said, "Sure thing," while keeping her eyes focused on her cell phone.

I, on the other hand, couldn't wait to get home. Tonight, I had decided it was going to be all about me and not about Mr. One, Two, Three, or Four. And in fact, I was looking forward to the time alone. The entire time that Alize was outside, I was thinking to myself about truly being alone until God finally sent him. And for the first time, I felt like it just might be possible.

After I made it home, I prepared a nice, steaming hot bath with my usual oils and fragrances to relax every part of my body. I lit my candles, turned on some soft rhythm and blues, and poured a glass of red wine. Then, as I sank into the bath and allowed the hot water to take effect, I thought about how it was just what the doctor had ordered. There was no one demanding my time and attention like Tyrone, no one making me feel less than like Charles had, or second best like Kevin. Then I closed my eyes and thought again about Will. As much as I hadn't wanted to admit it, Alize was right. I didn't see a future with Will and owed it to him to at least tell him that much. I wasn't in the business of hurting someone else, especially with the way I felt I had been hurt by men. So, I needed to tell him the truth sooner than later.

With that said, I told Alexa to mute the music and picked up my cell phone to dial his number. For some strange reason, I was extremely nervous and wasn't sure what to say once he answered, but I promised myself that I would be honest no matter what. The phone rang and rang, only to end up going to his voicemail.

"All right, Will. I'll give this one more try," I said, dialing once again and this time preparing myself to possibly leave a voicemail message. I knew it would be a little tacky if I'd taken that route, but I was determined to get the way I was feeling off my mind and my heart. To my surprise, I heard his voice after the second time around.

"Hello?"

"Will, hi. It's Mya."

"Uh, hey, Mya," he said with a strange hesitation in his voice. "What's up?"

"Are you busy? I wanted to talk to you . . . about yesterday."

"Oh, Mya, you don't owe me any explanations. You're a single woman and free to see whoever you like."

His statement had caught me a little off guard. He knew I was doing way more than *seeing* Kevin, but still kept his words classy and respectful. That in and of itself made what I was about to say even harder because deep down, I knew that I was about to let go of a perfectly good man all because of him not being a complete jerk like the men I was used to.

"I know, but still, it wasn't right," I said before hearing a soft voice in his background.

"Will, the movie is about to start," I heard her say, and immediately I became winded. Hearing this woman talking to him all sweet and gentle practically took the air out of me and made me feel as if I had been sucker punched in the gut.

"Uh, Mya, I'm sorry, but I—"

"You have to go." I finished his sentence for him. "Please, there's nothing to be sorry for. I guess I just caught you at a bad time."

"Yeah," was all he managed to say. "Um, but why don't I just give you a buzz sometime tomorrow?"

"Uh, sure, that sounds good," I said, trying to save face but also knowing that if he did call, I would more than likely not answer.

It was strange because with Kevin, I knew he'd asked another woman to marry him. I even looked this woman in the face that night, twice. And yet, I still had no qualms about playing second fiddle to her just to be with him. But with Will, it was something totally different. If he thought I was going to play second base to another woman, then he had another thing coming. Hearing her also made me wonder if she was simply someone he was entertaining because of what I'd done or if he was seriously into her. I also couldn't help but ask myself where she had come from. *Is she one of those women in the church last night who saw us together and now suddenly wanted to sink her claws into him?* I thought. Women were downright sneaky and conniving that way. She'd probably come in contact with Will a million times over but didn't want him until seeing him with another attractive woman.

Of course, I knew that I didn't have the right to be upset, but I was. And I also had the right mind to stroll right into that church on Sunday morning in my best Sunday's best outfit and plop my ass on the bench right next to him. Then I would see exactly who this *"Will, the movie's about start"* woman was. I was so irritated, plus my water was now lukewarm, that I decided to get out of the tub altogether. My relaxing vibe was over, all because of a man.

I cleaned out my bathtub, blew out my candle, and took my half-empty glass of wine into my bedroom. I was far from being sleepy and needed something to keep my thoughts from fucking Kevin as they were headed in that direction. Then suddenly, out of nowhere, I thought about the minister at Will's church and the passage he'd read yesterday.

"Seek ye first, seek ye first," I repeated to myself as I Googled those three words. Having never been the one to sit down and read my Bible word for word, I didn't know exactly where to find certain scriptures. In fact, the only reason I had a Bible was because my grandmother gave it to me before I went off to college. I could still hear her voice today telling me, "Now, Mya, no matter what you go through in life, every answer is inside of this book right here. Whether you need guidance, encouragement, uplifting, or just confirmation on the direction you're going, you can find it all right here. And if nothing else, fall down on your knees and pray."

I smiled as I thought about my grandma Mae. She was the one I would always run to whenever I needed anything—advice, a hug, a good home-cooked meal, or simply to hear "I love you." And it wasn't that I couldn't get those things from my parents, but my grandma was just someone different. She was special, and I felt like my world had been ripped away from me when she passed away four years ago.

After typing in those three words, the scripture was staring me dead in the face.

But seek first the Kingdom of God and his righteousness, and all these things will be added to you. Therefore, do not be anxious about tomorrow, for tomorrow will be anxious for itself. Sufficient for the day is its own trouble.

Reading the words over and over again, I tried my best not to be skeptical as I thought, was that really all that I had to do? *All I need to do is seek God and He will take care of the rest?* I asked myself. It seemed so simple, but also one of the hardest things for me to do. I was such an independent woman and prided myself on that. Trusting in a God I couldn't hear or see scared me. How was I to relinquish my control to simply trust Him? Part of me wanted to give it a try, just to see if all my heart's desires would suddenly be given to me if I lived my entire life for Him. But my grandmother had also taught me not to play with God. If I was going to be all in, then I had to be all in and not riding the fence, and honestly, I wasn't one hundred percent sure I was ready to be all in.

With that in mind, I deleted my Google search and headed to my social media. Scrolling through the various pictures and videos on Instagram, I just happened to come up on a video with the title *For Singles Only.*

Was this what Alize was talking about? I wondered as I clicked on to hear what they were saying. It was the host and a single man on Live with one another. I listened closely to her, asking question after question about what he liked, what type of woman he desired, and why he thought he would be a good catch. He had very intelligent responses and was actually fairly handsome, too. I almost thought about reaching out to him if I were the type to approach a man. But then he said he had five children by five different women and had never been married, and suddenly, I knew why he was single.

After that, I watched a few more people shoot their shot at a chance for love. Women wanting women, men wanting men, transgenders, and so forth. Then others with numerous children by numerous people. It was starting to be a bit much, but looking around my room and realizing my alone state just might be a normal thing, I said what the heck and decided to try my luck. I glanced at myself in the mirror before pushing the "go live" button and decided that I at least needed some lip gloss and to pull my hair back in a bun. I didn't want anyone I knew to possibly catch me looking a hot-ass mess, but then again, I really didn't want anyone I knew to see me on there at all. I looked at the time and thought how everyone I worked with should have been asleep, so hesitantly, I finally pushed the button. After about an hour of waiting to see if I would be chosen, I was about to disconnect when I heard her voice say, "Hey, love. Are you looking for love tonight?"

I could clearly see her face staring directly at me, but for some reason, I still couldn't believe I'd gotten on.

"Oh, wow. I can't believe you actually chose me."

"Well, believe it, because I did. Are you looking for love?"

"Um, sure."

"What's your name and where are you from?"

"I'm Mya, and I live in Atlanta."

She went on to ask me other questions about myself, like my age, zodiac sign, if I'd ever been married, and whether I had any children. Then, she got right down to the meat of things.

"Okay, Ms. Mya, so what type of man are you looking for?"

After the whole hour of waiting and watching others answer this same question, I thought that I had come up with the best answer. However, now that it was before me, I wasn't sure what to say.

"Um, I just want a responsible, lovable, charming, secure man."

"All right. So, does he have to look a certain way?"

"Uh, at least six feet or above, physically fit, and I'm more attracted to men with a darker complexion. And a full beard wouldn't hurt."

"Do you mind if he has children?"

"Well, maybe one or two, I guess I wouldn't mind, but I would really like someone that doesn't have children so that we can experience our *firsts* together."

"What about money? Does he have to make a certain amount?"

"I would think six figures, at least. I mean, how can you really survive in this world with anything less?"

"So, let me get this right," she said in a way that made me feel as if I was about to be reprimanded. "You want a tall, dark, handsome man that makes six figures with no children? Honey, that's what we're all looking for." She laughed.

I tried not to feel embarrassed or ashamed by her response, yet I did. Was I asking for too much, or was this type of man just not out there? I wanted to quickly end the call at that point and go hide under my covers, but I had to let her finish out.

"So, Mya, tell me, when was your last relationship?"

There was no way on God's green earth I was about to tell her about my one, two, three, or four, so I lied and said about three years ago.

"And when was the last time you've been intimate with someone?"

"Um, can I not answer that?"

"You can, I suppose, but at least tell me if it's been recent."

"Uh, I don't know. Maybe in the past couple of weeks."

"So why can't you be with that man?"

I searched my mind for the fastest, most appropriate answer, but there just wasn't one. And I definitely wasn't going to tell her that he'd just gotten engaged to someone.

"Uh, I guess we're just not compatible with one another as far as a relationship is concerned."

"But you're compatible enough to lay down with each other?"

Damn, I almost felt as if I was talking with my Grandma Mae, and even she wouldn't have been that hard on me.

"Hey, sex is sex, I guess," was all I could think to say.

Then, finally, it seemed I'd gotten to the finish line.

"All right, Mya, so tell us why a man would be lucky to be with you."

"I would just say because I believe I'm the whole package. I'm intelligent, I keep myself up and I think I'm attractive. Good career, financially stable, sweet, and I wouldn't mind catering to the right man."

"Well, there you have it, folks. If you want to get in touch with Mya, just hit up her DMs."

We ended, and at once, I could breathe. Although it was only a simple Live, it was one of the hardest things I'd ever done, even harder than any of my court cases. Coming out and saying what I truly desired without really knowing what I truly desired was a feat in itself. I immediately wanted to look to see if anyone had decided to DM me, but it was getting late, and I was tired as well as overwhelmed. So, I decided to turn out the lights and hope for the best.

CHAPTER 18

ALIZE

The car ride home from work had been quiet for the most part. Other than the sounds of Champagne and Hennesy playing with one another, there wasn't much conversation between Anthony and me. The minute we walked through the door and I had the children in their room, all of that changed. I walked into the kitchen to try to prepare a quick meal when Anthony followed me there.

"Zae, what's up? Why have you been so quiet?"

"No reason," I lied. "I just had a long day at work, and I want to cook, take a shower, and go to bed."

"Go to bed?" He walked over to me at the sink and put his arms around my waist. "So, no good loving for Daddy tonight?"

"Stop, Anthony, all right. I'm not in the mood." I pushed him off me.

"Yeah, I can tell, but what gives? What happened at work that's got you all upset?"

"I don't want to talk about it, so let's just leave it alone."

"But I bet I know exactly what—or shall I say *who*—it is. It's always that damn Mya saying some shit she has no business saying. How did she put her nose in our business this time? She had some shit to say because I'm back at home, didn't she? I keep telling you, Zae, that lonely chick just wants you lonely and miserable, just like her." He walked toward the back of the house as if he was totally right about what was bothering me.

Little did he know, he was the actual root of all my problems, but I surely had a way of fixing it. After Mya left and I waited for him to get there, I called my cousin, who was also like a big brother to me. I told him the short version of what was going on and asked if he would come by the house tomorrow and change my locks. Although Anthony didn't have a nine-to-five job, he was rarely home during the day. Then, without removing the access to his location on his cell phone, I told my cousin that I wanted him to basically be on call for me to go and pick up my car when I needed him to. I was sure that Anthony wouldn't know what hit him, but he would definitely find out.

After we managed to have a quiet and peaceful dinner without Anthony's constant bashing of Mya, I settled the kids and went to take a shower. Getting in, I let the hot water shoot into every crevice of my body. It was all extremely soothing as I tried to wash away the turmoil of the day. However, the second I started to feel at ease, Anthony opened the shower door and stepped inside.

"Anthony, what are you doing?"

"Trying to make you feel good. Baby, you know I hate when that friend of yours gets you all uptight and stressed like this."

"Look, it's not Mya, all right? And honestly, I just want to shower alone, so please . . ."

"Baby, come here," he said, trying to pull me close.

"No, just . . . just . . . move." I hopped out and wrapped my towel around me before going into the room with the children and shutting the door behind me. A rush of tears started to flow as I wanted so desperately to ask what the hell he was doing at an abortion clinic, but my pride wouldn't let me. I was going to be strong this time and not let my emotions or good sex block my train of thought. I was going to find my *inner Faye* to finally walk away from what was no longer serving me.

It took me at least an hour or so to calm my nerves, and once I did, I peeked out of the room to see where Anthony was. Thankfully, he had fallen asleep on the couch in front of the television.

"Yeah, I hope you're real comfortable because that will be your last opportunity to rest in this house," I said, looking at him with disgust all over my face. As I stared at him sleeping peacefully, I began to wonder why I stayed with him as long as I had. Had I been that afraid of walking away? Truth be told, I knew I wasn't as happy as I wanted to be, and I'd had this feeling way before Mya started preaching about marriage. Then, as I stared at him some more, I thought how I could practically kill him for getting another woman pregnant. He already had five children that he couldn't afford or help to take care of. In fact, the little that he was able to do for me and the children was the least he could do for me, taking care of the bills with everything else. I wanted and needed more than this, and Anthony was about to find out how serious I was.

I'd decided to sleep in the room with the children just in case he woke up and crawled into the bed in the middle of the night. I didn't want his body anywhere next to mine. Going into the girl's room, I wasn't all the way tired, but I didn't want to turn on any lights or television for fear of waking them. But I figured the minor light from my cell phone wouldn't do any harm. Pulling up my Instagram, I scrolled through the various pictures, laughed at some funny videos, and caught up on some news since that was my only form of news outlet.

Then I'd come across what had come to be my favorite, *For Singles Only*. It amazed me how people got on night after night, baring their hearts and souls while trying to find love. What was always the oddest thing were the very manly men who said they were looking for a man, but then I guessed love didn't have to have a gender. And what was even more shocking were the transgender people who you couldn't tell by looking were born a totally different sex. Watching it almost made me want to rethink things with Anthony because at least with him, I knew what I was getting and what I could deal with. There were so many men who had numerous baby mommas, no jobs, no goals or aspirations, and no problems saying that they were looking for a woman who could support them. Then, to top things off, you even had men who had someone and were looking for another woman to add to their polyamorous lifestyle. It was insane, to say the least, and made me cringe at the whole thought of dating once Anthony was gone for good.

Then, out of nowhere, I saw my friend's face pop up on the screen.

"Mya? Oh, my goodness. Girl, you really got on here?" I asked like she could actually hear me while I tried not to laugh too loudly.

My ears perked up at once so that I would hear her clearly, and there I lay, intensely tuned in, trying to answer each question just as I thought she would, all in my Mya voice. I heard the host ask, *"Okay, Ms. Mya, so what type of man are you looking for?"*

I was waiting for her to say a financially stable, good career, and extremely good dick type of man, but my mouth dropped open when all she said was, *"Um, I just want a responsible, lovable, charming, secure man."*

"Okay, so this is what we're doing, Mya," I talked to the screen. "So, you're just going to put on your proper voice and give these ol' stale-ass courtroom type of answers."

"All right. So, does he have to look a certain way?"

"Yes," I said before she even responded. "Tall, muscular, dark, a beard, and looonnnggg dick." And when I heard her answer, it pretty much confirmed how well I knew my friend, although she'd left off the long dick part.

"Uh, at least six feet or above, physically fit, and I'm more attracted to men with a darker complexion. And a full beard wouldn't hurt."

"Do you mind if he has children?"

"Well, maybe one or two, I guess I wouldn't mind, but I would really like someone that doesn't have children so that we can experience our firsts together."

"That's damn right, Mya. You know you don't want a man with a whole ready-made family . . . like my baby daddy ass. That type of man is only broke and probably still messing with the baby momma. Plus, you don't want to have to pay no man's child support for him."

"What about money? Does he have to make a certain amount?"

"I would think six figures at least. I mean, how can you really survive in this world with anything less?"

Man, when I heard my friend answer that particular question, I started hitting the air like I was high-fiving her ass. "Yes, bitch, yes. Six figures or more. Shit, what she thought? You're a whole damn attorney and can make six figures in your sleep, so the man definitely has to come with it."

"So, let me get this right. You want a tall, dark, handsome man that makes six figures and with no children? Honey, that's what we're all looking for."

Although I hated the way I felt like the host was trying to play my girl, I had to admit that she was right. One hundred percent of the women on earth were looking for that type of man. And I could tell that Mya had become easily embarrassed by the look on her face.

"So, Mya, tell me, when was your last relationship?"

With my hands formed in a praying stance, I pleaded to the heavens above, "Lord, please don't let her tell this woman about her one, two, three, or four. She's going to look like someone's average ho. I mean, I'm sorry, God, she's going to look loose." And that's when my girl came through.

"Uh, about three years ago."

"And when was the last time you've been intimate with someone?"

At that point, I simply put my head down and covered my face. Only I knew how much of a ho my friend truly was, and I was the only one that needed to know, not the whole damn world.

"Uh, I don't know, maybe in the past couple of weeks," she answered, and I couldn't have been prouder that she'd lied and said a couple of weeks and not a couple of days.

"So why can't you be with that man?"

"Now look, dammit, now you're asking too many questions," I talked to the screen as if I didn't know that question was about to come up. "What you got, Mya? What you got, girl?"

"Uh, I guess we're just not compatible with one another as far as a relationship is concerned."

"But you're compatible enough to lay down with each other?"

I couldn't wait to tell Mya how badly I wanted to fight the host at that point, and if I knew her location, I would suggest that we pop up on her.

"Hey, sex is sex, I guess," she answered, and I figured that was the best her discomfort would allow her to say.

Then, at last, the host came to the final question of the interview. *"All right, Mya, so tell us why a man would be lucky to be with you."*

"I would just say because I believe I'm the whole package. I'm intelligent, I keep myself up and I think I'm attractive. Good career, financially stable, sweet, and I wouldn't mind catering to the right man."

Immediately, I hopped up and started to dance around as if my friend had won a million bucks off that one response.

"Yes, bitch, you better let the whole world know who the hell Mya Anderson is 'cause you're that one, honey. You are that one. They better Google your ass."

"Well, there you have it, folks. If you want to get in touch with Mya, just hit up her DMs."

Laying back down, I couldn't help but think how much of a shit show that office building was going to be tomorrow. The thought of it, along with the show, had given me the much-needed laughter I needed for the evening and had taken my mind completely away from things with Anthony.

CHAPTER 19

MYA

"Oh my goodness." I covered my chest, and my mouth fell open the second I opened my eyes and picked up my phone to check the time. Right there on the front of it, I saw DM after DM scrolling across it. I couldn't even begin to count how many because it seemed like there were hundreds of them, from both men and women.

"Damn, it seems like the whole damn world was up watching this show last night." *What if someone from work saw this?* I thought to myself, but I figured a bunch of attorneys would never have time to watch a show like *For Singles Only*.

Quickly glancing at a couple of the messages, though, I saw some with just numbers, others with long paragraphs, and then there were some that actually included half or fully-unclothed pictures, again of both men and women, which I tried not to look at. However, instead of deleting them, I figured I'd keep them for whenever I needed a good laugh.

Amidst all the chaos of the DMs, I managed to see that I had some text messages on the screen as well. The first one appeared to be from Tyrone.

Hey, Ms. Anderson, what in the world was a woman like you doing on For Singles Only? You don't need that show. You got me.

"Yeah, I got you, but you don't know what the hell to do with me, youngster," I said back to the phone.

Then there was Charles. Wow, when I say that you have managed to surprise me yet again. The Mya that I first met would have never gotten on a ghetto-ass show like For Singles Only. This is what I mean when I say your friend is rubbing off on you.

"Oh, shut the hell up, Charles. No one cares what you think anymore." And that was when I reminded myself that I had to delete his number. There was no more debating about him being in my life after that phone call the other day.

There wasn't a message from Kevin, just like I suspected that there wouldn't be because social media just wasn't his thing. However, to my surprise, I did see a text from Will, which he'd sent thirty minutes before.

Good morning, Mya. I'm sorry to reach out so early, but I wanted to catch up with you before your day got busy. I wanted to explain last night if you allowed me to. Hope to hear back from you. Enjoy your day.

"How could you possibly explain last night, Will?" I questioned aloud. "You had a woman at your home in the evening hours to watch a movie. I don't need my law degree to decipher what that means," I said, wanting to be mad at him and hate his guts, but his holier-than-thou text had made it difficult to do that. So, I figured I would touch base with him when I was good and ready, if that ever came.

Having enough of my cell phone and social media, I threw it on the bed and tried to get ready for the day. However, in the back of my mind, I kept wondering if my Mr. Now or Never was buried somewhere in those DMs, or if they were all just a bunch of horny men and women that had nothing better to do with their time last night. With that thought, I hated that I'd ever listened to Alize and gotten on the show, and if I got the courage to tell her I'd tried it out, I was surely going to give her a piece of my mind.

I hadn't made it through the front door before Milton and Diane both had something to say.

"Hey Ms. Single and Ready to Mingle," Milton joked while holding open the door for me. "I would have never imagined you to get on a show like that, but I bet you got a ton of messages, huh?"

"I'm not exactly sure what you're talking about, Milton," I said, trying to play things off as much as possible. "I had a friend call and ask if that was me on some internet dating show, and I'm sorry to disappoint you guys, but it wasn't. I guess everyone has a twin in the world."

"Oh, c'mon now, don't be bashful, Ms. Anderson. We know that was you," Diane chimed in, pointing her finger at me like I'd been caught with my hand in the cookie jar. "That girl had a small mole above her lip, just like you do right there. And besides, it's nothing to be ashamed about. I thought about getting on there myself, but who's going to message my old behind?" She laughed.

"Listen, I'm telling you both that whoever was on there last night was not me, so can we please just give this a break, okay?"

"Whatever you say, boss lady," Milton said with a big smile across his face.

Then, walking to my office, I almost felt like I should have worn some type of disguise or at least a hat and sunglasses, because even if they didn't say anything, I still felt like everyone was looking at me as *that girl from the For Singles Only show*. I was positive that if Milton and Diane saw me on there, Alize surely did, so as I walked in, I tried my best to brace myself for whatever her reaction was.

"Hey, good morning, Zae," I said as I went inside and waited for her to give me the business.

"Good morning, girl. How are you today?" was all she'd said in a somber and kind of monotone voice. I was shocked to say the least, but also thankful that maybe she hadn't been on any social media last night like I thought.

"I'm good. I really could have used a couple of more hours of sleep, but I have my Frapp," I said, raising my cup and noticing the barista wrote *Ms. FSO* on the side instead of my name.

"What's got you so beat?"

"Just a long, sleepless night, that's all. It felt like by the time I got off to sleep, it was time to get up for work."

"I'm sure, but I would have thought you were tired from staying up and getting on *For Singles Only* last night. I saw you, Mya Anderson," she went on and on in her usual loud voice while pointing her finger at me.

"Would you please calm down, Zae? It was nothing, all right? I was bored and decided to log on for a few shits and giggles. That's it. Nothing serious."

"Nothing serious, my ass, Mya. I saw you with your hair all pulled back and lip gloss popping. And the way you answered that last question, why would a man be lucky to be with you? My girl said because she's the whole entire package. Now take that, bitches," she said and raised her hand to slap me a high five.

Although I desperately wanted things about the Live to die down, I felt like I couldn't leave her hanging. Plus, she was right. *I did answer the hell out of the question*, I thought as I finally obliged her high five.

"So, what made you get on last night?"

"Girl, I don't know. Maybe it was because part of me was bored and lonely, or maybe it had to do with hearing a woman in Will's background when I spoke with him. Either way, I'm kind of regretting doing it. I have a ton of DMs now but nothing from a quality man, I'm sure."

"But wait, wait, wait. Can we please back up to the part about hearing a female in Will's background?"

"Zae," I said, picking up my Frappuccino, walking toward the window, and looking out before taking a sip. I hated the fact that I'd said anything because it made me relive that moment all over again. "I called, basically to apologize for everything from the day before . . . leaving the church and for what he'd seen when he came by my house. I just wanted to make sure he knew I wasn't some ho, as you put it. But before I was able to get an apology out, I heard the woman's voice in the background, telling him the movie was about to start."

"Oh, wow, what did he say to you?"

"Nothing. I mean, there was more stuttering than anything, so I decided to end his misery and found the easiest and nicest way to get off the phone. He did leave me a text message this morning, though, in an attempt to explain, but I haven't bothered to call him back."

"Well, are you going to call him back?"

"I don't know. It's like, I know I don't really see a future with him, but I guess I just wasn't ready for him to *move on* so quickly."

"Well, I'm sorry to say it, Mya, but you know I'm going to always keep it real with you. I told you that if you didn't want that man, then some holy-holy woman would surely snatch him up."

"Thanks for not saying I told you so," I said sarcastically. "But anyway, that's when I decided to do the Live, and now it's turned into all of this."

"Girl, stop worrying, all right? I'm sure you and I were the only ones in this building to see it."

"Yeah, well, I wish that was true," I said as I set my half-empty cup back down on my desk. "But it seems that Milton and Diane were also up on social media as well."

"Not Milton and Ms. Old Diane?" She cracked up.

"Yeah, them too."

Before we were able to say anything more, Leslie made her daily appearance in our office.

"Hey, good morning, ladies."

"Good morning," both Alize and I said back dryly in unison.

"I saw you last night, Ms. Mya, on the *Singles* show," she said, smiling awfully hard at me. "Now, I'm sure that you probably got a lot of DMs, but I wanted to tell you that if nothing pans out, I would be more than happy to see if my friend has a friend or brother or cousin for you. He's a very well-off, high-profile type of guy, and you know what they say . . . birds of a feather flock together."

"Uh, you know what, Leslie? I only jumped on there for the fun of it all, nothing serious, so thanks but no thanks."

"Are you sure? Because I was already planning double dates in my head and everything. Oh, and we could make it a triple for you and your children's father too, Alize, if you want to tag along," she said.

I knew it was only a matter of time before those two went through their morning ritual with one another. Luckily and oddly enough, though, Alize didn't say anything. She simply gave her a weird smirk and went right back to focusing on what was on her desk.

"Trust me, Leslie, there won't be any double date planning necessary, all right? I'm fine."

"Okay, well, if you say so, but the offer stands whenever you're ready."

"I appreciate that."

She stood there for a moment or two before it looked as if she were about to head out, but out of the clear blue sky strolled in a manly creature practically sent from God up above.

"Damn," all three of us said in harmony as each one of our jaws reached to the floor. The term drop dead gorgeous was an understatement for him. He appeared to be at least 6 feet 5 inches in stature. His body was not too lean and not too bulky either, but just right like that of a Greek god. And as my eyes took a slow dance around this entire being, everything about him read striking. His skin looked like smooth caramel and butterscotch mixed together and good enough to eat. His baldpate showed off his Hades-black eyebrows, come-hither eyes that pierced straight through to your soul, his lordly nose, and full lips. His concave cheekbones rested on skin pulled tight like a bolt of fine cloth, and he had a marble jaw that was rugged and masculine, all wrapped in his salt-and-peppered beard.

"Um, hello." I was the first one to speak up while hopping off the edge of my desk and straightening my clothes and hair with my hand. "Hi, my name is Mya Anderson, and I am one of the family law and divorce attorneys here at New Horizons. How can I assist you today?" I asked, sticking my other hand out as an introduction but more so to get a sense of how strong his hands were.

"Hello." His voice echoed through the room, strong, deep, and powerful. "I am Mr. Carson Avery Reed, and I have an appointment today with Mr. Robert Buchanon. But, from the looks of it, I think I may have found myself in the wrong location because I'm sure none of you beautiful ladies could be Mr. Buchanon," he said, showing off his charming smile and debonair personality.

"Mr. Buchanon is actually on the third floor, which is my floor." Leslie smiled, extending her hand to introduce herself while jumping in front of me. "I would be more than happy to lead the way."

"Oh Lord, good grief," Alize tried to say quietly, but it came out louder than she must have expected.

"Um, sure, that would be great, Leslie. But I'm sorry, I didn't get your name." He looked over at Zae.

"Hi, I'm Alize," she said almost bashfully, which was totally outside of her normal demeanor.

"It's a pleasure to meet you, Ms. Alize. Like the liqueur, correct?" he asked with the word "liqueur" flowing off his lips all French-like and damn near made them good enough to taste. "I love the taste of a smooth Alize." We all started to laugh as Leslie tossed her rump from side to side as she escorted him out of the room to the third floor.

"Oh my goodness, Zae. It's him." I almost wanted to jump for joy.

"Him? Girl, what are you talking about? Who is him?"

"Carson! He's my now and forever. I mean, can't you see it? Mrs. Mya Anderson-Avery Reed. Don't you just love the way it sounds?"

"You really want to know what I think? I think that the whole *For Singles Only* has made you lose your marbles. You've only known the man all of five minutes and you don't know anything at all about him. Besides, who said he was interested in *you*? There were three of us in the room, you know."

"Alize, now, c'mon. Are you being serious right now? We both know that there's no way a man like that would be interested in Leslie. She'll run him away in a matter of a week." I laughed but didn't see a smile nearly begin to come across her face.

"And me?" she asked.

"You?"

"Yes, me." It seemed as if her voice raised an octave. "I mean, I may not be all well-educated, degreed, and proper-speaking like you, but would it be impossible to believe that a man like that would find some interest in me? You saw for yourself how he didn't want to leave until he met me, too, and heard him when he said he loved the taste of Alize."

"The liqueur, Zae. The liqueur is what he was referring to, and if you didn't realize it, he was teasing you, girl. None of that meant that he had an interest in you."

"But my question is why that would be so far-fetched, though, Mya. I'm beautiful, intelligent, and a woman with the whole package, just like you."

"Zae, yes, you are beautiful and intelligent. And yes, I do think you have the whole package, but not for a man like Carson. Besides, you still have a baby daddy that you go back and forth with practically every other day, not to mention four small children. I very seriously doubt a man like that wants to come in and take care of a ready-made family. I mean, we must be realistic here."

"Oh, wow, and this is coming from the mouth of the same woman that's been dealing with four different men at the same time for the past couple of years. Now *Ms. Indecis*ive knows what's best for everybody involved, huh?"

"Zae, I'm going to step outside for a bit and get a taste of fresh air. It's getting way too stuffy in here."

I walked out, almost knocking over Diane in the hallway and brushing right past Milton without all the banter. Alize had pushed me farther than I had been pushed in quite a long time, and I felt myself being on the verge of saying a lot more that I would have regretted. I already felt bad enough that I'd basically insinuated that she could never get a man like Carson, but the truth was the truth.

That man had a certain character and charm. He was mature and suave, classy and stylish, and needed more than a woman with caterpillar eyebrows and Edward Scissorhands-like fingernails. I mean, how on earth was he supposed to show up at important dinner meetings and functions with my friend, who was only used to eating wings and pizza and not fine-quality cuisine that she couldn't pronounce? And it wasn't that I was looking down on her at all, but I was doing this more for her protection. *Why can't she see that?* I thought.

After I took a couple more deep breaths to calm down, the man of the hour came walking out the door. Quickly, I tried to adjust my attitude so that he couldn't tell anything was wrong. He walked right over to me, and I simply wanted to melt in his arms.

"Hey, Mya. It is Mya, right?"

"Yes." I couldn't stop smiling. "Finished up with Attorney Buchanon already?"

"You sound surprised."

"I am, I guess. He's usually a bit long-winded."

"I guess I just know how to come in, state what I want, and get the job down."

"Oh, I see. Is that with everything?"

"Pretty much."

"So, what would you like right now, this very moment, if you could have it?" I asked, boldly flirting with him and hoping he took the bait.

"Honestly? Food. I haven't had much to eat all morning because of back-to-back meetings, and I am starving."

"Me too, actually. So why don't we grab a bite to eat?" I tried my luck, having never really approached a man and asked him out before.

"Oh, uh, 'we' as in you and me?"

"Yeah, I mean, you're starving, and I'm starving. So why not?"

"Well, Ms. Mya, that actually doesn't sound like too bad of an idea. I'll take you to one of my favorite spots, but first, you have to tell me that you're not just one of those salad-eating women, and you won't be ashamed to lick your fingers in public."

"What?" I looked at him like he was crazy as he went to open his passenger door for me.

"C'mon, get in, and I promise you won't regret it."

I was excited and nervous all at the same time, but happy too. Happy that I'd finally met Mr. Carson Reed.

CHAPTER 20

ALIZE

"Zae, the car is gone," Anthony yelled several times in my ear. "I'm here at my brother's house, and I know I locked the doors and turned the alarm on, but now it's gone. It's like whoever stole it had a damn key or something."

I calmly listened to him vent his frustrations while popping my gum and trying to fix one of my fingernails. I was already too upset with Mya for the things she'd said to me to turn around and get into it with Anthony over my car.

"Did you hear me, Zae? I said our damn car has been stolen, and you're as quiet as a fuckin' mouse right now. What's up?"

"Anthony, look, I'm at work and I'm busy. If the car was stolen, how would me getting all upset and panicky solve anything? All we can do is file a report with the police, but why don't we wait to do that? Let's just see if it'll turn up."

"See if it'll turn up? What, you think the thieves are going to just politely bring it and write a note saying, 'Hey, sorry I stole your car, but you can have it back now'?"

"Look, do whatever you feel necessary, but I have to go," I said after getting a text from Mya saying she was taking a very early lunch break and should be back soon.

Instantly, I ran downstairs to the front of the building, where Milton was sitting at the door.

"Looking for your boss lady?" he asked, and immediately, I knew he had some information that he wanted to share.

"Yeah, have you seen her?" I asked, acting as if I'd never received the text and had no idea where she was.

"I sure did. She left with that tall fella that was here to see Buchanon. Mya works pretty fast, I see."

"So, that bitch went behind my back and left with Carson, huh?" I said aloud to myself, with Milton thinking I was talking to him.

"Yep."

"She just had to have him to herself. She wasn't going to be good unless she had him and not me. Okay, Mya, but we'll see how long your boring, stuck-up, bougie ass can keep him interested."

I went back to the office hurt, upset, and furious with the woman I not only called my boss, but my friend. For the life of me, I didn't understand why she'd always felt like she was the one that had to have all the good and decent men while I was stuck with Anthony. Even when we'd gone out in the past and a nice-looking man approached us, she'd always made sure to tell him that she was the single one and I was involved. Not to mention the way she'd always talked about Anthony and me, as if I was stuck with him and couldn't do any better. He always expressed to me that he thought Mya was jealous, but I refused to believe that about my friend. In my eyes, we were both beautiful, intelligent women with a ton of things going for us. There was no room for either of us to hate on each other. But now, the more I thought about our past and the things she'd said when it came to Carson and me, I was rethinking things.

***

An hour later, she'd finally come back into the office all bubbly and giggly. I looked at her, wishing I could smack that smile right off her face.

"Alize, Alize, Alize. Girl, I feel like a teenager in high school. Carson is absolutely everything. I didn't even want to leave. And get this, girl. He took my prim and prissy ass to a spot that had hot wings and pizza. Can you believe it? I was all out in public licking sauce from my fingers with this man. But Zae, he was amazing. I mean, perfect. We talked about a little bit of everything, and the conversation was easy, you know? He was easy to talk to, he listened to everything I said, and he just made me feel comfortable. And I know I sound crazy with it just being one little lunch date, but Zae, I truly feel like this could go somewhere. The moment was so magical that I really believe he could be my now and forever." She'd said a mouthful without even stopping.

"Good for you, Mya," was all I said back.

"Good for me? What's wrong with you?" She looked at me strangely as if she really didn't know. "Zae, I know you're not still upset over our little disagreement from earlier."

"*Little disagreement* is what we're calling it now? Mya, you're supposed to be my best friend, and you basically called me ghetto and not good enough for a man like Carson, but yet you think that your stuck-up ass is?"

"Stuck up, really? And just so you know, I didn't *basically* have to say anything. I simply stated the facts, and I guess the proof was in the pudding because he invited *me* to lunch now, didn't he?"

"You sound so damn childish right now. Like, what are we . . . back in high school or something? We are adults, Mya, and we were supposed to be best friends. But the more I look at things, it seems like I've always been way more of a friend to you than you've been to me. I've had your back through everything you've gone through in life, whether you were right or wrong. And the sad thing about it is, I can't say the same for you. You've always, always acted as if you were better than me. Even Anthony saw it. But not me. I've always tried to give you the benefit of the doubt, but not anymore. For the first time ever, I'm actually seeing you for who you truly are."

"And who is that, Alize? Oh, you must mean the same woman that stuck her neck out on a limb and helped you get this position without any type of degree. Or better yet, the same woman that has helped you with a little extra on your bills whenever your baby daddy couldn't come through off his street job. Or maybe I'm the same woman that allows you to bring your children into a corporate office building every time you and their father get into it. That's who I truly am."

"Yeah, well, all I can say is, with friends like you, who the hell needs enemies?" I went back to focusing on my work but could literally feel her eyes pressed on me. I knew there was more she wanted to say, but I was also sure that my so-called *friend* knew me well enough not to mess with me anymore from that point.

On top of all of Mya and her nonsense, Anthony had still been texting and calling me back and forth, going crazy about the car, so I knew that there would be a lot more drama in store for me once I arrived home in the car he'd been searching for all day, with the locks to the house changed. But I was ready for it all.

CHAPTER 21

MYA

Ever since our argument, Alize and I had practically danced around the room, trying to stay away from one another. When I went to the copier, she would walk away, or if she went to the fax machine, I walked away. Leaving when I did only seemed like the best and most reasonable thing I could have done for both of us. The strange thing was that she and I had never once had an argument of that magnitude, so I wasn't quite sure what to make of all of it. It had me wondering if maybe she'd always had those feelings inside toward me, or if this was all about Carson.

Either way, I still couldn't understand it or the fact that her baby daddy had anything to say about me. I was floored when she said that even he felt I acted as if I was better than her. *Who the hell is he to think anything about me?* I thought. I may not have truly liked him or the way I felt he took advantage of Alize by leaving her to take care of everything, including the kids, with no help at all, but other than that, I'd never done anything to the man for him to feel one way or the other about me.

Now that I was home and soaking my troubles away in a nice hot, soothing bath, I wanted to take my thoughts far away from Alize and her man and began to center my mind around Carson and him potentially becoming mine. I wanted—no, I actually *needed* Mr. Carson Avery Reed in my life. I even had to laugh at the thought myself because although it had only been a few hours since we'd met, somehow it felt as if our worlds were destined to collide. Almost fate, even. It was like the stars had aligned perfectly for us to encounter one another when I think we both needed someone most. Lord knows, after dealing with my one, two, three, and four, and also the nonsense from the *For Singles Only* show, I needed Carson. All of me needed all of him and all that he had to offer.

As I reminisced on our lunch date in my head, I thought about how he possessed so much of what I desired in a man and potential mate that it was scary to me. I'd learned that he'd only been in Atlanta a year or so. He was a widow after his wife passed away from stage four breast cancer, and he didn't have any biological children of his own. I wanted to know more about him and his wife, but it seemed like he'd tensed up when speaking about her, so I didn't want to pry too much.

Looking at how he interacted with me and the way he conversed made me realize that he was nothing like the men I'd just had in my life. He was extremely mature and sophisticated, not young, inexperienced, or insecure like Tyrone. His nature was very laid back and down to earth, and he wasn't all stuck up and conceited like Charles. We'd talked about anything and everything that came to our minds, and he didn't come across as all withdrawn and inhibited like Kevin. Although I hadn't inquired much about his spirituality, I could tell that he wasn't a Bible thumper with no other balance in life like Will. Carson was an all-around perfect man, and I wanted to experience more of him in more ways than one.

Laying my head back, I closed my eyes and sank farther into the water. All at once, I suddenly saw Carson standing right in front of me, staring directly into my eyes. The only clothing that graced his muscular, six-foot-five physique was a white towel wrapped around his waist.

"Do you want me to get inside with you?" he asked as he smiled at me.

My eyes searched the room for some type of answers as to what was going on. All the lights were off, one candle was lit, and soft music played from the other room.

"What's going on? Is this real? Are you really here with me right now?"

"Yes, it's as real as you want it to be, Mya. So, tell me your fantasy. What would you like me to do to you right now?"

I could hardly look back at him. What was happening was all so strange to me, and I was somewhat caught off guard but aroused all at the same time. Instead of being bashful and shy, though, my mind and heart raced with excitement of the unknown of sharing my hidden desires with this still fairly unknown man.

"Um, I guess I would want you to bathe me, Carson," I said back to him softly.

"Is that it? Bathe you how? Slow? Gently? Where would you like for me to wash first? Your neck? Your breasts? Or your round, plump ass? Your every wish is my command."

I hid the sinful smile that had come across my face from his words, but he took my hand away and kissed my lips, soft and gently, and then his hand made its way to my breasts and began to squeeze my nipple.

"Is this what you want, Mya?" he asked with his tongue creeping in between my lips and gliding with mine, soft and slow. It was one of the sweetest kisses I had ever experienced in life, and I wanted more. I needed more.

"Carson?" I tried to speak, but I felt his hand move from my breast to my neck and begin to slightly grip it while his kisses became more passionate and intense.

For the life of me, I couldn't explain what the hell was going on at that moment. All I knew was he was having an effect on me that I hadn't experienced with any other man, and I wanted more of him in the worst way.

This is crazy, Mya, I told myself. *You barely know this man*, I thought, yet somehow there was a trust there that was indescribable. A trust that made me want to allow him to have his way with me in any way that he saw fit. I was ready to let him into my life, my world, and inside of me. Part of me, however, wished I could hold out and play a little hard to get, but my girlfriend between my thighs didn't feel at all the same. She wanted him badly, and needless to say, I allowed her to lead the way.

The next thing I knew, he stood me up. In front of him, water dripped from every part of my body, and I wanted to cover each portion with my hands. In a modest and self-conscious way, I allowed him to examine me with his eyes while praying that he liked what he saw. Although I'd always been a very confident woman, there was an insecurity there that wanted and needed his approval and satisfaction. Then, at once, our eyes met, but we didn't say a word to each other.

His eyes simply continued to travel up and down my body from head to toe until suddenly, I saw a small smirk come across his face. The little girl inside of me blushed. Finally, I knew that he was pleased, and I was relieved and happy all at the same time by his response. He took my hand and helped me out of the tub. Then he took me by the waist and drew me in close. I sighed with relief. Instantly, I felt protected, wanted, and even loved by him. There was a gentleness there that I hadn't anticipated. It felt so damn good. So much so that a single tear fell from my eye as he held me next to him. I could have stayed there in his arms forever. I felt just that safe. However, I pulled back to speak, but he quickly placed his finger over my lips and then kissed them again before taking my hand and leading me to my bedroom. Although it was his first time there, he glided through my home with ease, like he already knew where everything was. Then his powerful baritone voice said, "Lay down."

His words were bold, yet they weren't cold. They were warm and desiring. I did as I was told, eagerly following his lead and wondering what was about to happen next. He sat on the edge of the bed next to me and leaned over to kiss me once more. This time, it was much more passionate and forceful. Our tongues danced to the rhythm of our hearts beating as one. Then he stopped and looked at me again. There was that same smirk. I longed to know his thoughts, but he still didn't say a word. Instead, his lips made their way to my breasts. He kissed them, licked them, and even bit them at times. I started to moan softly as he caressed one while placing the other inside of his mouth. I had to stop myself from releasing everything within me at that moment because I needed more of him. Slowly, his hand went from massaging my breast and made its way to the lower portion of my body. I had been longing to feel his touch there, and I knew he could tell when he felt my warmth. He started to touch me . . . fast . . . then slow . . . then fast again. My heart felt like it was beating outside of my body. My back was arched. This man controlled all of me with one hand.

I called out, "Carson, please don't stop, please."

But then he replaced his hand with mine. I was struck with shock and surprise. What was happening? What was he doing to me? Then, slowly, I watched him walk over to my chaise, sit down, and light a cigarette. My mind was cluttered. I still didn't know what was going on until he said, "Finish."

My eyes stared at him with a slight fear within them.

"But—"

"Finish."

Suddenly, I began to stroke myself in the same manner that he had, and I started to hear his voice begin to guide my actions.

"Faster, now slow, insert one, now two, now three, go deeper. Now, think about my mouth where your hand is, and let go."

I did everything he said as I watched his eyes watching me. He never once took his eyes away from my hand that touched her. In fact, the only movement he made was to either take a hit of his cigarette or lick his lips like he could taste me all over him. It was all so crazy, but I liked every bit of it. I actually felt like I could feel his mouth right there. My body started to shake uncontrollably. It was telling me I was there. I was ready . . . ready to let go.

"Carson . . . Carson . . . I'm about to cum," I sang as my body shook so hard that I'd snapped myself out of my own wet dream.

"Oh, my goodness, Mya, what the hell is wrong with you?" I asked myself. It was almost like I'd gotten addicted, and Carson was my drug of choice. I was so ready to get high and never, ever come down from him. The attorney, more reasonable thinking side of me knew that it was crazy for me to feel this way so soon. Insane even. Yet, if Carson was anything like what I'd just dreamt, then I was determined to have him all to myself. And not any amount of time, past lovers, Leslie, or even Alize, was going to come in between me getting exactly what I wanted.

CHAPTER 22

ALIZE

"Open this damn door, Alize. I know you're in there, and you better open up before I bust this shit down!" Anthony had been yelling outside and banging on the door for at least the past twenty minutes since I'd arrived home. I kept debating with myself if I wanted to open it or just have his ass out there banging on the door all night. But I decided to go ahead and suck it up and say what needed to be said, especially since the kids were at my mother's house this evening. I'd had a feeling in my gut that things might turn out this way, so I'd already made the necessary preparations for them not to be home.

I wrapped myself in my cotton robe, slid my slippers into my house shoes, and trudged to the door without any sense of real urgency whatsoever. Then, I opened it up and stood there in the middle of the doorway and looked at him, blocking him from coming inside. He tried his best to go around me, but I stopped him by putting my hand up to his chest.

"What the hell is wrong with you, Zae? Let me in the damn house. And why the hell is my key not working in the damn lock? And what the hell is the car doing in the driveway if you had me thinking it was stolen?" His words spilled out while he stared at me like I was completely crazy. I stood, however, with my arms folded, calm, cool, and collected.

"You might as well know." I began to speak matter-of-factly, "I had the locks changed on the house, and no, the car was not stolen. I had my cousin come and pick it up for me."

"What? Your cousin? What's up, Zae? You had your cousin following me or something? What's up with that? Why are you doing all of this, and where are the children?"

"Don't worry. The children are fine. They are with my mother tonight," I said, ignoring all of his other questions. "Now, I can allow you to come in for a few minutes and gather your things, but then you have to leave. And you're not taking my car because if you do, I will report it stolen."

He threw his hands on top of his head, utterly confused as to what was going on. I almost wanted to laugh, but I still tried to have some level of respect for the man. I figured I would wait and do it when I wasn't directly in his face.

"Man, can you at least tell me why? Is this about that marriage shit again? Because I thought we worked that all out. I thought we were good, Zae."

"No, Anthony, this isn't about that '*marriage shit*,' as you put it." My voice started to rise because I felt like he was playing me like I was stupid. "This is about you being at the abortion clinic yesterday with some bitch. That's what this is about. So, who did you fuck around and get pregnant, Anthony? Is it Monique? Is that why you were with her the other day?"

He didn't say anything at first. He only looked at me as if he'd seen a ghost, and I was sure it was because he was trying to figure out how I'd come to know that information.

"Listen, I . . . I . . . I can explain, Zae," he fumbled around with his words, stuttering.

"No, I don't need an explanation at this point, Anthony. I've had enough excuses and explanations for the past seven years to last me a lifetime. Right now, all I need is for you to go. Go far away from me and leave me the fuck alone. The only dealings I want with you from now on will be with the children. We can come up with a schedule that will be best for the both of us."

"Zae, please. Just let me come in, and let's talk. We can work this all out, I promise. It's really not what you're thinking."

"Then what is it, Anthony? Tell me. What other reason could you have to end up in the middle of the day at a damn abortion clinic?"

"Okay, I was there, all right . . . with Monique, but—"

"You know what? Don't. Don't even finish because if you tell me some bullshit, there's no telling what I will do. I just want you to leave. Please." I felt a tear slide down my face, and I'd become more pissed because of promising myself I wouldn't cry over him.

"It's not what you think, Zae. All right. I love you. You and the girls. And I would never do that to you. But it's all good. If you want me gone, then I'll go. But don't call me when you need me because just like you're tired of the back and forth, so am I," he said before turning his back to walk away. But then he turned back around. "But you know why I won't ask you to marry me? This is why. You're this way one day and that way another. You're hot and cold. You don't have any real faith in me. You listen to your friends. And you're always throwing it in my face what you do. You pay the bills. You take care of kids. You, you, you. I don't feel like you truly want me; you need me. And the only reason you need me is for some consistent dick. That's it. And baby, I can give you that without the hassle of getting married."

He started to walk away, and I was completely stunned by his words. So stunned that I ran out of the house and began to hit him with both of my fists.

"Some dick, Anthony? You think that's the only reason I've hung around with your sorry ass through seven years and four children is for some damn dick? I love you, Anthony. I love you," I screamed like a mad woman. "And all I wanted was for you to love me back." I fell to my knees, drowning in my own tears.

"I did love you back, Zae, but it's never been enough. Let me know when I can see my babies."

He walked off, and there I was, outside, crying like a brand-new baby, half of me wanting to let him go, but the other half wanting to call him back to stay and work things out. My heart was practically torn in two, and at that moment, I wasn't sure what to do. I wasn't positive anymore that I could be just like Faye.

Forcing myself to get up and go inside of the house alone, I felt like I desperately needed someone to talk to. In fact, I wished I had my best friend, but then I remembered all the horrible things we'd both said to one another in the office. All I could see was the look on her face when I said the things I said. She was hurt, just as much as I was, but both of us were far too stubborn to break down and say "I'm sorry" first.

CHAPTER 23

ALIZE

"Listen, Mya, I'm sorry for the things I said yesterday. I think we both were extremely emotional and said a lot of things out of anger, and I, for one, regret it. I truly cherish our friendship, and I never want a man, or anyone, to come in between that," I said, breaking the silence in the room.

We had been there for the past hour without as much as a good morning to one another. And seeing that she wasn't going to give in, I decided to try to be the bigger person. At first, however, judging from her nonreaction a few minutes later, I almost regretted saying anything at all, until she finally spoke up in her true *Mya-like* way.

"I guess I forgive you, all right. And I guess I'm sorry, too. Believe it or not, I do love you, Alize, and I would never look down on you or think of you as any less than me. I'm not just saying that, either. I hope that you truly believe that."

"I do," was all I said as she came over and hugged me for the next few minutes or so. And to be totally honest, after what happened between me and Anthony, that hug was more than what I needed.

Without another second passing by from our little kumbaya moment, she brought up the one thing I was hoping not to discuss today—Carson Reed. It wasn't that

I was jealous over the fact that he'd chosen her, but I knew my friend. And I knew that without her realizing it, she would constantly go on and on about him, making me hate the fact that she would be the one on his arm and not me.

"Girl, I'm so happy we are talking again because I wasn't sure I could go all day without telling you about Carson last night."

"Last night? You let the man come over already? Please, Mya, tell me you didn't have sex with him."

"Well, yes and no—"

"What! What does that mean?"

She smiled in a very mischievous way before responding. "Okay, so yes, we did have sex, but no, I didn't let him come over already," she'd said, making me feel like I was playing some type of guessing game.

"C'mon now, girl, you and I both know that's not even possible. How on earth can you have sex with him without him being . . . wait a minute, did you have some type of wet-ass dream?" I questioned after putting all the pieces to the puzzle together while I spoke.

"Yes." She nodded her head in agreement with a completely satisfied look across her face. "Zae, I don't know what it is about him, but he has me so addicted, for lack of a better word. I mean, I literally feel like the man mind-fucked me yesterday at lunch, and it was amazing. So much so that I can't wait for the real thing. I think that's why I got so caught up while I was in the bathtub, and well—"

"Wait, wait, now that's where I draw the line, Mya." I put my hand up, halting her words. "I don't mind you telling me bits and pieces of your situationships, but I don't need to know all the dirty little details, all right? It's okay to keep some things to yourself."

"Whatever." She threw her ink pen my way in a playful manner. "But I'm serious. Carson seems so different than the men I've had in my life, and he's practically everything I desire. Who knew that by just considering letting go and letting God send me someone, He would act this fast?"

"Look, if there's one thing I know, it's that our time is not God's time. But even with that said, I don't want you to get yourself too caught up so quickly."

"What do you mean? Why would you say that?"

"I'm only saying that it's just been a day. So, give it some time to really get to know him. Go out on more dates. Inquire more about his background. And don't, I repeat, don't end up giving that man your goodies for at least the next thirty days. And I would say a little longer than that, but I know you. You're already having wet dreams, so I'm sure thirty days is pushing it."

"Don't worry, all right? I'm going to find out every little thing that I can about Carson Reed, but I know that nothing will change my mind. He is definitely the one for me, Zae. I can feel it."

"All right, *Ms. I Can Feel It.* I hear you. But before you go setting a wedding date, there is one little thing that's bothering me about Mr. Reed."

"What's that?"

"He's a little too perfect, and for me, it makes me wonder why a man so perfect is single."

"Oh, don't worry. I already know the answer to that. His wife, Lord rest her soul, passed away from breast cancer a couple of years ago, so he's just now getting back into the dating scene."

"I see. And two whole years, and he hasn't been involved with *anyone*?"

"Alize, where are you trying to go with this? Why don't you want me to be happy with Carson?"

"I do want you to be happy, but your *being happy* means that you throw all caution and reasonable thinking out the window. But you know what? I'm just going to shut up about it. If you're fine with what he said, then I'm fine too. You won't get any more pushback from me."

"Thank you."

"So, when will you talk to or go out with him again?" I asked out of mere curiosity.

"That's the funny part. I have no idea. You know my rule about not coming on to a man and letting him do all the up-front initiation. Well, I didn't get his phone number, and he didn't ask for mine, so I'm kinda just waiting in limbo."

"Wait, he didn't ask for your number? The man took you out on a wonderful lunch date, you two had all this amazing getting-to-know-each-other conversation, and he didn't ask for your phone number?"

"Something like that, Zae, okay?" she said, but I almost felt like she was trying to hide something.

"What's up, Mya? What aren't you saying?"

"Lunch wasn't actually a lunch *date*, all right. It was more just two people that were starving and went to grab a bite to eat together. I was the one that asked him if he wanted to get something. He was leaving the building, I saw him, and asked. That was it."

"Girl, what? You've been doing all this blushing and going on and on about your now and forever and having wet dreams over a man that you have no idea if you'll ever talk to or see again?" I tried hard not to laugh but couldn't help myself.

"Look, laugh now all you want, but I'm telling you it's only a matter of time, all right. Things were so great between us yesterday that I know for a fact that I'll see Carson Avery Reed again. Trust me."

"If you say so."

A few seconds later, we heard someone's footsteps coming down the hallway. I would have sworn it was the building's Evelina, but I knew Leslie's walk, and that wasn't it. It sounded more like a man's stride. My eyes immediately glanced toward the door when I heard them getting closer, and so did Mya's. And then he peeked inside, and instantly she lit up.

"Carson! We weren't expecting you here today," she said, glancing over at me in a way to say, *I told you so.* "To what do we owe the pleasure?"

"Hey, Mya, how are you? I had to stop by because I realized I forgot something yesterday."

I watched her movement as she walked over to her desk and retrieved one of her business cards from the holder. "You know, I realized, too, yesterday evening that I should have given you this."

She handed him the card, and I studied him as he tossed it around in his hands a few times.

"Uh, thanks, I'll definitely use this if I need to. But, um, I actually came by for you, Alize."

My eyes went from him to her and back to him, completely confused.

"For me?"

"Yeah, so look, I haven't done this in quite some time, so I hope that I'm not being too forward, but I would love it if you would have dinner with me one evening. I was so drawn to you and your energy yesterday that I couldn't stop thinking about you last night. So, there, I said it. But if you're married or already involved with someone, then please know that I'm not trying to be disrespectful of that."

"Oh, no, no, you're not being disrespectful at all," I said, blushing and grinning from ear to ear at this fine specimen of a man. I wanted so desperately to scream "Yes!" but not in front of Mya, whose eyes I could feel pressing directly on me.

"So, what do you say? Dinner?"

"Uh, sure. Dinner sounds good," I said hesitantly.

"Great, I'm really looking forward to it. But I have another appointment in a few minutes with Robert, or Attorney Buchanon, so I have to go. But it's Friday, and I love the weekend nightlife, so how does tonight around seven sound?"

"Um—"

"Alize, do you think you'll be able to find someone to watch your children?" Mya asked out of nowhere, and I knew right away that her jealousy was making an appearance. However, she was right. My mother had had the kids since yesterday, so I wasn't positive that I would be able to get her to keep an eye on them again. But then there was their father. Maybe I could get him to take them. Either way, I wasn't about to turn down dinner with Carson.

"Seven sounds great, Carson."

"Good. Here's my number, and you can text me your address. I'll be there at seven on the dot. Oh, and if you can't find a sitter, then I wouldn't mind dinner in." He smiled and walked away, and I just wanted to melt away right there in my chair until I heard her voice.

"What are you doing?" Mya stood there with her arms folded across her chest.

"What do you mean, what am I doing? I'm not doing anything. You saw for yourself that man came in here and asked me out to dinner. What was I supposed to do?"

"You were supposed to say no, Zae. You have four children and a man. You don't have time to be worried about trying to entertain Carson just to get back at me because of the things I said yesterday."

"Is that what you think this is about? Give me a break, Mya. Everything in life doesn't have to be about you, all right?"

"I'm not implying that it does, but you already have a man. What are you going to tell him about your dinner date?" she asked, and I'd forgotten that because of all the drama between her and me, I hadn't mentioned anything that had gone on between Anthony and me.

"I don't have a man anymore, okay?"

"Yeah, only because it's Friday. You two will be right back together in a couple of days. So, are you really going to play with Carson like that?"

"Damn, Mya, can you please stop thinking with your vagina and be my friend right now? I just told you that me and Anthony aren't together anymore. And no, there's no going back to him this time. I found out that he'd gone to an abortion clinic with Monique, and so I ended things. For good."

It took her a few minutes to process everything before coming over to me and putting her arm around me.

"Oh, Zae, I'm sorry. I had no idea this was going on with you and Anthony. Why didn't you tell me?"

"I don't know. I think I just wanted to make sure that this was what I wanted, and I wanted to handle things on my own without all the background noise."

"Yeah, I hear you. But now what? What about the kids?"

"Uh, they've been with my mother since yesterday. She's helping me through this as much as possible. And I imagine I'll just figure things out day by day."

"Are you sure this is what you want?"

"Honestly, no, but this is how it has to be. I've been with Anthony much too long for things to still be this way between us. We should be thinking about how to grow individually as well as together and as a family. I shouldn't be concerned about if he's cheating on me with someone or got someone pregnant. I just can't do that anymore. So, as much as it hurts, I'd rather go through the pain now.

"Wow, an abortion clinic, huh? I can't believe him. What was he thinking?"

"Clearly, he wasn't, but it's cool," I said, trying not to sink into a depression thinking about my problems with Anthony. "I'm going to go on this date with Carson and have a wonderful time and not think anything about Anthony."

"Zae, do you think that's the right thing to do? I mean, getting fresh out of something with Anthony and going straight to Carson in a matter of days? Don't you think you need time to heal? And how fair is that to Carson?"

"Mya, it's dinner. I'm not looking to marry the man tomorrow or anything. I'm just going to enjoy him. The same way you were."

"And when he wants more, then what? Because Carson is the type of man that's going to want more. He's not going to do the same back-and-forth thing you've been used to with Anthony. They are two totally different men, and you're going to have to handle him differently."

"Look, I know you're the *Carson Reed expert* as of yesterday, but I know how to handle a man like him. And well, if you don't believe me, just watch."

CHAPTER 24

ALIZE

Excited wasn't the word to describe the way I felt at that moment about my date with Carson. It was more like I was in seventh heaven or on cloud nine with just the mere thought of it. I couldn't wait to be in his presence outside of that office and truly learn the type of man he was. However, I also couldn't deny that there was an extreme amount of nervousness and anxiety that lay within me as well, because I hadn't been on a real date with a man in the past ten years.

After the first couple of years of dating, Anthony had stopped taking me out the way he had when we'd first met. In the beginning, we always went to the movies, out to eat, bowling, out for ice cream, or anywhere that crossed our minds. But it seemed like once we'd become official, and especially after having Champagne, all of that ceased. Our dating from that point on only consisted of a Netflix-and-chill kind of evening in the house with the kids. Needless to say, I was quite overdue for some real adult time and conversation.

Before I even got that far, however, I figured I'd better swallow the huge lump in my throat and call Anthony and ask him to watch the children for the night. Inside, my gut told me that this was not going to be an easy hurdle to get over, especially with how things ended last night. But with this whole situation about to become our new normal, I suspected that this would be as bad as it would ever get. It should only get better from here. I dialed, and he picked up on the first ring.

"Yeah," was all he said, and I could tell right off exactly how this call was about to be.

"Hello, Anthony. It's Zae. How are you?" I asked nicely and softly, trying to be as feminine and polite as I could.

"Yeah, I know who it is. What's good?" he asked, completely dismissing my asking him how he was or having the courtesy to ask me back.

"Um, I'm good too, Anthony," I answered sarcastically. "But anyway, I was wondering if you would mind having the kids tonight. I mean, if you're not somewhere that there will be any conflict."

"No, Alize, I'm not at Monique's if that's your way of asking me. I'm at my brother's house. And where are the girls now? Why can't they be at home with you?"

"I wasn't concerned about whether or not you were at Monique's, all right? And right now, they're at my mother's, but she's had them since yesterday, and I wanted to give her a break, especially with this being the weekend."

"All right, but why can't they stay home with you?"

"I'm not going to be at home this evening, Anthony," I fumbled and stuttered my words, reluctant to say anything about having a date.

"I see. Well, my girls are always welcome to come and spend time with me. So what time should I get them?"

"Uh, it will be good if you can swing to my mother's and get them. I'll tell her you're coming around six thirty if that will work for you."

"Why can't I get them from the house? It's closer to where I am."

"Because I told you they're at my mother's, and I didn't want to bother her with bringing them all the way here. I just thought it would be easier if—"

"Hey, don't worry about explaining. I'll pick them up from Mom's." He cut me off.

"Thank you, Anthony. I really appreciate this."

"Yeah, well, you can keep your thanks, Alize. They're my children, and I will never abandon them, no matter what's going on between me and you."

He hung up in my face, but I didn't care. Instead, I took a huge sigh of relief after thinking that although it wasn't the best call, it went a lot better than I had imagined. Plus, my overall mission was complete. Now that that was over, the only other thing I had left to worry about was what to wear. I knew that with a man like Carson, I couldn't dress the same as I did with Anthony. With him, I always had some skin showing if I wasn't damn near half-naked, and he loved it. But with Carson, I wanted to look sexy and sophisticated without appearing old and stuffy. I wanted to look classy and elegant, not cheap and tacky. So, with Anthony getting the girls from my mother's house, I knew I had enough time to put together the right outfit in peace. Aside from that, Anthony wouldn't at all be aware of my date with Carson.

Thirty minutes later, however, as I reached the house, I pulled up only to find my mother parked in the driveway. I got out of my car and went straight to her driver's side door.

"Momma, what are you doing here? I arranged to have Anthony pick the girls up around six thirty from your place."

"Listen, I don't know what you and Anthony have going on, but he called and asked me to drop the girls off and said he would get them from here. Besides, I'm telling you just like I told him. I don't know what's going on with you two, but I have a life of my own, and I'm nobody's babysitter or go-between. You two are adults and should know how to parent these girls whether you're together or not. Now, I've had the girls for two days, and it's time for you to take your kids back. They are your responsibility, not mine."

"Momma, I'm not sure what he told you or why he did that, but thank you for everything. Thanks for keeping them the past couple of days and bringing them back home," I said, feeling somewhat defeated. Anthony knew exactly what he was doing, and I was about to say fuck all this nice stuff and tell him what was truly on my mind this evening.

My mother handed me the twins in their car seats, and Champagne and Hennessy got out of the car and ran inside the house. Before she left, though, she let her window down and looked at me.

"Zae, what's going on with you two? You don't seem like yourself, and he's all angry and uptight. Why can't the two of you get it together?"

"Momma, look, it's just a lot that you don't know, and I really don't want to get into all of it right now. Anthony and I are adults, and we have to figure this out on our own."

"Okay, I can live with that. But I'm going to say this before I leave. You and Anthony have been together for seven years and have four beautiful children together. You both need to stop behaving like teenagers and start being the adults that you say you are. Now, I've told him that he needs to man up. I told him he needs a steady job and needs to help you more with the girls. And now I'm telling you that, no matter what, these girls need their father just as much as they do their mother. I know that we, as women, get tired of dealing with certain things from these men. I sure did with your father. But honey, they're the men that we chose to be with and have children with. And once I had you and your siblings, your needs became way more important than my own. And I knew that no other man was going to love you all and care for you the way your father did. Just like no other man out there is going to love your girls the way their father does."

"Yeah, I know that, Momma, but what about me? I need love, too."

"Girl, hush. That man loves you. Anthony just has to figure out how to love himself enough to become the man that you and the girls need him to be."

"And what am I supposed to do in the meantime, wait another seven years for him to do that? I don't know if I can, Momma. I just don't believe I have enough left inside of me to give," I said, walking inside of the house, ready to call off my whole date with Carson.

After getting the girls settled, I figured I would call Carson to let him know I wouldn't be able to make it. My mother had given me her whole guilt trip about Anthony and me, and the girls' needs being first and foremost, so I'd decided that seeing Carson probably wasn't the best idea—at least not so soon and with things being up in the air with me and Anthony. The part I hated the most about this whole situation, and what I didn't want to admit to myself, was that it was beginning to look like what Mya said was probably true. I had way too much going on in my life, and there was no way that a man like Carson would want to step foot into a situation like this. It was time I faced the fact that without Anthony, I was doomed to be a single woman with four small children, and finding a decent man who wanted to take me as a package deal would almost be impossible. Taking a deep breath, I dialed his number, and he answered immediately.

"Alize, hey. I'm about to leave out soon. Are you dressed?"

"Well, that's kind of what I'm calling about. Carson, there's a lot you aren't aware of when it comes to me, and a lot that you probably don't want to deal with."

"What are you talking about? You got some type of criminal record that I need to know about? Or some long-lost husband?" he asked in a joking manner.

"I wish it was just that simple, but the thing is, Carson, I have four small children. Their father and I are no longer together, but our breakup was fairly recent, and well, I don't want to put you in an uncomfortable situation."

"What would be uncomfortable about the fact that you have children? And if you say that you and their father are no longer together, then I trust that. I mean, unless he's some crazy killer or something." He laughed again behind his words.

"No, he's not. He tries to act tough, but he's pretty harmless. But you really don't mind that I have kids? You don't have in the back of your mind that I'm trying to drag you into a ready-made family?" I used Mya's words.

"Alize, look, I like you, and I'm interested in getting to know you and everything that comes along with that, including your kids. I'm not some jerk that will throw a good woman away just because she has children. I mean, what if I had kids? I would want you to accept me as well."

"Wow, I guess I didn't expect you to respond this way."

"Yeah, well, I told you, I'm a very laid-back, new-age type of guy. I know that most women my age probably already have children, and I'm fine with that."

"This is unbelievable," I said, smiling so hard that he could probably see it through the phone.

"What's that?"

"You just seem, I don't know, nothing short of amazing. I mean, to be honest, Carson, I haven't connected with a man outside of my children's father in quite a long time. And then to meet someone like you at a time when

I needed to most has caught me by a complete surprise. It's exciting but a little scary, too."

"Please, there's no need to be afraid with me. Alize, I am looking forward to getting to know every bit of you, with or without kids, with or without an ex. And when it comes to being amazing, I think it's because it's from the eyes of an amazing woman."

From there, we simply began to talk about a little of everything. He asked about my likes and dislikes, my favorite food, and my favorite color, and even wanted to know my wildest dreams. I'd even shared with him my hope of wanting to open a clothing boutique one day, and he immediately encouraged it, unlike Anthony, who always thought it was way too far-fetched. It was truly refreshing to have someone's genuine support. I liked Carson, and I wasn't afraid to admit it anymore.

As we spoke more, my eyes glanced over at the clock, which read well after six thirty. Anthony should have come to get the kids by now, but my gut had already told me when he asked my mother to drop them off that something would come up where he would cancel. With that, I decided to bite the bullet and go ahead and tell Carson that I needed to cancel.

"Carson, I hate to tell you this, but it looks like I don't have a babysitter tonight. So unfortunately, I don't think I'll be able to go out. Their father was supposed to pick them up, and since he hasn't shown up or called, I'm taking it that he's not coming."

"Oh, I see. Well, we have forever, right? And I'm going to be waiting on pins and needles for my opportunity to take you out. So, please don't think you're going to get rid of me that easily."

"Trust me, I never want to get rid of you, Mr. Reed."

"Good."

With or without getting the chance to go out with Carson, it seemed that the night was turning out exactly the way it was supposed to. Anthony may have very well thought he'd thrown a monkey wrench in my plans when he asked my mother to bring the kids home and not showing up to pick them up, but he'd better think again. I was going to live my life with or without him in it and despite having four little ones. I was finally dealing with a grown-ass man who wanted nothing more than to spend his time with me, unlike Anthony. And honestly, I wanted to spend all my time with Carson, too. He accepted that tonight wasn't going to be the best time for us to go out, so we ended up simply talking on the phone like two high school teenagers.

THREE WEEKS LATER

CHAPTER 25

ALIZE

It had been three weeks or so of dating Carson, and I hadn't tired of him yet. He was so much more than I could have ever imagined, and I was truly enjoying every moment I was able to spend with him. He stopped by the office practically every day to take me to lunch. We had picnics in the park, walked around the mall hand in hand while admiring clothing boutiques, and sometimes just sat in his car shooting the breeze about much of nothing at all. He kept me laughing, kept my spirit peaceful without all the unnecessary drama, and even pushed me to be a better version of myself. I loved every second of it and had to admit that I was falling hard for this man. So hard that I really didn't care about what Anthony did or didn't do. I felt in my heart that he knew I was seeing someone because it seemed that every time Carson and I planned a date, Anthony would stand me up with coming to get the kids. Little did he know, though, that it was making him look bad in their eyes instead of doing any harm to me.

As I sat at my desk, I continued to daydream about Carson and the life that we could have together. With Mya having a full day in court, I was happily in my own thoughts, fantasizing about one day being Mrs. Carson Reed. At least, that was until my baby daddy's name began to scroll across the front of my cell phone.

"Hello?"

"Alize, what the fuck is going on?"

"What do you mean what's going on, Anthony? What's going on with what?"

"I stopped by your mother's house to see the girls earlier, and Champagne said something about not wanting you to talk to *the man* anymore. Who the fuck is 'the man,' and what has he done to my daughter to have her so afraid of him? Or better yet, why the hell are you chasing up behind any man when you need to focus your energy on being a mother to our kids?"

"Are you done now? Because I'm honestly not trying to hear you going off about anything that I do in my personal time. And Champagne is not afraid of anyone, and no one has done anything to her. She's a child who misses her daddy and is saying whatever she has to to get his attention. That's it."

"That's it, huh? You know, this is the problem with most women now. You all run off the good men in your lives and bring some lunatics around your children because you're more concerned about your own needs than your kids."

"Are you fucking kidding me right now, Anthony? I wouldn't be single if the father of my children stood up to be a real man instead of some low-life bum who wasn't man enough to ask for my hand in marriage. And my kids wouldn't be around some random man if they had both of their parents in the home and not one who wanted to go hang out all the time. So, don't go pointing the blame over here."

"Oh, so it's my fault that they don't have both of their parents in the home? I could have sworn that you were the one who put me out, Zae."

"Yeah, I did, because you were so much more concerned with going to an abortion clinic with your baby momma instead of being home with us. But you know what? I don't have time for this with you. I gotta go."

"Alize, don't you dare hang up this phone. We're not done with this until I say so."

"That's where you're wrong. I'm done. Goodbye, Anthony," I said, hitting the end button and getting up, going over to Carson when he walked through the door. The second I reached him, I simply laid my head on his chest as the tears began to stream down my face.

"Hey, hey, hey, what's wrong?" He held me tight.

"It's my children's father. He's accusing me of putting you before the children. He also thinks that Champagne is afraid of you and basically called me an unfit mother."

"Okay, so why are you crying?" He pulled me away and looked into my eyes.

"What do you mean why?"

"Alize, you know that none of that is the truth. You know you're not placing me before your kids. You know you're not unfit. And we both know that Champagne hasn't really been around me to be afraid of me. So why are you allowing yourself to get emotional about things that aren't true? Fuck Anthony," he said with an immediate sense of aggression. "He ain't shit, and in my opinion, never will be shit, so you're not about to listen to anything he has to say."

Carson quickly turned from sweet to furious in a matter of seconds and spoke as if he almost knew Anthony personally or something.

"I'm sorry, Carson. I didn't mean to get you so upset over this."

"It's not you. I just hate men like Anthony and the way they fuck with women's minds. But trust me, Alize, he's going to get his one day, sooner than he thinks. That's just the way that bitch karma works."

As I looked into Carson's eyes, I could have sworn I saw red inside of them. It was like he had some personal vendetta against Anthony instead of simply speaking about men in general. And true enough, Anthony had pissed me off with his words, but I still didn't want any harm to come his way. I wasn't sure how I felt about Anthony *or* Carson at that very moment, until Carson walked closer to me and began to kiss me. His lips felt good. The kiss was a little forceful yet soft. It was tender and warm. More importantly, it was what I needed to take my mind and heart completely away from Anthony and back to him. I wanted Carson in the worst way but kept trying to contain my composure so that I wouldn't look like an average ho. Plus, I hadn't been with anyone in that way but Anthony in so long that I wasn't exactly sure if I was ready. But as his hand began to make its way up my thigh and closer to my pussy, I was afraid I might just give in a lot sooner than I thought.

CHAPTER 26

MYA

After finishing up my weekend errands, I got back home and decided to relax for the evening while reading the latest novel by Kennedy Ryan. I hadn't sat down to read in quite a long time, but this seemed like as perfect a time as any. Normally, my days would have been filled with trying to go between Charles or Kevin or Will or Tyrone. But strangely enough, I hadn't heard a sound from anyone in the past few weeks, and honestly, it was quite refreshing. However, I still hadn't been able to pull my mind away from Carson Reed.

Out of all the people in the world, I was still in complete shock that he wanted Alize and not me. And even more shocked that it seemed things were actually going well between them. Immediately, I tried to run down the qualities that Alize might have over me. And besides her flamboyant style of dress, some fake lashes, hair, and nails, nothing stood out that would make me think he'd choose her before me. Then I thought about that smug look on her face when he first approached her in the office. She'd tried to act so innocent and pretend like she wasn't gloating, but I knew my friend almost better than she knew herself. And I'm sure the fact that she'd been going on lunch dates with Carson day after day made her feel as if she were winning.

Trying my best to stop thinking of either of them, I contemplated calling Kevin. If I were to see anyone, it would for sure be him. We hadn't spoken since the night I told him I loved him. And quite frankly, I missed him and his dick even more. But I wasn't sure if it was enough to call. I still had so many questions about *her*, why he'd proposed to her, why he didn't love me back, and so much more that I knew he wasn't going to answer. So, I poured one of my favorite wines into my favorite glass, pulled out *Before I Let Go*, covered up with my blanket, and started reading. I just prayed there weren't any over-the-top, explicit sex scenes, or I might just go back on my own word.

I was fully happy and content by the time I'd made it to chapter five when my cell phone started to ring. It was a number I'd never seen before, so I decided to decline it, figuring it was nothing more than a bill collector. At least, that was until they called back-to-back three more times.

Who the hell could this be? I thought.

"Hello?"

"Hey, Mya. Um, it's Anthony. I got your phone number off the company's website. I hope you don't mind."

"Uh, no. I guess I don't mind, but what's up? What can I do for you?"

"Well, I was hoping that we could meet, or I could come by and speak with you. I'd rather not over the phone."

"Um, I'm not busy or anything, so I suppose it would be all right if you came by. I'll text you my address."

"All right, cool. I'll see you in about fifteen minutes or so."

We hung up, and instantly, I sat up and shut my book as my mind started to race. "What on earth could Anthony, of all people, want with me? And why haven't I heard from Alize?"

I started to call her, but with my attorney senses on one thousand, I attempted to put the pieces of the puzzle together first. Clearly, if he'd gotten my number from the website and not directly from Alize, then that meant she didn't know anything about the phone call. Then he'd said he didn't want to talk over the phone. So, that more than likely meant it could be something illegal that he didn't want to be traced back to either one of us.

"What the hell have you done, Anthony? What is this all about?"

All at once, some of the worst suspicions went through my head. Had he gotten himself caught up with whoever he was with at the abortion clinic with? Since Alize put him out and he didn't have a job, had he robbed someone or something? Had he possibly put his hands on Alize for putting him out in the first place? But I knew that couldn't be it because he wouldn't live to see the next day. But whatever it was, it was driving me crazy trying to figure it out, and he couldn't get to my home quickly enough.

A short time later, I heard a knock at the door, and when I opened it, Anthony basically barged his way in and began pacing my living room floor back and forth.

"Anthony, can you please explain to me what's going on?"

"Explain to you? You want me to explain to you? I came here so that you could do the explaining to me."

"Explain to you about what? I have no idea what you're talking about."

"Cut the crap, Mya, and let's keep things real. You've never liked me. From the very day we met, it's always seemed like you had it in for me."

"Wait, you came here because you think I don't like you?" I asked, making my way to the couch to have a seat.

"I want you to admit it. For once, I want you to finally be honest about it."

"Anthony, look, I don't dislike you, okay? Honestly, I do, however, hate the fact that I feel like my friend has to take care of everything on her own. I mean, you don't have a nine-to-five. She had to waste money on a sitter instead of you watching the kids. She takes care of the house, the bills, and everything all by herself. So, yeah, if there's something I don't like, then that's what it is."

"I see, and I guess that's why you hooked her up with some guy that my daughter is afraid of? Because you think she can do so much better without me?"

"What guy are you talking about? And who's afraid? Wait a minute, are you possibly referring to Carson? You met him?"

"I stopped by Alize's mother's house to see the girls, and Champagne mentioned some man that Zae has been talking to and said she was afraid of him . . . well, in so many words. Knowing Alize the way I do, my gut told me that it more than likely came from you. That you hooked her up with this guy because of your dislike for me. Because Alize is not out there just meeting random men."

"Listen, Anthony, did I know that Alize and Carson have been dating? Yes, I did. But was I the reason behind it or in favor of it? No, I wasn't. Carson was someone that came into our office for one of the other attorneys. I actually wanted him for myself, okay? But he was interested in Alize, and well, she was interested too. I had nothing to do with any of it, and I'm offended that you came here, barging into my house and accusing me of such. I'm not who you need to be trying to take your anger out on. You need to be talking to Zae."

He stopped pacing and stood there quietly while he thought to himself. Then came what seemed like the real question he'd been wanting to ask this evening. "Mya, I'm sorry. I shouldn't have stormed in your home the way I did, accusing you of anything. But I'm just so furious with this entire situation, mainly because Zae is trusting this man. I mean, what do you know about him, Mya?"

"Uh, I don't know. I had lunch with him the first day he came into the office, and he appeared to be a good and decent man. He's widowed with no children and very laid back. That's as much as I was able to learn."

"No, no, there has to be more than that. Mya, kids sense things that we, as adults, sometimes don't. And we both know how friendly Champagne is with people. She wouldn't say that she didn't want her mother talking to this man for no reason at all. He has to be hiding something."

"I don't know, Anthony. I mean, how much could Champagne have sensed from him? Alize has only been seeing Carson for a few weeks or so, and as far as I'm aware, she hasn't really had the kids around him like that. Are you sure you're just not coming up with this because he's with Alize, and well, you're not?"

"Think what you want, Mya, but I'm telling you something is not right. My child isn't crazy, and I don't want him around her or any of my children."

"Well, seeing that Alize really likes him, I think it's a little too late for that. Besides, I'm not the one that you should be expressing this to. You need to be talking to Alize."

"I tried. Trust me, I have," he said before turning around as if he were about to leave.

"Anthony, before you go, I'm not trying to pry, but why were you at an abortion clinic? I mean, that is the very reason why all of this transpired between you two, right?"

"Listen, you're probably going to think I'm lying just the same as Alize, but I didn't get anyone pregnant, okay? My son's mother, Monique, ended up pregnant by some jerk of a guy. When she told him about the pregnancy, he didn't want anything else to do with her, and she didn't

know what to do. She already has three children by three
jerk-ass guys, and that's including myself. So, when she
said her only choice was to have an abortion, I almost felt
obligated to support her. I surely can't tell the woman
what to do with her body, but she asked me to go with her
because she didn't have anyone else, so I went. I mean,
what was I supposed to do? She's the mother of my son,
and no matter how much Alize hates her, I have to be
there for her just as I would Zae. It's just that simple."

"Well, if that was it, why didn't you just explain it to
her? I mean, it sounds reasonable enough."

He shot me a look as if to say, "You know your friend,"
and I threw my hands up in surrender.

"Okay, okay, you're right. We are talking about Alize.
But Anthony, it seems to me that all of this could be fixed
with just a simple conversation."

"Yeah, but she was right the other night. We have been
through so much and gone back and forth for so long that
I don't think either of us knows if it's right anymore. It
just might be time to move on."

I heard his words that came from his mouth, but I
also felt his love and pain that came from his heart. It
was the very first time that I'd seen Anthony in a totally
different light, and, for once, he appeared to be a good,
down-to-earth, and decent type of guy. He still might
need a job and all and need to stop smoking and whatnot,
but he was a good man who loved my best friend with all
his heart. That's all I could ever hope for with Alize, and I
just hoped she figured it out for herself.

"Hey, before I go, you said that this guy is a widow?"

"Uh, yeah. He said his wife passed away from cancer."

"You know anything else that I may need to know?"

"Unfortunately, I don't, Anthony. But since you feel
so strongly about things and especially about how
Champagne feels, then I promise I'll keep an eye on him."

"Okay, cool. Thanks. That's all I ask for. Anyway, take care, Mya, and again, I'm sorry for barging in and interrupting your evening."

Anthony left, and I continued to think about everything he said, especially the part about how something didn't seem right about Carson. *What could Champagne possibly sense about Carson that isn't right?* I thought to myself. Normally, I would have my senses in tune, especially in my profession. But I had to admit that I may have dropped the ball a bit the second I'd seen him. He appeared so perfect to me, Alize, and even Leslie. But now, I was beginning to wonder from what Anthony said if he was really that perfect or if it was just what we wanted to see. I figured it was time for me to do some digging and make sure Carson Reed was who he really said he was, for Alize and her children's sakes.

CHAPTER 27

MYA

For the rest of the weekend, I hadn't been able to stop thinking about what Anthony said. I'd even tried doing a little digging on Carson myself by Googling his name, but there wasn't much that had come up. That was odd because I'd assumed I would have at least found something about his wife's death, but once again, there was nothing. So, I figured my best bet was simply to talk to Alize when she arrived at work.

Moments later, she sauntered in, looking nothing at all like the Alize I'd come to know. There was no flamboyant attire, long blond wig full of horsehair, or claws for nails. In fact, this particular Alize appeared very stylish, sophisticated, refined, and classy. I wasn't sure what to make of it.

"Alize?" I asked, trying to make sure it was her and not a clone.

"Good morning, Mya. How are you today?" she asked back, not at all sounding like her normal self either. Even her tone and diction came across as more refined and polished.

"Girl, what is up with this whole change? Your outfit, the way you're talking? What gives?"

"Nothing is up, Mya. I just came to the reality that one should dress and talk and behave like the person she is trying to become. It's about maturing and elevating. The Bible even says, 'When I was a child, I talked like a child, I thought like a child, I reasoned like a child. When I became a woman, I put the ways of childhood behind me.'"

"Oh, my goodness," I said, almost feeling sick to my stomach. "Girl, who are you right now? All this elevation just suddenly happened in a matter of a few short weeks. Give me a break, Zae. We both know that this has everything to do with Carson and nothing at all about your sudden maturing. And why are you allowing him to change you like this? When he first expressed his interest in you, I'm sure it was because he liked *you*, Zae, exactly for who you are, not for this person in front of me that you're basically pretending to be."

"Mya, look, he's already told me that people wouldn't be able to accept the change in me and that they would want me to be the old Alize in order to keep me at a standstill. But this is who I am from now on, so you're just going to have to accept it, whether you want to or not."

She sat down at her desk, and I couldn't help but continue to examine her, wondering if she'd lost her mind. Maybe I had dodged a bullet by not dealing with him if this was going to be the after-effects. However, I still needed to find a way to talk to her about what Anthony said without letting her know that he'd come by my house.

"Uh, Zae, all jokes aside, I really need to talk to you about something important."

"Of course. What's that?"

"I've been thinking over the weekend. Remember how when I thought that Carson was interested in me, you told me that I really needed to take my time and get to know him better—that he might be a totally different man than what he appears to be?"

"Yeah, and?"

"Yeah, and well, I think you should probably take your own advice. I mean, just look at how he's trying to change your whole personality and identity by having you dress and talk differently."

"Mya, all he did was have a conversation with me and remind me that I'm a beautiful, intelligent woman who has a lot going for herself, and I should want others to view me that way. He's only trying to help me grow. What's wrong with that?"

"What's wrong is this isn't who you truly are. I mean, can you honestly say that you're a hundred percent comfortable the way you are right now instead of how you normally dress? Plus, I can tell you're trying to watch every word you say to make sure you're saying things correctly. And not to mention, I think it's way too soon to have the man anywhere around your children, especially if one of them has expressed their dislike or displeasure," I spat out of frustration, not realizing what I'd done.

"Wait a minute. How do you know anything about Carson being around my kids—which, by the way, he hasn't—or if anyone has expressed dislike? The only other person that would have known that information is Anthony. Have you talked to him or something? Did he call you?"

I tried to remain quiet, but her looks were threatening death toward me with each passing second.

"Answer me, Mya. How do you know?"

"Zae, please calm down, all right? Anthony was only concerned when he reached out to me about you having him around the kids so soon, and well, I kinda agree."

"You know what? You and Anthony both have a lot of nerve. What I do in my life and who I want to have around my children or not is my damn business, and nobody else's." She got up and stormed out of the office before I had a chance to say another word. I still couldn't believe that I'd let it slip about talking to Anthony, but deep down, I felt like she was bound to find out sooner or later anyway.

The second she left, our daily unwelcomed guest came in, and, honestly, I was in no type of mood to deal with her.

"Hey, Mya, was that Alize?"

"Yes, that was her, Leslie," I answered nonchalantly.

"Why is she all dressed like she's Olivia Pope from *Scandal* and not her usual self?"

"I don't know, Leslie. Maybe she's having some type of identity crisis, but anyway, what's up? What can I help you with?" I asked, and I could tell that she finally sensed I wasn't in the mood.

"Oh, well, I only came down to say good morning to you two. But is something wrong between the two of you? I mean, the way she stormed out of here was crazy. You guys having a little office squabble?" she asked, attempting to joke and make light of the situation.

"I'm sorry, Leslie, but I have a ton of work right now, and I can't get into all of that at the moment. I'm sorry."

"No apology necessary, Mya," she said, frowning down at her cell phone.

I felt obligated to ask, "Is everything okay?"

"Yeah, everything's fine, I guess," she said, but I could tell by her resistance that there was something more to her lack of words.

"All right, Leslie, but if you need to talk about anything at all, I'm here," I offered.

"I know, but you're busy and all, and I don't want to lay my troubles at your feet."

Instantly, I began to feel bad for trying to brush her off the way I did. There was clearly something on her mind, and knowing that she had no other family or real friends in Atlanta, I wanted to provide a listening ear or shoulder to cry on if needed. With that in mind, I got up, closed the door to the office, and pulled up a chair.

"Here, why don't you sit down? Now, Leslie, I know we're not the closest of friends, but I also want you to feel that you can talk to me if you need to, and whatever you say will remain between us . . . strictly confidential."

She hesitated for a moment or two before finally putting it out there. "It's just the guy I've been dealing with."

"Not your *Mr. Wonderful*?" I asked and tried to make her crack a smile.

"Chile, *Mr. Pathetic* is more like it, okay. See, he made himself out to be this amazing man that had so much potential and so much going for himself, but Mya, honestly, he's far from that."

"Really? How so?"

"Girl, every time I turn around, he's hounding me for money or has gotten himself in this kind of bind or that one. The man almost even had his truck repossessed and needed help with that. And I'm sorry, but one thing I don't do is take care of a grown-ass man. I mean, my mother didn't raise any fools, all right? Then, on top of his financial issues, he's so demanding and always says how I should dress and behave more appropriately to be with a man like him. And lately, I've had to listen to him vent about his ex and how he had to cut her loose because she just couldn't hold up to his standards. His exact words were, 'She wanted to continue to hang around with ghetto-ass women.' But hell, I wanted to ask what he truly thought about me because I can be a little ghetto myself at any given time. Anyway, I've had to look at myself and wonder what I ever saw in the man and how I got hooked up with him in the first place."

"Wow, he almost sounds a lot like someone I know," I said, thinking of Charles, of course, but I knew there was no way on earth that the two of them would be linked together. Instead of drifting my thoughts to him, though, I tried to remain focused on her and her situation.

"Look, Leslie, you are a very beautiful woman who I feel could have any man she wants. The last thing you need to do is settle for some loser who can barely take care of himself, let alone give you the world. Besides, you don't need a man that's going to tell you how to dress or what type of people to be around. You are your own woman," I said to her matter-of-factly but also reminding myself.

"Thanks for that, Mya. I really needed to hear that. But what's so messed up about the whole situation is that I'd really thought I'd finally met the one, you know. And I liked this guy, but I swear, this will be the last time I meet some random man that pulls up in our work parking lot after hours, all right? I am officially and completely done with Charles's ass for good."

I heard the name, but I knew there was no possible way that she could be referring to *my* number one. But then again, with her saying how much of a jerk he really was, I was positive she was talking about him. I thought about telling her, or better yet, calling and giving him a real piece of my mind, but that would be giving him too much energy that he wasn't even worth at that point. The only thing it did was confirm to me that he needed to stay a thing of the past. Besides, I had more issues on my mind with Alize and Carson than to be worried about Charles.

"Look, Leslie. I'm sure from what you've told me that whoever this Charles guy is, he's not worth having you. There are tons of men out there that will treat you far better than him."

"Yeah, but where do you find them?" she asked. "Because I'm definitely not going on that *For Singles Only* show like you did. Girl, that was a hot-ass mess," she said, and we both burst out laughing. "Anyway, I better get back upstairs before Mr. Buchanon comes to hunt me down." She rolled her eyes to the back of her head as she stood up.

"Okay, but um, before you go—" I stopped her in her tracks as soon as the thought crossed my mind. "What's up with Robert and Carson? Are they old friends or something?" I tried to pry whatever information I could out of her.

"Oh, girl, no. Mr. Buchanon can't stand the man, but money is money, you know? So he's never going to turn down a client, no matter how grimy he is."

"He can't stand him? Grimy? Really? He seemed like an amazing guy."

"Yeah, he did all of the ten minutes that he was down here, but all I can say without saying too much is that he's not what you think. Trust me."

I had a million more questions that I wanted to ask, but I knew that she was bound by confidentiality and Leslie was never going to do anything to jeopardize her job. But I needed to know exactly what she meant by grimy.

"Wow. Well, I guess I won't be going on any dates with him," I threw out there, hoping she would somehow catch the bait.

"I wouldn't if I were you, Mya. Leave trouble right where he is, okay? Like you just told me, there's plenty of others out there that you can deal with."

"I know, but he had me feeling so sorry for him for the death of his wife, with the cancer and all."

"Cancer? Trust me, his wife didn't pass away from cancer. But like I said, I can't say much of anything else, and I need to get back upstairs. Thanks so much for being a listening ear. Maybe one day I can return the favor."

"It's no problem, Leslie. I actually enjoyed our conversation."

She left, and immediately the thoughts in my head started spinning. *What did she mean that his wife hadn't passed away from cancer?* I asked myself. I knew for a fact that I'd remembered him telling me that. So, with no other choice, I felt I needed to call Anthony to help me get to the bottom of things.

"Hello?" he answered.

"Hey, Anthony. It's Mya. Do you have a second?"

"Yeah. What's up, Mya?"

"I'm calling because I found out some news about Carson that's pretty disturbing to me. Now, I don't know all the details, but he's working with the attorney upstairs, and his secretary made it seem that he's not who he really makes himself out to be. In fact, she called him grimy. Then, on top of that, I know that I remember very well that he told me his wife had passed away from cancer. But the secretary just told me that's not the case. Now, of course, she couldn't actually go into detail about everything because of confidentiality, but I think we should find out what we can before it's too late."

After everything that I'd said, all I heard was complete and utter silence on the other end of the line.

"Um, hello? Did you just hear me, Anthony? I said that Carson isn't who he's made himself out to be."

"Yeah, Mya, I heard you, but what do you want me to do about it? I mean, I thought about it, and your friend put me out of my home—the man she's been with for the past seven years and has children with—and let this guy in. If she thinks he's that much better than me, then she's welcome to do what she wants, and she'll get whatever's coming her way."

"Anthony, you can't mean that. Don't you still love her? And what about the children? Do you really want a man that's labeled as grimy around your kids?"

"Look, as long as the punk doesn't do anything to my girls, then I'm good. I can't say anything about who she has around them, no more than she can say anything about who I have around them."

"So, that's it? After all you and she have been through together, you're going to just say fuck it and let things be? Even after everything I just told you?"

"She made her choice. She's the one that has to deal with it, not me. But I'm in the middle of something right now. I gotta go."

He was in the middle of something, all right, because before he hung up, I'd heard a woman in the background giggling. At that point, I didn't know who I was more upset with, me or him. Him for not giving a damn about my friend's well-being, or me for actually believing he had a little sense of decency about him. Now I knew exactly what Alize had been going through with him with all the back and forth over the years.

On top of all of that, I was becoming even more frustrated because I'd been putting all my energy into Anthony and Alize while I still had no one. And honestly, all I wanted to do was call up Kevin and enjoy an amazing and satisfying evening of his dick being all up and through me because I couldn't take another night with my rose and not the real thing.

CHAPTER 28

ALIZE

"Can you believe that, Carson?" I asked him after giving him an earful of what just happened between Mya and me. "After all this time of her hating Anthony and telling me that I could do better, she actually let him call and fill her head with a bunch of nonsense about you. But no matter what she says, I don't think that her concern is strictly based on what Anthony said. I believe this stems only from the fact that I'm dating you, and she's not."

"What? What are you talking about?"

"You might as well know, if you didn't already, that she was interested in you, Carson, and she thought you were interested in her. At least, that was until you came back to the office for me."

"Is that right? Because we went to lunch together?" he asked.

"Yes, because you went to lunch. She came back to the office practically head over heels in love with you," I said, not caring about what came out of my mouth at that moment. Any other time, Mya and I had always been sure to stick to our girl code, and the things we'd said in confidence remained between us. But I felt that that code was broken when she talked to my children's father behind my back. She very well better hope I didn't say anything to Carson about her wet dream.

"Wow," was all he said at first. "Listen, why are you getting yourself all worked up over this? Didn't we already talk about this? What they think doesn't matter at all. Your children's father or Mya can't stop what we have going on between the two of us. They can try all they want, but Alize, I don't plan on going anywhere, so I hope you don't either."

His words made me blush from ear to ear. I didn't know what he'd seen in me that made him want me as much as he did, especially over Mya, but I was overjoyed that he'd chosen me—so happy that I felt I was finally ready to give him what I'd been holding out on for weeks.

"Carson, what do you think about coming over to the house tonight for some time alone . . . just me and you?"

"Some time alone, huh? Are you sure about that?"

"Of course I am. I can see if my mother or even their father can watch the kids. I think I want to finish what almost started in the office the other day."

"Wow, I think I'm liking the way this sounds."

We hung up with one another, and I couldn't believe the effect he'd had on my mood. When I'd first gone outside, I was furious and practically ready to blow a gasket over my argument with Mya, but just talking with him for five minutes had put my mind at ease. I knew I was ready to go back inside, and nothing Mya had to say would matter to me one bit.

Back in the office, Mya tried her best to pretend that she hadn't seen me come in, but I knew better. I could also tell that she had more on her mind that she was itching to let out, so I braced myself for another round in the ring with her.

"Zae, can we talk, please? Without all the anger and hostility between us."

"What now, Mya?"

She got up and closed the door before speaking. "Look, I just want you to be careful with this man, okay? There are some things that you don't know about him. Hell, I still don't really know everything. But it doesn't sound good, and I don't want you to end up with any regrets."

"Are you serious, Mya? Is this more of what Anthony said, or is this simply because he chose me and not you? Because I'm beginning to think it has more to do with the latter."

"All right, clearly you're refusing to listen to anything I'm trying to tell you, but everybody is not lying on this man. I asked Leslie, and—"

"Wait, so now you're discussing my business with the one person you know I can't stand?"

"No, I wasn't discussing your business. She doesn't know anything about you and Carson dating. But I did ask her about him since he's working with Robert. She thought I was asking for myself. But anyway, Zae, she said the man is not who he portrays himself to be. And on top of that, I know that I remembered Carson telling me his wife passed away from cancer, but she also said that's not true either. Something is up with him, Alize, and I don't like the thought of it."

"Mya, you have really outdone yourself this time. First listening to Anthony, and now Leslie? The same woman that's fucking your no-good ex Charles, or whatever he was. But I bet she didn't say a word about that, now, did she? Girl, please, just stop with the accusations already because they're tired, and not to mention, we both know they wouldn't exist had he been dating you."

"Alize, how do you know anything about Leslie and Charles?" she asked, obviously stuck there, and I couldn't help but laugh under my breath.

"I know because she met him the same day he came to pick you up for that dinner meeting. He'd gotten her

number right before you pulled up. Oh, and you want to
know why I really hated his guts, Mya? Because when
you first started dating him, he came on to me the same
way he did to Leslie. You had left work early that day.
He'd just missed you. But he came in here like he owned
the place. Anyway, I was standing at the copier, and he
walked up close behind me, put his arm around my waist,
and told me how good I smelled. The second I realized
what he was doing, I pushed his ass off me so hard that
he fell down. Then when he hopped up, he called me a
dumb ghetto bitch and ran out. I wanted to tell you then,
and I know I should have told you. And maybe I should
have said something about Leslie, too. But out of respect
for our friendship and because you were so in love with
him at that time, I kept quiet both times. I knew a man
like him would eventually tell on himself sooner or later.
So, how about you do the same for me this time? I'm
happy seeing Carson, so just let me be that. And if he's
hiding something, which I doubt very seriously, I'll find
out on my own.

"All right, Zae, if that's how you want it, then fine. I
won't say anything else about it. But when you're done
having your head in the clouds, find time to ask him
about his wife and her death and see what he says."

CHAPTER 29

ALIZE

My pussy jumped for joy at the thought of being with Carson. We were so close to fucking on my desk the other day, but I didn't want our very first time to be that way. Plus, although I hated it, I couldn't tear my thoughts away from the fact that I hadn't been with anyone but Anthony. Speaking of him, I was about to go crazy at the fact that I'd called his cell at least ten times, and he wasn't answering. I had no one else to watch the children, and with him being their father, he owed me that much. Then, finally, after three more attempts, he picked up.

"Yeah, what's up? It's Ant." I could already hear by his tone that this wasn't about to be a pleasant exchange.

"Anthony, you already know this is Zae."

"What you need, Alize?"

"Before I get to what I need, can you tell me if we are ever going to have a decent relationship where we can truly co-parent these children together, or is it going to always be like this?"

"Look, I don't have a lot of time. Are you going to tell me what you need or not?"

I took a deep breath to try to release all the frustration that was starting to build inside of me. "Okay, I was wondering if you'd mind getting the girls this evening. I have plans, and so I was hoping they could come and stay the night with you."

"You have plans? Well, I'm sorry, I have plans too, and you can't just call me up last minute expecting me to drop everything because you suddenly have plans. I'm sorry."

"You know what? I should have expected this from you. Just because you've made up in your mind that I'm some horrible person for asking you to leave, you want to make my life a living hell. But you're the one that went to an abortion clinic with another woman, Anthony, not me."

"I don't have to make your life a living hell. You've done that all on your own. But like I said, I've got plans, so I can't get them. If things change, then I'll call you, all right?"

He hung up without giving me a chance to say another word, and I'd become so angry that I could have thrown my phone against the wall. Instead, I tried to think of an alternative. I called my mother, but she said no. I wanted to call Mya, but we weren't speaking, and besides, she wouldn't know what to do with four small children. I even tried a couple of friends that I hadn't talked to in months, but it seemed that everyone had something to do. Finally, I realized that I would simply have to give in, and tonight was not going to be *the night* for me and Carson. With that said, I dialed his number while still trying to come up with a sitter.

"Hey, beautiful," he answered on the first ring.

"Carson, hi. I, um, kinda have some bad news."

"Really, what's that?"

"I hate to say this, but it looks like we're not going to be able to get together tonight. I've been having trouble finding a sitter for the girls."

"Oh, I see," he said, and I could immediately hear the disappointment in his voice, along with the dead silence afterward. "Okay, well, what about Plan B?"

"Plan B? What's that?"

"Plan B is I order some pizza or something, whatever you like, come over, and we—meaning me, you, and the girls—watch a movie together. We can even watch something the children will enjoy, and maybe this may be an opportunity for Champagne to get comfortable being around me. And I can promise you that I will be a perfect gentleman. I won't even try to touch any parts of you when the lights are out, so you better not try and touch me either."

We laughed, and once again, I couldn't believe how amazing and understanding he was.

"Wow," I said, smiling from ear to ear. "I guess I didn't expect this type of response, but all right, pizza and movies it is. You already have my address, and you're welcome to come whenever you like. I'm just going to freshen up a bit and hop into something more comfortable, and I'll be waiting."

All of forty-five minutes later, I opened the door, and it practically felt like Christmas time. Carson stood there with several boxes of pizza, bags of groceries, toys, and other goodies for the kids. Not to mention the fact that he looked and smelled so good that I wanted to eat him up. He was definitely my personal treat.

"Carson, what is all of this?"

"Well, it's a night in, right? So, I wanted to make sure that you and the children wouldn't want for anything."

"Oh my goodness, you know you didn't have to do all of this. The pizza would have been just fine," I said, walking him into the kitchen.

"I know, but it was my pleasure." He set everything down and stood there staring at me the same way he had at the office.

"Well, thank you. Thank you so much for understand-ing my situation and being so kind," I said, reaching up to his tall frame to hug him. Without any hesitation, his muscular arms gripped my body, and immediately I thought about how good it felt. It was so warm and inviting and instantly made me feel safe, and I didn't want to let go. But before I knew it, my little busybody friend came running into the kitchen.

"Mommy, where's Daddy? Where's Daddy?" Cham-pagne asked, more than likely thinking that Carson was her father at the door.

"Uh, honey, Daddy had something come up, so he can't come and get you guys like I said, all right? But maybe sometime over the weekend. I promise he'll come and get you guys and then do something really special with you, okay?" I lied for him, hoping I wouldn't have to make it some type of habit. But instantly, she started to cry, and her tears practically broke my heart.

"Sweetie, don't do that. C'mon and just look at all the goodies Mommy's friend brought you and your sisters." I picked her up in my arms. "Champagne, this is Mommy's friend, Mr. Carson. And Carson, this is my oldest daugh-ter, Champagne."

He picked up her little hand and tried to shake it, but she snatched it away from him. I had to admit that I was totally shocked by her reaction because out of all the girls, she was my friendliest and normally took to everybody, but surprisingly, not this time. I figured it was just because she had her hopes up on spending the evening with her father, but I also couldn't stop thinking about what Anthony said either. Suddenly, I found myself second-guessing myself and wondering if I'd made the wrong decision by having him come by.

"I'm so sorry, Carson, for her response. She's usually much friendlier than this."

"It's okay. It's her first time meeting me, so I completely understand. I would feel the same way if I were her age, meeting some strange man who wasn't my father."

"You're quite understanding about everything, Carson, and I can't thank you enough for that," I said to him, also wondering why Anthony couldn't have been more like him. "But listen, I'm sure if you just give her some time, she'll quickly become your best friend, especially if you keep bringing her and her sisters treats like this." We both laughed as I began to prepare the living room and food for movie night.

The first movie we started up was Carson's idea, *The Little Mermaid*. All of fifteen minutes in, the girls were in complete awe. Carson still didn't have Champagne wrapped around his finger with the movie choice, but at least she'd stopped crying, and I saw a smile cross her face. All their eyes watched the screen in wonder, including his, and I couldn't help but think to myself that this was what family life was supposed to be like. It was exactly what I needed to give me the peace I'd been longing for, although that peace seemed very short-lived when I heard the knock at my door.

"I'm sorry, Carson. I wasn't expecting anyone, but maybe it's my mother. Maybe she changed her mind about coming to get her grandchildren."

I got up to answer the door, and the second I opened it, there was Anthony standing there, gaping at me.

"Anthony, hey, um, what are you doing here?"

"What do you mean what am I doing here? You asked me to come and get the girls, and I told you if anything changed, then I would drop by."

"No, you said you would call. So, when you didn't, I assumed you weren't coming. Um, so my friend and I decided to have movie night here with the girls." I tripped and fell over every single word that came from my mouth.

He stepped inside and just continued to look for a minute. "Your friend?" was all he asked while basically mean- mugging Carson, who'd gotten up and reached out his hand to him.

"Hey, man, I'm Carson—Carson Reed—and it's nice to finally meet you. I've heard a lot about you. And you and Alize have some beautiful little girls here," he said to him.

However, Anthony didn't flinch or show him a single ounce of love in return. All he did was try to get the girls' attention. "Champagne, Hennessy. Hey, babies. Daddy's here," he called out to them, but their little faces hadn't moved one second from the television screen to give him the normal attention he was used to. "Uh, Alize, I need to talk to you outside for a minute," he demanded more than asked.

"Carson, do you mind? I need to take care of this for a second."

"Of course, go right ahead."

I went onto the porch with Anthony, and he wasted no time letting me know exactly what was on his mind. "What the fuck is wrong with you, Alize?"

"What's wrong with me? No, the question is, what's wrong with you?" I said, trying my best not to raise my voice. "You were supposed to call if you had a change of plans, not just drop by. And then you show up here hours later and expect our kids to be thrilled to see you. That's not how this works, Anthony."

"Oh, so having my girls around some random perverted man is how it works, Zae? Do you really even know this joker the way you think you do?"

"Here you go. You're on the same nonsense that Mya's on. But listen, I know him well enough, and that's all that matters."

"Right. So, in other words, you don't know this cat, and you have him in my house around my girls? Is that why you put me out, Zae? So you can entertain some lame-ass old dude in our home?"

"See, that's where you're mistaken, Anthony. Maybe you've forgotten, but the deed to this house is in my name. Mine. I just allowed you to lay your damn head here because of my kids. And you know good and well why I put your ass out, and it didn't have anything to do with Carson but everything to do with you being at the abortion clinic with some random-ass bitch. So, if you wanna be upset with somebody, be upset with your damn self because you're the one who fumbled the fucking ball. Now, I'm going back to watch *The Little Mermaid* with my girls. You can pick them up tomorrow if you like, but please do me a favor and call before you come."

I went back inside and slammed the door, fuming at the audacity of that man. How dare he act as if I was doing something wrong when the fact of the matter was that we were in this whole predicament because of his actions—nothing more, nothing less. As I stood at the door, taking a few deep breaths to calm down, Carson walked over to me and took me in his arms.

"I'm sorry, Alize. I didn't mean to start anything between you and your children's father. I can leave if you need me to."

"No, please don't. I want you to stay, Carson. Honestly, I need you to stay," I said, holding him as tightly as I could.

"Okay. I'm not going anywhere. I promise."

CHAPTER 30

MYA

I was happy to finally be home and in my safe place. The tension in the office between me and Alize today was so thick you could have cut it with a knife. The fact that we had yet to settle our differences had made it difficult for me to absorb and focus on any of my work. I truly missed my friend, not to mention the fact that I had a million other thoughts swimming around my mind that refused to allow me to concentrate. I couldn't seem to stop thinking about what type of secrets Carson might have been hiding, especially with lying about the death of his wife. Then there was Charles and Leslie and the fact that Alize knew all about them and never told me. Plus, in my heart, I'd truly started to miss Kevin, while in my panties, my pussy had begun to miss him long ago. All of it was more than a notion, so leaving an hour early seemed like the only reasonable thing to do.

Now that I was home, I wanted to do the one thing that would bring me the most pleasure and satisfaction—call Kevin to stop by. However, seeing that I hadn't heard from him since telling him I loved him, I needed to get a feel for where his mind was exactly. I decided to shoot him a vague text just to see what type of response I'd receive.

Hey, Kevin . . . thinking of you.

Normally, he would have responded within a few minutes of my text, but after twenty minutes or so, there was still nothing. I began to give up hope and prepare to read the last novel by Ashley Antoinette instead. She always brought the drama and excitement in her novels, and that was exactly what I needed at the time. At least, that was until I heard my phone alerting me to a text. My heart started to skip a beat at just the thought of being with him again, but the second I read the words on the screen, it did just the opposite. It quickly sank into the pit of my belly instead.

Hi, Mya. I wanted to reach out and see how you were. I hope you're doing okay. God bless.

Really? I thought. Here was Will texting with his holiness and blessings when my mind was in the complete gutter. I almost responded, but the second I prepared myself to do so, the text that I'd been waiting for had finally come through.

What's up? was all he said, and since that whole incident that had occurred with his fiancée, I'd learned to be as vague as possible and put the ball in his court when responding.

Nothing much.

Want some company tonight?

Sure, was what I texted back, yet I was literally jumping around doing my happy dance and shouting "Yes, yes, yes!" in my bedroom. I couldn't wait to have that man back inside of my bed and, more so, back inside of me.

He shot back that he'd be over in a matter of fifteen minutes, and that gave me more than enough time to take a quick shower, light some candles, turn up the Pandora station, and wait for a much-needed dick session.

Shortly after, the house was warm and inviting, I was warm and inviting, and all that was needed was the man of the hour. Fifteen minutes tops, and there he was knocking at the door. When he entered the house, I assumed that it was safe to say he missed me just as much as I did him. He didn't waste any time and got right down to business, too, by taking off my robe and his clothes. He didn't say one single word—not a "hello," "how are you," or anything of the sort. He simply undressed and then laid me down on the bed and put his face right between my legs as if I was about to be his last supper.

At first, I was enjoying every bit of it, but then the craziest thing happened. Suddenly, out of nowhere, Will, his "God bless" wish, and the Bible verse I'd heard at his church all crossed my mind. I knew that there was no way I could be having those types of thoughts at a time like the present, but the more I tried to put them out of my head, the more prevalent they became.

Repositioning my lower body, I hoped that if he'd hit a different spot, the thoughts would somehow fade away, but they didn't. In fact, they'd become so dominant in my mind that I was no longer enjoying what was happening. Kevin was none the wiser, however, when he stopped and got on top of me. He was so into everything that he was doing while I only lay there, distant and in a whole different world. Quickly, I wondered if the fool was so oblivious to my lack of interaction that he couldn't take a hint.

"Kevin, Kevin. Stop, please. This isn't working."

"What's not working?" he mumbled, still in full motion.

"I asked you to stop already. Please."

He stopped, rolled off me, and stared like I had three heads. "What's up with you, Mya? You called me over here."

"I did, and I'm sorry, but I just can't do this tonight."

"Do what, Mya? Fuck? This is what we always do, so what kind of games are you playing with me?"

"Look, I'm not playing any games, Kevin. It's just that I have a million things in my head right now, and something doesn't feel right this time. There's a disconnect, and I'm just not enjoying things the way I normally would."

"You know what? I don't have to deal with this, Mya. Shit's becoming way too complicated just for some pussy," he said, getting up and throwing his clothes and shoes on.

I, on the other hand, was completely outdone because he'd never really been that insensitive towards me. *Did he really just have the nerve to reduce me to just some pussy?* I thought to myself, although I honestly already knew that was the case. It hit a lot different hearing the words come directly from his mouth, though.

After getting dressed, he started walking to the door as I trailed right behind him. "What do you mean *'just some pussy'?*" I questioned, needing to hear his explanation clearly.

"Mya, you knew what this was from day one. I don't know why you keep acting like you didn't, but we were supposed to be having fun. That's it. But every time I come over now, it's something different. And it's too much for me to deal with. I have a whole fiancée at home that I could be laid up with right now, doing what I thought I was coming here to do. I'm sorry."

"So, that's it? After all this time, is that really it? And you're talking about a whole fiancée, so why are you over here then?"

"Listen, I'm sorry, all right. I thought we could keep this going, but it's starting to look like we can't," he said before kissing my forehead and walking out the door.

I wasn't sure who I was upset with the most: him for actually saying the truth, or me for knowing the truth and keeping up with the whole façade as long as I had in the first place. The one thing I did know was that Will and Bible scriptures and all kinds of spiritual thoughts were floating around in the forefront of my mind, and I wasn't sure why. *Why hadn't I been able to concentrate on anything else?* I asked myself, trying to make sense of everything.

After Kevin left, I walked back into my bedroom and picked up my cell phone before I talked myself out of what I was about to do. I dialed the number, and he answered on the first ring as if he'd been waiting for my call.

"Hey, Will. It's Mya. How are you?"

"I'm good, Mya. How are you? I figured when I texted earlier that you would more than likely text back. I never expected you to call."

"Yeah, well, I've never been big on the whole texting thing," I lied, just to keep the conversation going smoothly.

"Well, I wanted to reach out to you again and apologize for that night when you called me and we were interrupted by my guest. I didn't want you to have the wrong impression of me."

"Will, there's no way I could have had the wrong impression. You're an adult, and it's not like we were exclusive. You are more than free to see whoever you like."

"That's true. But I'm very mindful of my behavior and how I represent myself as a Christian man. I just didn't want you to think I was out here trying to be some lady's man." He chuckled behind his words. However, I couldn't help feeling like that was almost a jab at me because I practically felt like a ho from the day he'd come by and Kevin had shown up.

"Listen, your reputation is still squeaky clean in my eyes. I didn't think you were trying to be a lady's man just because you moved on."

"Moved on? I didn't move on, Mya. It was simply two old friends watching a movie together. That's it."

"I'm sure," I let slip out of my mouth.

"Wait, why would you say that? Do you not believe that two adults could enjoy one another's company without there being anything romantic or any intimacy involved?"

"Uh, honestly, it's not what I think that matters, Will," I said, but in the back of my mind, I wanted to say a resounding "hell no."

"I know it doesn't matter, but I would still love to know your thoughts. Or better yet, why don't we do this? Allow me to take you out. And not to church this time. And it doesn't have to be called a date or anything. Just two friends hanging out, and I promise it will be the time of your life . . . without any intimacy involved whatsoever. I mean, unless you want to give me a hug as a thank you."

I was tickled and flattered all at the same time. And although I still had my reservations, something made me want to take Will up on his offer.

"Okay, sure. That sounds good," I told him.

We talked a while longer after that. Actually, at least an hour or more after, and, to my surprise, our exchange was good and refreshing. It turned out to be exactly what I needed, and better yet, I hadn't thought any more about what had happened between Kevin and me.

Immediately I started to think that maybe this was God's way of showing me something different than what I'd become accustomed to. Maybe it was even His way of getting me closer to my now or never. Either way, I couldn't escape the fact that I was going to bed with a smile on my face that had nothing at all to do with sex. And for the first time in forever, I was ready to do something different and do things God's way.

CHAPTER 31

ALIZE

Mya had left early, and I assumed it was because we hadn't said as much as a word to one another during the day. I wanted so badly to at least try to start a conversation with her, but I simply couldn't find the words. Most of it was because I felt like she and Anthony were basically teaming up against me and Carson. Anthony, I would have expected, but never Mya. She was my dearest friend, and all I truly wanted was for her to be happy for me the way I would have been for her.

Now that my day was complete, though, I couldn't wait to get home and have some much-needed time alone with Carson, of course. Tonight, we'd finally planned a dinner date out, and it was the one thing I was looking forward to. The only thing I had to worry about, though, as usual, was finding a sitter. My mother had already told me that she couldn't do it, so it seemed like Anthony would be my only option, and that was only if he'd come through for me after our last argument.

I ran downstairs to pack some things into my car before leaving, but before heading back to the second floor, it dawned on me that I hadn't seen Milton at all during the day.

"Hey, Diane, where's Milton been today?" I asked before she headed out herself.

"He took the day off today, Alize. He normally does each year around this time. Today is the anniversary of his divorce, and he usually wants to be alone."

"Oh, okay. Thanks for letting me know."

Milton had been there so much for me over time that it bothered me to hear that. All I could think was that he was home alone in grief and despair over his divorce from Faye. I couldn't let that continue to happen. Somehow, I had to find a way to break the cycle and bring some happiness into his life around this time each year. Then it dawned on me. Instead of having a heated argument with Anthony about having the children tonight while I went out with Carson, I could see if Milton wanted some company. He absolutely adored the kids, and I was positive that Champagne and Hennessy would give him all the love and joy he needed to lift his spirits. Plus, Moet and Moscato wouldn't be a problem because I would give them a bottle, and they'd be out for the count for the evening.

With the go-ahead from Milton, I'd made it home, gotten dressed, packed the kids up in the car, and headed toward Milton's house. He was overjoyed and more than welcoming when I called and asked if the kids could come and keep him company this evening while I went on a dinner date. In fact, it seemed that his entire mood shifted from when I first called, so I knew in my heart that this was exactly what he needed. I was relieved as well that he was so accommodating because the last thing I wanted to do was ask Anthony to keep his own children again while I went out with Carson for the evening. I didn't have time to argue with him about my whereabouts or who I would choose to have my children around. And I especially didn't have time for him to run and have any more private conversations about me with my Mya. Besides, until he fully explained why and with whom he went to an abortion clinic, he and I had nothing further to discuss other than how we were going to coparent the girls.

After twenty minutes or so, we were finally pulling up to his home. Never once having stepped foot inside before, my eyes bulged and my jaw dropped simply from the outside, looking nothing short of a mini-mansion and much too big for one person. I realized that he must have purchased it when his wife and daughter lived with him and wondered why he never downsized once they divorced. A second later, I saw him coming out on the porch to help me.

"Alize, I'm so happy you asked me to watch the girls this evening."

"Well, I'm happier that you accepted, Milton. But I had no idea your home was so elaborate. It's beautiful," I said, walking inside. It was just as gorgeous as the exterior was.

"Yeah, it was Faye's dream home when we were together, and I can't seem to part ways with it."

"Well, you have four little ones here that would love to come spend time with you in this place anytime you like."

"And they are welcome anytime as well," he said, fixing up a little spot for the children in what appeared to be his family room. "And where are you off to, might I ask? You and Anthony need some alone time for a bit tonight?"

"Uh, no, not exactly. I'm having dinner with my new friend, not Anthony." I hesitated while his eyes glared at me, saying he knew there was more to my words than what I was saying.

"Okay, now, I might be an old fool, but I wasn't born yesterday, Alize. Who are you going out with tonight?" he questioned, sounding a lot like my real father.

"You don't really know him, Milton. His name is Carson. He came to the office a couple of times to see Attorney Buchanon."

"That same guy that went to lunch with Mya and now the one that you've been going to lunch with almost every day? Yeah, I've been watching his car pull up, and then you run out and hop inside."

"Listen, Milton, before you think I'm doing anything behind Mya's back, she knows all about me dating Carson now. Besides, it's not like he asked her to lunch that day anyway. They just somehow ended up together."

"I hear you, Alize, and I'm not trying to get all in between what you girls have going on. But let me ask you this: what do you really know about this man? I mean, really know about him?"

"Well, of course, I'm still getting to know him, but so far, he seems like a really good and genuine man with a lot going on for himself. Plus, he doesn't seem to be about all the drama that Anthony was about. And not to mention that he loves the girls, and Champagne is just as crazy about him," I lied.

"Now, who are you trying to convince, honey, me or you? And why are you rushing so soon to have him around these girls? You don't even know this man other than what's on the surface. And I have to be honest that it still bothers me that one day he's at lunch with Mya, and then the next he's with you. I mean, that doesn't mean anything to you, or woven a web in you all's friendship?"

"Milton, you almost make me seem like a horrible friend or something. I had nothing to do with them having lunch together, and as for me and him, he approached me."

"Listen to me. Be careful with this man. If I remember correctly, that day when he and Mya left together, I didn't like the look in his eyes. There was something strange or sneaky about him that I didn't like. And besides that, don't be in such a hurry to dismiss these kids' father from your life. Now, I know that you and him have been together for years, and he hasn't been the man he needs to be. I agree wholeheartedly with you that he needs to step up, but give him the chance to do that. Tell him what your requirements are for you two to be back in the house together, and trust me, if he truly wants the relationship, then he'll do it. And don't be demanding, either. Be straightforward. There's a difference between the two."

With tears in my eyes, I reached up to hug him. I knew deep down that everything he'd said came from a good place. Although I still felt that everyone else had all these negative things to say about Carson, I believed they just didn't know him the way I did. And as for Anthony, although I still loved him, I truly felt in my heart that I'd given him more than enough of my time and energy. It was now time for me to do something different.

CHAPTER 32

ALIZE

Pulling up to the restaurant that Carson and I agreed to meet at for the evening, I checked my makeup in the mirror and made sure that everything was perfect. I'd decided to wear something very simple, so I pulled out my little black dress that had been in the closet for years and some black heels. Other than that, I dressed it up with some gold accessories and made sure my hair and makeup were on point. In my mind, I always felt that a person embodies the fashion they wear and not the other way around.

As I got out and looked at the name of the restaurant, I realized that it was the exact same place that Leslie strolled into the office bragging about a while ago. I also recalled her suggesting that Anthony could never bring me to a spot like this, and I couldn't wait to throw in her face that I'd been here. It would be all the revenge and satisfaction I needed to see the look on her silly face, especially when I revealed it was with Carson.

Then, out of nowhere, I heard a voice from behind me.

"Hey, gorgeous, can I be your date for the evening?"

I smiled without even turning around, knowing exactly who it was. "Only if your name is Carson Reed."

He took my hand and spun me around to face him. "Damn, girl, you look good enough to eat. You make me want to say fuck this restaurant and take you home now."

"Carson!" I playfully slapped him on his chest. "You promised me a good meal, and that's what I want tonight."

"Don't worry, you're going to get your good meal. But what do I get in return is the question."

"Be a good boy, and we'll definitely find out," I joked back with him.

After all the fun-loving antics, he placed my arm in his, and we walked inside. I almost felt like we were celebrities or movie stars the way everyone stared at us as we strolled past them. I had to admit that they were probably gaping at Carson just as much as they were at me because the man did look fine as wine. His tailored suit fit perfectly on his long, strapping build. His caramel skin was smooth as silk, and his full beard was trimmed to perfection. Not only did the man look good, but he smelled good, too. I hated comparing him to Anthony, but every time I thought about both of them, Anthony didn't stand a chance.

Carson had given the maître d' his name for the reservation, and he escorted us to our table. Once there, Carson pulled out my chair for me.

"I can't believe how beautiful this place is," I said, looking around still in amazement.

"Yeah, it's pretty cool."

"Pretty cool? Hello? Are we in the same restaurant?"

"Yes, Alize, we are. But I've been here several times now since they opened, and I'm not that impressed with it anymore," he said. "I'd much rather be eating some wings somewhere with sauce so good that I have to lick my fingers."

That's what I liked about him the most: the fact that he was so laid back and down to earth. That in itself made me comfortable around him enough to where I didn't feel like I had to be all fake and phony. However, as I looked at the table, I was somewhat embarrassed because there was so much in front of me that I wasn't sure which glass or silverware to pick up with each course. Then, while glancing over the menu, I didn't think I could pronounce half of the items on it.

"Um, Carson," I said with a look of desperation written across my face, which he must have picked up on immediately. He placed his hand on top of mine before speaking.

"Don't worry, okay. I'll order for the both of us. And this is your salad fork, and this one is your dinner fork, all right?"

I had no idea how he'd known, but I was thankful that he'd saved me the humiliation. After he ordered us some appetizers and the main course, along with a bottle of wine of our liking, he started a conversation that I honestly wasn't in the mood to discuss. Instead of us having a wonderful evening, it seemed he was more curious about Anthony and his reaction when he came to the house. In fact, it almost appeared as if he were taking some type of satisfaction from Anthony's displeasure. I, on the other hand, hadn't concentrated on much of anything he said because now my mind was more focused on the kids and even Anthony's well-being.

It was crazy because I'd gone through so much just to get to this point with Carson, but since we'd sat down, he was the furthest thing away from me. And then, out of nowhere, thoughts of what happened to his wife popped into my mind. Mya's words hadn't escaped me ever since she'd said them, and now seemed like as good a time as any to try to clear up any confusion or misinterpretation. I had to get right down to the truth to prove her wrong.

Completely dismissing anything he was talking about at that moment, I interrupted his words. "So, Carson, you were married before, right?"

"Uh, uh, yes I was," he stuttered with his words and looked at me oddly before putting his face in his salad as if that was the end of the conversation.

"So, what happened?" I asked, not exactly sure where to begin with my questioning.

"What do you mean what happened?"

"With your wife. I take it that you two got divorced, right? But why?"

"Um, she, um . . . I'm sorry, Alize," he said with his eyes shifting around and looking as if he were trying his best to muster up some tears. "It's always a little difficult for me to discuss my late wife. But she passed away. We didn't divorce. Her untimely death took me and her family by a complete surprise."

"Oh, I'm so sorry to hear that. I wasn't aware that she passed," I answered, behaving as if I was totally clueless. "Do you mind me asking what happened?"

"Well, it was a horrible car accident," he mumbled between mouthfuls of lettuce. "Yeah, an accident. She was the athletic type, you know . . . always in the gym. And one evening, on her way home, it was raining cats and dogs outside. I was told by the police that her car just kind of lost control. They pronounced her deceased at the scene."

"Oh wow." My mouth stood open, more shocked at the elaborate tale he'd come up with instead of what he'd told Mya about his wife dying from cancer. "I'm truly sorry to hear that, Carson. I'm sure that had to be tough to deal with."

"Yeah, it was. Hardest thing in life I ever had to go through, actually. And now I think about her practically every day. Especially since everything reminds me of her, including you. You resemble her in so many ways. I guess that's why I took to you so quickly."

"I see."

"Anyway, it's been a couple of years or so, and I'm finally beginning to get my life back on track. I've had counseling to try to heal from the suddenness of it all. I'm opening myself up to dating again, which is why I love that I met you, and the insurance I received left me a nice little nest egg to live from so that I don't have to go back into anyone's office anytime soon. So, life is getting better now."

"I see," I said again, not really knowing what to say. I couldn't help but wonder, though, what he was trying to hide, and for the very first time, I believed I'd seen what everyone else had seen, with something peculiar lying behind his eyes. But then, the more he gazed at me, the more I started to see the softness and tenderness I'd come to know within them. It made me wonder if maybe all of us had him mistaken. Maybe he'd told different stories about her death because it was private and personal to him, and he just wanted to keep the truth to himself. By all means, it was his right to do so. Maybe he'd said whatever came into his mind at the time about how she'd died, simply not wanting to relive that tragic event.

It was at that very moment that I decided to let myself go ahead and give him the benefit of the doubt. I no longer cared about what Mya, Leslie, or Anthony had to say. In fact, I didn't even care about Milton's warning. I liked Carson, and he made me feel extraordinarily good, and that's all that mattered. Although I was still nervous and a bit cautious about this new start, I was even more excited and ready for whatever was in store for me or us.

CHAPTER 33

MYA

It had now been an entire month since Alize and Carson started seeing each other, and nothing had changed. I would have thought by now that he would have shown his true colors, and things would be over between them, especially when I shared with her what Leslie said. I assumed she would have taken heed to my suspicions, cut him loose, and things would go right back to normal with her and Anthony, yet it was the complete opposite. He'd been having flowers delivered to her almost every other day. She continually showed up with a new piece of jewelry around her neck or wrist. And she constantly stayed on the phone with him, giggling throughout the day.

Plus, she'd still been coming into the office every day in what had now become her usual attire: business suits, dresses, or skirts and blouses. There was no more flash or flamboyance to her style anymore. Her nails were cut down to a short active length, and she'd actually been wearing her real hair. When I thought about it, it sickened me that this man had that much control over her the way he did. It seemed from her appearance to the way she talked and behaved, and even down to her thinking, had been groomed by him. Not to mention, it was beginning to seem less and less like she and I were best friends, let alone immediate supervisor and employee. But instead, it was more like we were simply distant associates who just happened to work together. Of course, it honestly bothered me, but since she'd given the impression that it was her and Carson against the world, I refused to say anything.

"Hey," was all that I did say when she finally decided to stroll in late to work yet again.

"Hey," she said back nonchalantly in what had become her new tone when speaking to me. "Um, I'm going to have to leave about noonish today. Carson is taking me somewhere special."

"Uh, Zae, we're going to have to talk about that. You know that I have a very important case coming up, and I need your assistance. Besides, for the past month, you've been sauntering in here late a lot and leaving whenever you feel like it. Something's got to give. I mean, if you're no longer happy here or feel that your personal life now supersedes your position, then I need you to tell me so we can figure out an alternative."

"An alternative, huh?" was all she said with a slight snicker behind her words.

"What's so funny, Zae? I'm being completely serious with you."

"What's funny, Mya, is you. I mean, I don't know whether to take you seriously right now or if this is possibly coming from the fact that I'm happy with Carson while you're no closer to getting your now or never than the man on the moon."

I had to admit that I was perplexed and hurt all at the same time. Her words hit me to the core, but I wasn't going to give her the satisfaction. Instead, I'd decided to take a more soft and gentle approach.

"Alize, where is all this hostility for me coming from? I mean, yeah, I talked to Anthony that once, and yes, I felt something strange about Carson. But honey, if you like him and truly feel that he's the one for you, then who am I to say anything? But it shouldn't have any bearing on our friendship or work relationship."

"Look, no one is hostile, Mya. And you're absolutely right. My relationship with Carson doesn't have any bearing on my relationship with you. But I still don't feel right that you chose to listen to Anthony over me. And since I feel like you picked your side by going against me with Anthony, then, well, I've chosen mine too. And by the way, to be painfully honest, I'm not happy here any longer in this mediocre position. I have huge dreams and aspirations, and like Carson has been telling me, life is much too short to not go after them."

Once again, her words were an utter slap in my face. *How dare she consider this a mediocre position after everything I went through for her to be here?* I thought, especially with her not having any type of degree or formal education outside of her high school diploma. Now, all of a sudden, it was mediocre. And once more, it all was rooted in none other than the devil in a suit, Carson Reed.

"You know what, Alize? At this point, do whatever you believe is best for you. I think it might be time for us to go our separate ways anyway and for me to find someone more fitting for this position."

I left the office to go outside and get a breath of fresh air while using my cell phone. I thought I would give Will a call and see if his day was going any better than mine. Oddly enough, he had become a very pleasant outlet for me ever since I'd let him take me out a month ago. Our interactions hadn't been really romantic or anything, yet I enjoyed spending time with him. It surprised me, too, that I hadn't even thought about sex much since we started hanging out. Although I still longed for love and a form of intimacy with a man, I was content with where things were. Besides, Will was always happy and encouraging, always willing to lend an ear or helping hand, and he taught me spiritual things that I hadn't gotten from any other man. It didn't even bother me any longer that he wasn't a white-collar man because he seemed to be very well off financially. He was perfect, yet I still wasn't convinced that he was perfect for me.

"Hi, Will. How are you?" I asked when he answered on the first ring.

"Hey, I'm good, and how are you?"

"Honestly, I've been better."

"Really? What's up? What's going on?"

"I don't know. It's just this whole situation with Alize. I already told you that she hadn't acted like her normal self ever since she started dating Carson. I always thought that if she ever dated someone other than her children's father, that it would be good for her. But . . . but I can't let go of this feeling that something isn't right about Carson, and I think it's doing her more harm than anything. Plus, I'm not so sure that she's fully over her children's father. I think this is just her way of getting back at him for what she thinks he did to her."

"Listen, I know that's your best friend, and I know that you're concerned about her, but, Mya, she's a grown woman, and she's going to do exactly what she wants to do. And I'm afraid that the more you push, the more she'll pull away. So, my best advice would be to pray for her."

"Pray? That's it? But what if this guy could be so lowdown and corrupt that he ends up harming my friend or her children?"

"Look, prayer is truly all she needs. You pray that her eyes are opened to whoever he truly is. Pray that his real character and intentions are revealed before it's too late.

And trust me, God will handle the rest. If this man is hiding something and not meant to be in Alize's life, then he won't be. So, yes, that's it. Prayer is the very best thing you can do for her right now. And if you want, I'll pray with you."

"Wow, you always have a way of just making things all better."

"That's not me. That's the God in me."

"So, you promised me a good meal and movie some-time this week. I could really go for it tonight, but honestly, I don't feel like going out."

"No problem. If you don't mind, I could pick us up some takeout and stop by."

I took a quick second to think about his offer, and even though it sounded great, I wasn't so sure. I may have been content over the past month with no sexual activity, but my hormones still had a way of reminding me that I was human. And I didn't want to violate the man or make him do anything that would compromise his beliefs.

"Um, Will, we've always done things outside of the house. I don't want to—"

"Mya," he cut me off, "you don't have to worry. If I ha-ven't shown you by now, I am a Christian and gentleman before anything else. This won't be my first time being alone with a woman, and I know how to conduct myself. So, what do you say?"

"Okay, why don't you come over around seven thirty?" I said after hearing his words. But little did he know, it wasn't him or his actions that I was worried about.

CHAPTER 34

ALIZE

"Hey, Carson, I just told Mya that I needed to leave early, so I should be heading out in the next thirty minutes or so. I'll fill you in then on what happened between us."

"Oh, okay. But Alize, I'm sorry . . . I had something just come up. Do you think we could just hook up later tonight?" he asked, not really sounding like himself and seeming very preoccupied.

"Sure, tonight is good. But is everything all right?"

"Yeah, everything's good. But how about I come to your house around seven or so? And is it possible that we can be alone this time and the children not be there? Maybe take them to your mother's or something?"

"I can probably arrange that. Let me try to find them a babysitter now, and I'll just see you later."

"Cool."

We hung up, and I tried my best to process what had just happened. I wanted to be excited about sharing my news with him, which was basically that, since Mya was more than likely letting me go, now was as good a time as any to try to open my own boutique. However, something wasn't sitting well with me with the tone of his voice. He hadn't sounded like himself. Then, there was his request for me to find a babysitter, which he never directly came out and asked. I kept trying to tell myself that none of it meant anything and that I was only making myself paranoid, but still, I'd always been one to trust my gut, and this time, it was telling me that something was off. That's when I saw the one person who might have been able to help me peeking in the door, but the second she didn't see Mya, she turned to walk away.

"Leslie, Leslie," I called out. "Please, come in."

She stared at me like I had three heads.

"Um, look, Alize, today is not the day, and I was only looking for Mya to talk to her."

"Hey, I'm not trying to go back and forth with you like usual either. I just had a quick question, and well, I think you're the only one who can possibly answer it for me."

"Really? And what's that?" she said, continuing to look at me strangely.

"It's about Carson Reed. Now, I know that we are all bound by confidentiality, but I was wondering, is there any way at all that you can tell me what happened to his wife?"

She stood there, appearing to be at a loss for words. I, on the other hand, hated that I was desperate enough to ask my archenemy, but it was what it was. If anyone had an answer to help me, it was her, and I was basically at her mercy.

"Alize, like you said, we are bound by confidentiality, and anyway, I just don't think I should get involved in anything pertaining to Mr. Carson Reed."

I walked over and closed the door so that no one could hear me plead my case to her and so she wouldn't be able to leave.

"Leslie, please. I just need to know anything that you can tell me. I've been seeing Carson, and well, lately, it feels like something hasn't been adding up. I don't want to be overly suspicious, but honestly, I am. I'm asking for your help despite how either of us feels about the other."

"Listen, I don't feel one way or the other about you. I've always come at you a certain way because of how you always came at me. But I guess I'll go ahead and say this without feeling like I'm undermining my position. Carson Reed isn't one to be trusted, okay? I can't provide you with all the details of his wife's death, but I really don't think it was a mere accident or something that simply happened. From what I've gotten from Mr. Buchanon, her death was very intentional, and I believe it was at the hands of Carson."

"Are you serious? Do you mean he killed her?"

"I'm as serious as a heartbeat, honey. And no, I don't think he actually killed her, but I believe he very well knows who did because he was the mastermind behind it. From what I gathered, he swept her off her feet . . . somehow like he's doing you . . . and then he married her all within a matter of thirty days, and now, two years later, she's dead, and he collects on a large insurance policy. So, you do the math. But anyway, you can take that bit of information and do with it what you will. Just be careful, though, okay? I mean, we've never really gotten along, but I don't want anything happening to you. These men are not always who they appear to be. Trust me, I know. Plus, I personally think that you can do a million times better than him anyway. You're a very beautiful girl, and I've always looked up to you."

"Really? You think I'm beautiful?"

"Chile, hush. Anyway, I better get back upstairs before Buchanon comes looking for me. But can you tell Mya I came by?"

"Sure, I will, and Leslie, thank you so much. I appreciate you more than you know."

"I got your back, girl, and who knows? You might just luck up and find a folder on your desk by mistake before the end of the day with everything you need to know about Mr. Carson Reed."

I didn't say another word but simply winked my eye at her instead. It was crazy how all this time she hadn't been my favorite person, and we were always at odds simply for what happened all that time ago. But now, she was the one coming through for me in a major way.

Then, my thoughts immediately went to what she'd said about Carson. *Did he really have his wife killed for insurance money? And if so, what are his intentions with me?* I asked myself. I wanted so desperately to ask Mya what she thought, but then I remembered I already knew exactly how she felt. Plus, I was sure that my attitude toward her earlier wouldn't place her in the best mood to help me. So, I knew I was on my own on this.

"Carson, please just let this all be some huge misunderstanding. Please be the man I've known you to be for the past month."

CHAPTER 35

ALIZE

Thankfully, once again, Milton was overjoyed when I asked if the children could hang out with him for the evening. He was a pure godsend whenever I needed someone to keep an eye on them. My mother had put her foot down until Anthony and I got things figured out between us, and dealing with him lately had been more like pulling teeth. He hadn't really seen the children much on his own, and when I did pressure him to get them, there was always some type of argument that ensued. He felt that as the mother of four girls, I needed to be home with them twenty-four-seven and not entertaining some strange man that I hardly knew. Those were his words. Yet, after everything I'd learned from Leslie earlier, I was beginning to wonder if I truly knew Carson the way I thought.

Right before I left for the day, she'd come back downstairs and handed me a manila folder filled with papers, all on Carson. She told me to guard it with my life and give it back to her after I'd seen what I needed to see. I decided against looking at it at that moment, though. Hoping he and I had established a good enough relationship, I expected that we could talk about our pasts truthfully without me having to sneak behind his back. I still wanted to believe in my heart that this was all some

huge misunderstanding, and that he wasn't this horrible
man that everyone had made him out to be.

Heading into the house, I set my purse and the folder
down on the table by the door and headed to take a
shower before Carson arrived. Hoping to celebrate my
news of starting my boutique, I figured I would put on
something special for him. With that in mind, I pulled
out a black satin nightgown and robe set that I purchased
a long time ago.

"Wow, Anthony, I was going to wear this for you on
our anniversary," I said aloud to myself while shaking
my head and wishing in my heart that things could have
turned out so much differently for us.

I was running my bath water when I heard Anthony's
ringtone, along with his name scrolling across the front
of my phone. Dreading what was possibly awaiting me on
the other side, I almost decided not to answer, but a huge
part of me wanted to hear his voice as well.

"Hello?"

"Zae, where are the girls?"

"Well, hello to you too, Anthony," I said sarcastically.
"The girls aren't here right now."

"Where are they? Your mother's?"

"No, they're with a friend because I'm going to be a
little tied up tonight. Why?" I asked. "I know you're not
suddenly trying to see them."

"Alize, look, we've been playing this game with each
other for the past month now. Can we give it a rest? All I
want to do is see my babies."

"And like I said, they're not home right now, but you're
more than welcome to come by tomorrow."

He hung up in my face, and I sat on the edge of my
bed for a second, thinking about things between me and
him. I missed Anthony. In fact, I missed him like crazy. I
longed to see his smile, to feel his embrace, and just be

near him. But something wouldn't let me get past the fact
that he'd been at an abortion clinic with another woman,
no matter how he tried to explain it. And the kids—although I knew inside that he was a wonderful father, they
were my only way to get back at him. It was probably
horrible for me to not nurture their relationship, but that
was his fault for choosing another woman over us.

Trying to take my thoughts away from him, I turned
on some music, drank a glass of wine, and soaked in my
bubble bath, anticipating Carson's arrival. For the past
month, I had been holding all this built-up energy inside,
but tonight, I was going to be free. And if that meant
getting closer to Carson, then so be it. I was ready for all
that the evening had to offer.

An hour had gone by when I finally heard the knock
at my door that I'd been waiting for. I gulped down the
last sip of my wine, smoothed my nightgown down, and
headed to open it. When I did, there he stood, his normal
handsome and charismatic self with a dozen red roses in
hand.

"Hey, Carson." A smile immediately came across my
face, and all thoughts of Anthony disappeared.

"Hey, beautiful," he said, kissing my cheek and handing
me the flowers.

"Now you know you don't always have to bring me gifts,
don't you? I mean, of course, I love them, but you're
going to spoil me, and it's going to be something I look
forward to all the time."

"Well, that just means I'm ahead of my game then,
huh?"

Both of us laughed, and I gave him another smooch on
the lips before walking into the kitchen to put the roses
in a vase while he took a seat on the sofa. Then I spoke to
him from inside the kitchen.

"Would you like a glass of wine, honey?"

"Sure. If you have red wine, that would be great."

"You know I already know you like red instead of white wine."

"You know me best, don't you? So, where are kids?"

"Oh, I got my co-worker, Milton, to keep an eye on them again. He just loves them and loves having their company, and they feel the same way."

"Really? He sounds like a good guy."

"He is. I just hate the fact that he's alone all the time. That's pretty much the reason why I try to take the kids to him as much as possible."

"I see. And what about your children's father?"

"Anthony? What about him?"

"Where is he?"

"Not here, of course. He's probably either at his relative's home or his crazy-ass baby momma's house. Either way, I don't want to talk or think about him this evening if that's all right with you."

I didn't hear anything after that, but I started talking about a bunch of randomness to keep the conversation going until I joined him in the living room.

"Baby, have you had anything to eat? I have something that I could throw into the oven really quick if you want. Carson? Carson?" I called out because it had remained extremely quiet without any response from him. That was until he popped up in the kitchen doorway, just standing there looking at me.

"What's wrong? I thought you fell asleep on me in there or something," I joked as I went ahead and put the food in the oven.

"No, not sleeping, but curious, though."

"Curious? About what, baby?"

"Why do you have this?" He pulled the manila folder from behind his back and flashed it at me. "What the fuck are you trying to find out, Alize?"

"All right, look, don't get upset, okay? I can explain everything," I said, suddenly starting to feel numb. My hands began shaking from the enraged look behind his eyes. "It's . . . it's . . . it's just that the things you said about your wife weren't quite adding up completely. You told Mya she'd died from cancer and then me from an accident. I . . . I . . . I just wanted to know the truth."

"You wanted to know the truth, so you got my file from Attorney Buchanon instead of asking me?" he asked in a calm and cool way, walking closer to me.

"Baby, I wanted to come to you. Believe me, I did, but how do you come right out and ask someone if they had anything to do with their spouse's death? I didn't want you to hate me or stop seeing me because of it."

He cracked a slight smile on his face while continuing to move toward me. "Alize, you know what? You remind me so much of my wife in so many ways," he said, now standing right up to me.

His tall stature against my small frame started to make me a bit fearful. He continued talking as I searched my mind for an exit strategy if needed.

"You're beautiful like she was, your sassy and exuberant nature is like hers was, and the fact that you're too fucking nosey for your own damn good is what got her in the predicament she's in," he said, putting his bare hand around my neck, massaging it before he started to squeeze it tightly. I couldn't believe what was happening, and I tried to force words to come out between the pressure of his grip.

"Carson . . . what . . . are . . . you . . . doing?"

"Don't worry, baby," he uttered with his grasp getting tighter, and I felt like I couldn't breathe. "I'm going to give you just what the fuck you deserve, just like I did her."

Struggling to fight my way from his hold, I remembered I'd just put a skillet in the sink. I reached in without him realizing it and struck him over the head as hard as I could. As he released his grip and grabbed his head with both hands, I ran to the bedroom at the back of the house, closed the door, and locked it.

I could hardly think of what to do next when I heard him banging on the door and yelling for me to let him inside. I almost pissed myself when I saw the door beginning to break down.

"Please, stop Carson, please," I yelled at the top of my lungs. "You don't have to do this."

Before I knew it, he'd torn the door off the hinges and lunged at me, knocking me straight to the bed. The weight of his body was much more than my small frame could bear, and he immediately knocked all the wind out of me. I kept trying to wiggle myself from underneath him, but his massive size on top of mine wouldn't let up.

"You ghetto-ass bitch!" He went in on me right away, giving me a hard blow to the face. I was stunned and still couldn't fathom that this was happening. He was far from the gentleman who had come through my door just a little while ago or who I'd known for the last month. He was exactly who Mya, Leslie, and Anthony had warned me of.

I kept trying to block any punches coming my way, yet still, a couple landed, and I found myself dazed and confused, making it difficult for me to fight back. I just knew in the back of my mind that I would eventually succumb to his torture and that this man would possibly kill me tonight, so I did the only thing I knew to do. I started to pray nonstop in my head that God would deliver me from this maniac, and that was when, all at once, everything stopped. There I lay, staring at him and him looking back at me, when we both heard someone beating on the front door.

"Who the fuck is that? Were you expecting someone?"

"I . . . I . . . I don't know who it is, Carson. It might be Anthony. He . . . he . . . he called me earlier wanting to come by," I confessed. Deep down, I wanted so badly to scream just in case it was Anthony, but there was no telling if he would hear me or what Carson would do to me in return.

"Get your ass up and get rid of him." He yanked me from the bed and pushed me toward the front door. "And don't you dare try anything funny, or you will definitely get what's coming to you," he said right before pulling a gun from behind his back.

I peeked out the peephole and saw Anthony standing there. I knew that once he saw me, he would know that something was wrong, but I prayed in the back of my mind that he wouldn't try to be my hero. The last thing I wanted was for him to get hurt by this lunatic. He pushed me again to open the door, and I peeked out, not allowing him to see my full body or face.

"Hey, what's up, Anthony?" I tried to say without crying or seeming like anything was wrong.

"Look, I know you have company, but there are some things I need to get out the house, and plus, I want to know where the kids are so that I can pick them up tonight."

"Um, I'm sorry, Anthony, but tonight is not a good time right now, okay? Maybe you should just come back tomorrow." I hurried to try to close the door when I felt the pressure of Carson's gun in my back, but Anthony stopped it with his hand.

"Hey, what's going on? What's wrong with you?"

"Nothing. I'm good, but it's not a good time. I'll call you later."

I closed the door before he could ask anything else, but I could tell from the look on his face that he was aware something was wrong. That's how experienced we were with each other. So, whatever he was going to do, I needed him to do it quickly before it was too late because the minute I closed the door, Carson had pushed me so hard that I fell to the floor. Looking up at him, I wasn't sure what his intentions were before the night ended, but I knew it wouldn't be good.

CHAPTER 36

MYA

"Thank you so much for bringing dinner by, Will. I was starved, and Italian is one of my favorites," I said, making myself comfortable on the sofa next to him.

"It was no problem at all. I actually look forward to us spending time together now. It's become my favorite pastime."

"Mine too," I said, blushing. We both laughed together before he leaned over and attempted to kiss me. However, without truly realizing it, I turned my head away from him.

There was an odd silence in the room before he finally spoke up.

"All right, Mya, what's wrong? Is my breath foul? Are my lips crusty? Have I picked up the wrong energy between me and you, reading too much into things?"

"Will, honestly, I really don't know what's wrong. I mean, trust me, I absolutely love hanging out and spending time with you—"

"But?"

I hesitated a few minutes before answering. "I think it might be the fact of your spirituality."

"My spirituality? What does that have to do with anything? he asked, looking completely confused.

"I really don't know, but it's like I get the overwhelming feeling that I'm doing something wrong every time I think about any kind of intimacy or affection between me and you."

"Mya, you do know that God isn't going to judge or condemn us simply for a hug or a kiss, right? And you have to believe that I wouldn't let it go any further than that."

"I know that. It still doesn't stop the way I feel."

He was about to reply when my phone started buzzing across the coffee table. I saw Anthony's name, and although I wanted to press ignore, my curiosity got the best of me. I knew that it had to be something urgent for him to call.

"You don't mind if I get this really quick, do you?" I asked Carson first.

"No, no, go right ahead."

"Hey, Anthony, what's up?" I questioned as soon as I hit the talk button.

"Mya, thank goodness you answered. I think something's wrong with Alize, but first, do you know where our girls are?"

"Wait a minute. Wait. What do you mean you think something's wrong with Zae? And you don't know where the kids are?"

"Listen, I just stopped by, and she didn't look or sound right to me. I know that guy is in there, but my gut is telling me something isn't right. Plus, I've been asking about the kids all evening. She said they're not home and they're not with her mother, so besides me or you, I don't have any idea where else they could be. But I've called my brother to come by with me. I've got my weapon on me, and I'm getting inside of my house even if I have to kill somebody to do it."

"Kill somebody? Anthony, please don't. Look, just wait before you do anything. I'm on my way over."

"Oh, shit!" he yelled out of nowhere before I hung up, and my heart felt like it was about to jump out of my chest at what was possibly happening.

"What? What's happening, Anthony?"

"Mya, I knew there was something odd when I saw that guy. I think he might be related to my son's mother."

"What? That doesn't make any sense. What are you talking about?"

"Listen, I can't remember if it's him or not, but if it is, I know for sure Alize isn't safe."

We disconnected the call, and Will stared at me for answers.

"Will, I told you earlier I felt like something wasn't right, and now I know it isn't. Please come with me and drive because I'm a nervous wreck. I don't know what I'll do if something happens to my friend." I started to cry.

CHAPTER 37

ALIZE

"Carson, please tell me why you're doing this," I pleaded with him as he pulled me off the floor, threw me in a chair, and started to tie my hands with zip ties from his pocket. It was at that very moment that I knew he'd planned to do this tonight.

"Shut the fuck up, Alize."

"Look, I don't care about what happened to your wife, okay? That's why the folder was just lying there. I hadn't even read anything in it. I was going to talk to you tonight instead. I promise I'm telling you the truth."

He began to laugh as he started to pace back and forth and waved his gun around. "Your dumb ass really thinks this has something to do with my wife, don't you? This isn't about her, Alize."

I was completely confused by his words. "I, I don't understand. If this isn't about you killing your wife, then what is this about?"

He stopped pacing and smiled down at me before speaking. "That crazy-ass bitch of a baby momma that you referred to earlier when it comes to your baby daddy. Yeah, those were your exact words, right? Well, I'm Monique's cousin, and she sent me to do a job."

"Monique?" I was sure the expression on my face matched the confusion of my words. "Her cousin? Carson, I don't understand. How could—"

"See, Alize, it's because of you that she's not with her son's father, basically leaving him fatherless all these years. It's because of you that she has to face him asking her things like, 'Why don't I have a daddy?' And the very reason she ended up getting herself knocked up by yet another loser. And as much as I hate Anthony, I was tired of hearing and seeing my cousin cry over his ass."

"Wait, but none of this still makes any sense. If you're Monique's cousin, he had to have seen you before. Plus, you came to the office for Attorney Buchanon."

"Yeah, see, that's the crazy part of all of this. It was like it was all meant to happen this way. See, the first time you put him out a few weeks ago, he ran to her house, only for him to come running back to you less than twenty-four hours later. That was when we devised this whole plan. Anthony had only met me once or twice when he and Monique were together, and trust me, I look completely different from back then. I knew there was no way he would remember me. And as for Buchanon, well, he owed me a huge favor for some money I loaned him when my wife died. So, it was the perfect opportunity. I came up there for Buchanon and bumped into you. The only thing was, all three of you women were so damn desperate for a man that it was a little hard to just settle for your pathetic ass, especially after I took Mya to lunch, because any fool could tell that she was the better option out of all you ladies."

"So, what were you going to do, Carson? Get me all in love with you and then kill me so that your cousin could have Anthony all to herself? Do you honestly plan to take a mother away from four little girls?"

"If it means seeing my cousin happy again and not all depressed the way she's been for years since Anthony left her for you, then yes. And don't worry about your girls. I'll make sure that Anthony and Monique take good care of them. Besides, they're still small anyway. They'll get over it, just like you expected my baby cousin to get over not having his father around."

Tears were streaming down my face like a river as he stood there, pointing his gun at me. At that point, I started praying so hard in my head that this entire nightmare would end. I prayed that either I could talk him out of doing what he planned to do or that Anthony would save me before it was too late. That was when, out of nowhere, we heard another knock at the door.

CHAPTER 38

MYA

"Alize? Alize, honey, are you okay?" I yelled from outside, praying that she could hear me."

"What if I go around to the back of the house to see if I can get in the back door?" Will suggested.

"Yes, please, but be safe, Will."

"Zae, honey, it's Mya. I know you and Carson are in there, and you need to let her go, Carson. I've called the police, and they'll be here any minute. If you let her out now, then this does not have to end badly for you."

Still, there wasn't a sound, and then Will came running from around the back. "Hey, I was able to see in from a side window. Looks like he has a gun and has her tied to a chair."

"A gun? Oh my goodness, Will. What if he tries to shoot her? We have to get inside."

As we attempted to think of the best and safest way to get in, suddenly, we saw the front door open. There, Carson stood with Alize in front of him as he held a gun to her head. "I should have known you, of all people, would show up here. You really need to learn how to mind your own damn business."

"Carson, please don't do this. Like I said, the police are on their way, and this can all end peacefully if you just release her."

"You must think I'm crazy or something. If the police are coming, there's no way things are going to end peacefully. So, it's going to be me or Alize because I'm damn sure not going back to jail. Say goodbye now to your little friend."

A second later, a ton of police cars, a fire truck, and an ambulance all came speeding around the corner, and then, before I knew it, Carson slammed the door shut. The officers hopped out of their cars and immediately asked Will and me who was inside. I'd told them that as far as I knew, it was only Alize and Carson but that her children could possibly be in there too. But as I spoke to them and they were about to negotiate with Carson to get him to come out, we heard a gunshot go off inside. Immediately, my heart sank at the thought of him possibly shooting Alize.

A second after that, Anthony pulled up, hopped out of his car without stopping completely, and ran over to us. "Mya, where's Alize? What's going on? Is she all right? I'm going inside," he spoke a million miles a minute, but a police officer stopped him in his tracks.

"I'm sorry, sir, but until we make our way in and secure the scene, no one is allowed inside."

"Mya, what the fuck is going on?" he questioned as we all watched the police try to force their way inside of the house.

"Anthony, we heard a gun go off just a second before you pulled up."

"What? Did he shoot Zae? Is she—"

I stopped his words and threw my arms around him as we both feared the unknown. We all stood there on pins and needles for what seemed like an eternity. But that was when we saw a male officer walking out of the home with Alize wrapped in a blanket. We all ran over to her.

"Everything's all right, okay," the officer responded. "Your friend is a little beat up and most likely in shock, so the paramedics are going to take her to the hospital to give her a thorough examination. It seems, however, that the deceased male in the home turned the gun on himself."

"Oh my goodness, thank God you're okay, Zae." I threw my arms around her, not wanting to let her go.

"Mya, oh, Mya, thank goodness you're here," she cried, hugging me back. "I'm so sorry for everything. You were right all along about Carson, and I should have listened to you."

"Hey, don't you dare apologize to me. Everything is good with me and you, all right?"

"Would you mind coming to the hospital with me?" she asked through her tears and heavy, deep breaths.

"Girl, I'm not leaving your side. I am right here as long as you need me."

"Okay." She nodded her head.

But then, before we got into the ambulance, her eyes went directly to Anthony. Neither of them said a word to the other, but as he walked closer to her, she simply kissed him, long and hard, letting him know that things were all good between them.

Will finally walked over and immediately put his arms around me, and it was the one time I refused to turn away his affection.

"I can't thank you enough for everything, Will."

"There's no need to thank me. I just thank God that everything turned out the way it did."

That's when we both looked over and saw them bringing the body of Mr. Carson Reed out of the house. Instantly, I thought back to the very day he walked into our office. Nothing could have ever told me that the perfect man who we both thought would be our now or never would turn out to end this way.

SIX MONTHS LATER

CHAPTER 39

MYA

One of the very things I always loved and admired about my best friend was that she was going to bounce back from anything that life threw at her and accomplish anything and everything she'd set her mind to. And as I walked into InFashion by Alize and looked around, I couldn't have been prouder of her. She'd always had dreams of opening her own clothing store, and here it was today, right in front of her—her grand opening. I believed that all she'd gone through with Anthony and Carson had actually given her the fuel and motivation she needed to make this very dream come true.

It had only been six months or so since that fatal night, but we'd all moved on like it never happened, though I was positive that we would never forget Carson Reed. Alize told me that she pleaded with him not to kill himself, but he said he'd rather be dead than spend any time in jail. It was truly unfortunate that he'd lost his life, but truth be told, we were all at peace that it was him and not Alize. However, the one person who did find himself behind bars was Attorney Buchanon after the police discovered his relationship with Carson and his interaction with Carson's' wife's death.

It also seemed that that evening was just the wake-up call that Anthony needed to get his life in order. He'd actually gotten a nine-to-five job with UPS, been helping Alize as much as possible with the kids, had cut his hair into a clean-cut type of look, and I believed he even stopped smoking marijuana. He was finally becoming the man that my best friend needed, although he still hadn't made her his wife. In fact, they weren't even living in the same house together. Since that night, Alize and the girls had moved in with her mother, while he stayed with his brother until they "figured things out." Their figuring things out may also have something to do with the fact that he'd gotten full custody of his son since Monique was serving time for setting up the whole incident with Carson and Alize. I don't think that my best friend was quite ready to take on being a stepmother to the son of the woman who tried to have her killed.

Walking in and seeing Diane and Milton standing across the room, I headed their way to speak.

"Hey, Diane. Hey, Milton," I said, giving both a hug.

"Mya, we were just wondering where you were," Milton said back while handing me a glass of champagne.

"I had some things to take care of, but I didn't miss anything, did I? Where's Alize?"

"Oh, she had to tend to one of the girls really quick," Diane said. "But isn't this place gorgeous? It's completely Alize."

"Yes, it is," I agreed, and we all laughed.

"Hey, y'all," she said in her boisterous way, with the girls following right behind her. "I'm so glad you all could make it. Thank you so much for coming."

"Now you know we wouldn't have missed your grand opening for anything in the world." I hugged her and kissed all the girls.

"I know."

"The woman of the hour," we heard a very familiar voice say loudly while heading our way. As she strolled over, I still couldn't believe how far she and Alize had come. My friend had matured in such a major way, and I almost shed a tear as I watched them embrace one another.

"Hi, Leslie. I'm glad you made it," Zae said.

"Girl, hush. I wouldn't have missed your big day for anything in the world. And everything looks great. I can't wait to purchase some of these fashions by Zae."

"Well, I hope you've got your Black Card, girl." They gave each other a high five, and the only thing that crossed my mind was the day they were rolling around on the ground, trying to hurt each other. We were far from that day, and I wondered if they knew how much alike they truly were.

After the greetings and salutations, we all stood around laughing, talking, admiring the items in the store, and, of course, shopping. Everything was simply amazing. However, I quickly noticed that one key person wasn't in attendance. With that in mind, I discreetly pulled Alize to the side.

"Hey girl, where's—"

Before I was able to finish, I was completely shocked by the voice behind me.

"Hey, baby." Dexter hugged and kissed Alize. "I'm sorry, I'm a bit late, but everything looks amazing. I'm so proud of you," he said and left her cheesing even harder than I'd seen all night. I yanked her arm, though, and pulled her toward me because, after seeing him and their interaction, I surely needed some answers right then and there.

"Uh, Dexter, do you mind if I steal Alize really quick? I need her help with something." Pulling her to the side, I went in with my interrogation immediately.

"Zae, what in the world is going on? Anthony isn't here, but Dexter, the doctor from the hospital who took care of you, is. And what's up with him calling you baby and giving you that big ol' smooch on the lips? I thought you two were just being playful in the hospital."

"We were, Mya, but once I was released to go home, he said there was no way he was allowing me to leave without promising him at least one date, and it seems like we've been inseparable ever since. And I honestly wanted to tell you, but I also didn't want to jinx things, you know?"

"Okay, but what about Anthony?"

"Look, I still love Anthony with all my heart, and it's amazing how much he's changed. He's finally becoming the man that I always needed him to be. But the truth of the matter is he had seven whole years to get it right, and he didn't get his act together until Carson left me for dead. There wouldn't have even been a Carson Reed in my life if he'd done things the way he was supposed to a long time ago. So, I didn't want to go back to what I wasn't happy in just because we have children or because we'd been together so long. I didn't want to be together simply because we struggled together or based on principle. I want love, and well, I'm trying to see if I can have that with Dexter now."

"Are you sure? I mean, are you truly happy, Zae?"

"Yeah, I think I am."

"Okay, you know what? I'm going to stay out of it because who am I to say anything when I'm still single Sally myself? So, girl, if you're happy, then I'm happy. Do your thing, best friend."

We reached in to hug one another, but Dexter pulled her away as he started to speak to everyone there. "Everyone, excuse me. Can I have your attention, please?" He tapped on his wine glass. "Um, first, I want to congratulate this beautiful woman right here for going after her dreams and doing what she needed to open this store today. I tried to help in any way possible, but she wouldn't let me. She was determined to do this all on her own, and I'm proud of her for it. But now, I'm determined to do something, too."

He directed his attention to her, "Alize, I know we've only been getting to know each other for a few months now, but you have been my happiness, my joy, and my peace that I've been in search of for a long time. I thank God for bringing you into my life that night, and it doesn't take a man long to know when the right woman has entered his life. So, I wanted to make your special day even more special by asking if you will be my wife." He got down on one knee and extended a massive ring.

I watched Alize's face light up and tears begin to build in her eyes as she looked around at everyone in the room. Then, I suddenly saw her glance at the front door to see the person that was standing there. Anthony's face looked defeated seeing Dexter on bended knee.

The room became silent, so quiet that you could hear a pin drop. Everyone was hanging on and waiting for Alize's answer, including Anthony. I watched her eyes go from Dexter to Anthony to the kids and then back to Dexter. And then, just a few short seconds later, she softly spoke.

"Dexter, I'm sorry, but I can't," she said as she walked quickly toward the door and kissed and hugged Anthony as passionately as she could. Instantly, you could hear the gasps and chatter as everyone began to talk amongst themselves.

I, on the other hand, was relieved that she hadn't made a horrible decision. Although it had taken some time, I knew Anthony was best for her and that they were truly made for each other. Quickly, my eyes shot over to Dexter, who stood there for a moment or two, appearing to be in a state of shock. Then, a second later, he simply walked out without another word. Zae, however, didn't seem to care one bit. She was still kissing her man and finally experiencing her now or never unapologetically, *with* her children's father. And although I didn't have mine yet, I was sincerely happy for my best friend.

ONE YEAR LATER

CHAPTER 40

MYA

The past year had been extremely quiet yet very productive and self-rewarding for me. I may have still been manless and sexless, for that matter, but things were peaceful, and my mind was clearer than it had been in quite a long time. I'd become so much more focused on loving and bettering myself that the fact that I wasn't married, or let alone had someone to date, was no longer as huge a factor as before. Instead, I'd begun devoting my time and energy to things that made my heart, mind, and spirit happy.

In fact, I'd actually found myself a church home and began attending on a regular basis. Of course, I'd always heard that the people *are* the church, not the building. But I felt like being there in the atmosphere amongst fellow worshipers was extremely important for spiritual growth, at least for me anyway.

It just so happened that I started attending the same church that Will attended, but luckily, things weren't odd or uncomfortable for either one of us when we saw one another, which was often. He always greeted me with open arms, even when in the presence of his new girlfriend, Paula. In my eyes, she fit him perfectly, and I was truly happy that they'd found one another in the church. Anyway, he and I discovered that we were much better friends than anything else, and I found myself often calling him when I wanted spiritual advice on things.

Besides Will, oddly enough, I sometimes kept in touch with Tyrone. It wasn't for him to come over and do that little thing I liked either. Instead, I'd assisted him in studying to get his GED so he could find decent employment to better help with raising his children, especially after his grandmother passed. Without having her to lean on, he had to step up and be the man he needed to be for his little ones. I didn't mind helping at all either, and sometimes, I even took the children to the playground on Saturdays or worship service with me on Sundays. It honestly gave me something to keep my mind from being idle, as well as the opportunity to work on my motherhood skills in case it ever came about in the future. I realized that maybe that was the reason he and I were meant to be in each other's lives, not for anything sexual.

The two men that I had cut all ties with were Charles and Kevin, and rightfully so. After discovering that Charles had been dating Leslie, I wanted nothing more to do with him at all. I was really over his alter ego altogether after the dinner meeting with the Tates, but dating her behind my back was the icing on the cake.

The funny thing, however, was that after she found out about his dealings with me, she didn't want anything to do with him either. I tried even telling her that I wasn't bothered, and if he was her one, then so be it, and she should keep seeing him. However, she expressed that he wasn't the *Mr. Wonderful* that she thought he was. Although he'd come across as having his shit together, she said he was broke, in a ton of debt, barely hanging on to his job, and was about to get his car repossessed and his house foreclosed on. To make things worse, he'd started to try to get her to cover his expenses, which she was not having. So, all in all, it seemed as if I'd dodged a huge bullet when it came to my number one.

Then there was my lover man, Kevin, my number two. I still couldn't believe that I had settled for that whole situation simply based on the good sex. Well, I take that back. Yes, I can believe it because that was the mindset that I was in at that time in my life. Did I sometimes miss him? Yes. Did I miss our amazing sexual encounters? Hell yes. But that hadn't been enough to go back to subject myself to being someone's part-time lover. And more importantly, I didn't want to hurt another woman the way I had Sasha, his now *ex*-fiancée. Once she found that he'd still been dealing with me amongst other women, she sent all of us a group text letting us know that she was leaving him and that we were more than welcome to fuck him as often as we liked. The crazy thing was many of the women thought they were the only ones in his life, and at least two others had been proposed to as well.

Needless to say, I was more than grateful and thankful to God that I'd gotten myself out of that situation with nothing more than a broken heart. When I thought about the things that could have happened, like being harmed by a scorned lover or possibly getting an STD, I thanked God every chance I got that things never went that far. That was it for my one, two, three, and four, and now all I needed was the one, God above, in my life, who would one day send me my earthly one.

Other than that, my self-care journey had also included a whole healthy eating regimen along with a workout routine that had my body looking absolutely amazing, if I said so myself. Whenever God did send the one, I wanted to be looking and feeling my absolute best for both of us. I couldn't wait to shed a few more pounds while toning a bit more to get the look I'd always dreamed of having.

So, that was what now made up the new Mya. Work, church, and working out had become my new routine, and I was loving it. I even found joy and inner pleasure in my latest new pastime. As of late, I'd taken up learning to make healthy vegan meals, and not only had the dishes been good to me, but they were also good for me financially. After I'd taken a few dishes to Alize for her to try out, she'd gone crazy at how good they were and healthy all at the same time. In fact, she went as far as to tell me I should allow her to sell them inside of her store, which had really panned out for me—so much so that I was contemplating opening my own vegan establishment.

Thinking of food, my stomach had been rumbling, and my mouth salivated at the thought of the vegan Philly cheesesteak eggrolls I'd come up with recently. I glanced over at the clock on my nightstand, which read eight-thirty. It was a bit late to even consider going to the grocery store, but knowing exactly what I wanted, I figured I could quickly run in and run back out.

A few minutes later, I threw on some oversized sweats and a crop top and tied my hair up into a messy bun. Then, instead of putting on any makeup whatsoever, I slid on my glasses to help me see better in the evening dusk. As I grabbed my wallet, I chuckled a little from thinking how I would have never walked out of the house like this before. However, not having a man in my life or even looking for one made me almost have an *I don't care* type of attitude. The only thing I was concerned about was grabbing the ingredients for the weight loss salad I'd seen all over TikTok, getting what I needed for the eggrolls, and then getting back home to relax.

Shortly after, I found myself slowly creeping down aisle after aisle, reading labels for the number of calories on items. I couldn't believe how quiet and peaceful everything was this time of the evening. I'd grown so accustomed to doing my shopping early in the day with all the hustle and bustle that that's the way I thought it was supposed to be. But now, the quietness and freedom of not bumping into others in the aisles made me think that I could make this time a part of my normal routine.

Making my way over to the fruit and vegetable section, I began to examine the strawberries and bananas for their freshness to put in my daily smoothies.

As I stood there, I suddenly heard a strong and deep voice speaking. "Excuse me, miss?"

I was so caught up in my inspection of the produce that I hadn't even acknowledged that he could have possibly been speaking to me until I heard him once again.

"Excuse me, miss? Can I bother you for a second?"

Finally, I looked up with my glasses sitting on top of my nose, my messy bun as messy as could be, and old gym clothing, as I admired the most handsome specimen of a man standing in front of me.

"Um, are you talking to me?"

"Of course." He smiled and looked around as if to say we were the only two people standing there at that moment. "I was wondering if I could ask for your help on picking out the best mango."

"Picking out the best mango?" I repeated, looking at him with the words "*yeah, right*" written across my forehead. He must have sensed my suspicion because he immediately began explaining.

"Listen, please let me explain so that you won't think I'm some freak trying to creep you out in the middle of the grocery store. I, um, normally don't do this . . . shopping, that is. I have been recently divorced for about a year and a half now, and I've had about all the fast food that I can take. So, lately, I've been trying to shop and do my own cooking at home, and well, sometimes I need a little help. That's it, that's all. So, I hope you don't think I'm some kind of weirdo."

"Uh, no, no, I don't, not at all. It's fine, and to answer your question, I think that this one would be best," I said, picking up the mango and handing it to him as I noticed his large, massive hands grip hold of it.

"Oh, thank you, and um, by the way, my name is Ezekiel." He stuck his hand out, and as I placed mine in his for a quick shake, I almost melted at how it covered mine up completely. The man was more than perfect to look at, and I didn't want to take my eyes off him, but I also kept thinking about what a total and complete mess I must have looked like in front of him. So, I hurried to introduce myself in return in hopes of leaving as quickly as I could.

"Um, I'm Mya, and it's a pleasure to meet you. But I should go and finish my shopping, so I hope you enjoy your mango." I tried to rush off, but something inside made me think to myself. *Am I really that vain? This could very well be the answer to my prayers to God—to send me a mate when I least expected it. Yet, here I am, about to run away from him because I don't appear as perfect as I could be.*

"Stop it, Mya," I said out loud as I dipped down another aisle so he wouldn't see me talking to myself. "Get ahold of yourself. Don't let your loneliness attach you to the first good-looking stranger you bump into in the middle of the store. Like Alize said, when it's God, you'll just know." I tried talking myself out of making my way back over to Mango god. At least, that was until I'd headed over to the self-checkout and found him there a couple of people ahead of me. I kept trying my hardest not to stare at him, but that was a lot easier said than done. He was simply gorgeous. Even in a mere pair of jeans, a graphic tee, and some sandals, the man was truly a sight to see.

I saw him pay for his items and leave, and finally, it was my turn at the machine. Trying to remain focused on the task at hand, I moved quickly, thinking I could somehow catch him in the parking lot. But, when I made it outside, and there wasn't a sight of him anywhere, all I could do was kick myself.

"Dammit, Mya. All you had to do was stand there and talk to the man, but you walked right away from him because of the way you looked."

As I thought to myself while putting the groceries into my trunk, out of nowhere, a black Range Rover pulled alongside me, and slowly, the driver's window slid down. To my surprise, Ezekiel smiled his pearly whites at me.

"Hi again, Mya. I'm sorry to pull up on you like this, but I really didn't want to pass up the opportunity. Um, do you think it's possible that I leave my business card with you, and you can call me if you like? I mean, only if you're not already spoken for, that is. I hope you're not already spoken for."

I smiled at him, blushing over the fact of him being so concerned about whether I was with someone. "Um, no, I'm not spoken for, and sure, I can call you," I said, hoping I didn't seem too eager but not truly caring either. There was something about Ezekiel that spoke to my soul. I couldn't pinpoint whether it was his dark eyes, his warm smile, or just the way he made me feel comfortable. I actually looked forward to getting to know him better.

"Great! Well, I hope to hear from you soon, and maybe we can get together one day and have lunch or something. Anyway, you be safe getting home, and thanks again for your help in the store."

We waved goodbye, and my stomach did flips. Not only was he handsome, but he was also very articulate, charismatic, and polite. I actually wanted to call him the second I made it home, but again, I didn't want to come across too eager. I figured I'd wait and give him a buzz sometime tomorrow.

The second I walked back into my home, I went straight to the kitchen to put up the groceries as well as pour myself a glass of wine. Taking a second, I leaned against the counter as I took a sip of my red wine, and my thoughts traveled straight to Ezekiel. Closing my eyes, I spoke to God as sincerely as I could.

"God, please let this man be decent and nothing like the men I dealt with in my past. If he should be part of my life, please reveal it to me and make it plain. I don't want to waste any more time on someone that was not sent by You."

As I continued to speak to God, my phone began to buzz. I figured it was only Alize calling because we were meeting the next day to go over some details for the wedding, so I answered without clearly opening my eyes.

"Hey, girl. What's up?"

"Uh, Mya?" I heard his voice speak to me, and chills immediately went down my spine.

"Ezekiel, hi. I didn't expect to hear from you tonight."

"Yeah, I know, but I couldn't help myself. I wanted to make sure you made it home safely . . . and to hear your voice again."

"Well, yes, I did make it home safely, and thank you for checking on me. I'm also glad you called because I actually wanted to talk to you, too."

"Good. But can I ask you something before things go any further?"

"Um, sure, of course."

"Mya, I don't want to waste your time or mine. I believe in letting my intentions be known upfront. I am not at a stage in my life where I am simply looking to date for fun. I date with a purpose. With that said, I see who I want when I want until things become exclusive with me and one person. Now, that's not to say I'm being intimate with everyone, because I'm not. I want to wait until I'm in a committed relationship for that. But I'm very interested in getting to know you better, and if everything I said is fine with you, then I would like for us to go further."

"Wow." My mouth fell wide open, thinking how God truly has a way of answering our prayers on speed dial. "Uh, I'm almost at a loss of words. I feel exactly the same way, and I don't want to waste either of our time. Ezekiel, my spirituality and God are the most important things in my life right now, and I don't want to do anything or be with anyone that will compromise that."

"Man, it seems like we're in total agreement."

We talked some more, and I was in complete astonishment at how easy-flowing and satisfying our conversation was. After all this time, I thought I needed great sex to be fulfilled, but this type of conversation was more fulfilling than I could have ever imagined. We talked about our hopes, dreams, future goals, and even our insecurities, and everything was just easy and comfortable. In fact, I could have very well had an orgasm from this man's words alone.

It was getting late, yet neither of us wanted things to end. We were like two high schoolers on the phone late at night. So, I grabbed my whole bottle of wine and glass, turned out the kitchen lights, and headed toward my bedroom. I was just about to undress; however, the second I was about to slide my joggers off, I heard my doorbell ring. My eyes quickly caught a glimpse of the time on the clock on my nightstand, which read almost one in the morning. Not knowing exactly who it could be, my heart began to race a million beats a second. Maybe it was Tyrone, but he'd never just popped up at my home. I knew it wasn't Will, and Charles surely wouldn't have the gall to come by after everything that had happened between us. Then, I thought about it. The only person who would have the balls and audacity to come to my home this time of night without calling was my number two.

While still listening to Ezekiel talk, I tried my best to gain control of myself. All at once, I felt a rush of emotions come over me from anger, confusion, excitement, and, although I hated to admit it, even a bit of arousal.

Removing my joggers, I grabbed my black silk robe, tied it around me, and quickly headed to the door. The entire time, I kept saying things like, "yes," "I know," "really," and "wow," like I'd caught every single word Ezekiel had been saying. I knew I probably should have gone ahead and ended the call, but he was going to be my excuse for not letting Kevin inside—inside of my door or inside of me.

I placed the call on mute as I prepared to snatch the door open, ready to let him have it. I couldn't wait to see his face or hear him explain himself since I'd cut all communication with him after Sasha's group text message. I said a quick prayer in my head, hoping that I would be able to focus on anything that came out of his mouth because, at once, my fleshly desires were taking over as my mind was more on having him inside of me than anything else.

"What in the world are you doing here, Kevin?" I yanked the door open and asked. Although, after seeing the person standing there, my eyes practically bulged out of my head.

"Michael?"

"Hey, Mya."

I felt like my eyes were staring at a ghost. A very handsome ghost, but still a ghost nonetheless. Michael hadn't changed one bit, other than looking a little more mature than the teenager I once knew. He was still attractive, still in shape, and still had the power to make my pussy dance around without even touching it.

I pressed the mute button on my phone and interrupted Ezekiel's words. "Um, Ezekiel, can I please give you a call tomorrow? I don't mean to end things so abruptly, but I need to handle something." The second I heard him say sure, I disconnected and placed my attention back on the man I once loved.

"Look, I know it's late and all, and I know that you and I haven't spoken in forever, but I was hoping that we could talk."

He was right. It was late, and we hadn't spoken since that tragic night that landed me single, betrayed, and in handcuffs. I really shouldn't have had anything to say to him, but beyond my better judgment, I allowed him to come in. I only prayed that it would end there and that before the night was over, he wouldn't cum inside of other places of me.

He walked past me as he came in, and I got a whiff of his cologne. It was masculine, yet clean and refreshing, and just like something he would wear. My eyes followed him as he took a seat on the sofa. In the back of my mind, I kept wondering to myself, *Mya, what are you doing? This man betrayed you and left you for the school's tramp. Don't be stupid.* But as I examined him, I realized that he wasn't the same person, just like I wasn't the same woman that I was six months ago. He was a grown man now and not that little boy from back then. Even with the negative things I'd heard regarding him and Tasha's marriage, I didn't truly know what went on behind closed doors, which was why I decided to give him the benefit of the doubt.

"What do we need to talk about, Michael? Better yet, how did you think you could just pop up over here as if we just talked yesterday?" I asked while sitting on the arm of my couch with my arms folded.

"I know, I know. I was taking a real chance on you possibly cursing me out, but I had to see you, Mya. My life hasn't been the best lately, or for a long time, for that matter. And well, I almost feel like it's my karma for the way I treated you in the past. That whole thing with Tasha, I should have been completely honest with you about it, but I was just a dumb jock back then, and I guess my hormones were all over the place. I just needed to come and look at you face to face and apologize because this has been eating me up inside."

There was silence as I tried to let what he said sink in. I wanted to believe that he was being sincere, but my gut kept telling me that there was something more to this unexpected visit. The attorney side of me needed to investigate more and wouldn't allow me to believe that this boiled down to a mere "I'm sorry."

"Um, I appreciate the sentiment and your desire to make things right between us, but I guess, why now, Michael? Why, after all this time, did you find it necessary to do this now?"

"Because I've put it off long enough. I mean, I'm sure you heard that I married Tasha, and we had children and a whole family together. But that ended, and well—"

"And well, you thought I would simply let you back in with open arms? You have to know that if I heard you were married, that I also heard you cheated on her as well, and that's why your marriage ended," I said very matter-of-factly.

"I didn't cheat, Mya. One of Tasha's friends saw me out with my secretary and ran with a story that was never true. But just like I tried to tell her, my secretary is very happily married, and there's no attraction between us . . . especially not like it's always been between you and me," he said, getting up, coming over to me, and having me stand up. Then he wrapped his arms around me. "I've missed you, Mya, more than you'll ever know."

"I've—I've missed you too, Michael, but—," I said between breaths while feeling safe inside of his strong and powerful arms.

Slowly and gently, I began to feel Michael's lips interrupt my thoughts and my words and press against mine. I began to have flashbacks of our time in the past. His kisses felt good, soft, tender, and damn good, and I wanted more. But then, as our tongues collided with one another, I instantly began to visualize myself on the ground, rolling around with Tasha while he ran to protect her and not me. Then, a second after that, I saw myself with handcuffs on. It was at that moment that I recalled promising myself that I would never be that stupid for Michael or any other man ever again. Well, I'd broken that promise to myself after dealing with One, Two, Three, and Four. And as I remembered where I was at that point in my life, I was not about to break that promise again and go back to what I didn't want or need in my life. All at once, I pushed his body away from mine.

"I'm sorry, Michael, but I can't do this."

He stood there staring at me with the most astonished and offended look on his face, as if I'd actually done something wrong to him.

"Michael, I'm not the same teenage girl that I was way back in high school, who would have taken you back even after you chose Tasha over me. I've grown so much mentally, emotionally, and most of all, spiritually that I know you are not who God has for me. So, I think it would be best if you turned around and walked out my door, and we'll both act like you never came back here tonight."

"Mya, you can't be serious right now. I mean, are you really about to let go of what we both know is still very much alive between us?"

I heard his question as my mind traveled to my relationship with God and then to the man I'd just met, Ezekiel. True enough, I had no clue what was in store for me and him, or if he could possibly be my *now and forever*, or *never*—only God knew that. But I knew who wasn't. So, with that thought, I simply smiled at him and said, "I'm not letting it go, Michael. You did, all those years ago. So, I would suggest that maybe you go to Tasha's tonight and see what you can probably salvage as far as your marriage is concerned. I think you owe her and your children that much."

I pushed his back toward the door, and as he stepped out and turned to me, still with a look of amazement, I kissed his cheek and closed the door on him and what we had all those years ago. And as I leaned my back against the door, I looked up to God and plainly said, "Thank you."

A few seconds later, I heard my phone alert me to a text message. I ran to pick it up, and looking down at it, I read,

Mya, I hope everything was all right. But I wanted to take the chance to tell you that I'm glad we met, and I can't wait to get to know you better. Anyway, sweet dreams, and I'll talk with you soon.

I closed my eyes and held my phone against my chest. For the first time in a long time, my heart was truly happy when it came to a man, and it didn't involve sex, money, or anything of the sort. Although neither of us knew where this was about to go, something inside about it felt good to me, and that was all the confirmation I needed. Only time would tell from here if he'd one day become my now and forever.

THE END

The Author

After attempting several different career paths, Hazel Ro embraced and followed her passion and God-given talent as a fiction romance author and entrepreneur.

Her love for writing started at an early age, when, at times, she felt misunderstood, and she found release in journaling her thoughts. Hazel Ro would take whatever negativity from her reality and build her own world by drawing from her imagination and creativity.

However, never in a million years did she imagine her writing manifesting into her first self-published Novel, *For Better or For Worse*. Its storyline uses an entertaining yet effective way of dealing with real-life issues such as cheating and adultery, betrayal, lies, broken relationships, spirituality, and so much more. Hazel Ro's ultimate objective through this first piece and others is to promote and encourage healthy African American relationships.

Aside from writing novels, Hazel Ro is passionate about anything related to the arts. She co-produced her first stage play, *For Better or For Worse*, in 2012 and loves music, poetry, and singing.

Hazel Ro is a graduate of Lindenwood University, where she earned her MA in mass communications. She has her BA in sports and entertainment management from Fontbonne University.

Hazel Ro is originally from St. Louis, Missouri, but has found her home in Chicago, IL, since April 2015.

~~Ro Chamberlain~~

Find *Now or Never* and other novels by Hazel Ro by visiting www.hazel-ro.com.

There, the author can be contacted for discounted book purchases for large orders, group discussions with book clubs, speaking engagements, and much more!

Thank you again for your support!